2027

MASUCCIRACING

dal 1916

MASUCCI™

RACING

MASUCCI™

RACING

**This is the story of a very unusual friendship.
On one side, Vic Cooper, racing driver and time traveler.
On the other, the Masucci family, the most controversial
and successful racing dynasty in the world.**

**This book series celebrates the daring Masucci machines
that Vic raced between 1916 and 2615,
and the machines of his strongest rivals.**

Vic Cooper's first challenge is the 2027 Endurance Cup.

Welcome to The Timeless Racer.

Daniel Simon

Voici l'histoire d'une amitié hors du commun. D'un côté, Vic Cooper, pilote de course et voyageur intertemporel. De l'autre, Masucci, à la fois une famille et une écurie de course, qui suscite des controverses à la hauteur de ses succès. Cette série d'ouvrages célèbre les audacieuses créations Masucci que Vic pilota entre les années 1916 et 2615, ainsi que les machines de ses principaux rivaux. Premier défi pour Vic, la Coupe d'Endurance 2027.
Bienvenue dans le monde du Timeless Racer.

Dies ist die Geschichte einer ungewöhnlichen Freundschaft. Auf der einen Seite Vic Cooper, Rennfahrer und Zeitreisender. Auf der anderen die Masucci Familie, die erfolgreichste Renndynastie der Welt.
Diese Buchserie stellt nicht nur die Masucci-Boliden ins Rampenlicht, die Vic Cooper zwischen 1916 und 2615 gefahren ist, sondern auch die Maschinen seiner stärksten Rivalen. Vics erster Ritt: der 2027 Endurance Cup.
Willkommen bei The Timeless Racer.

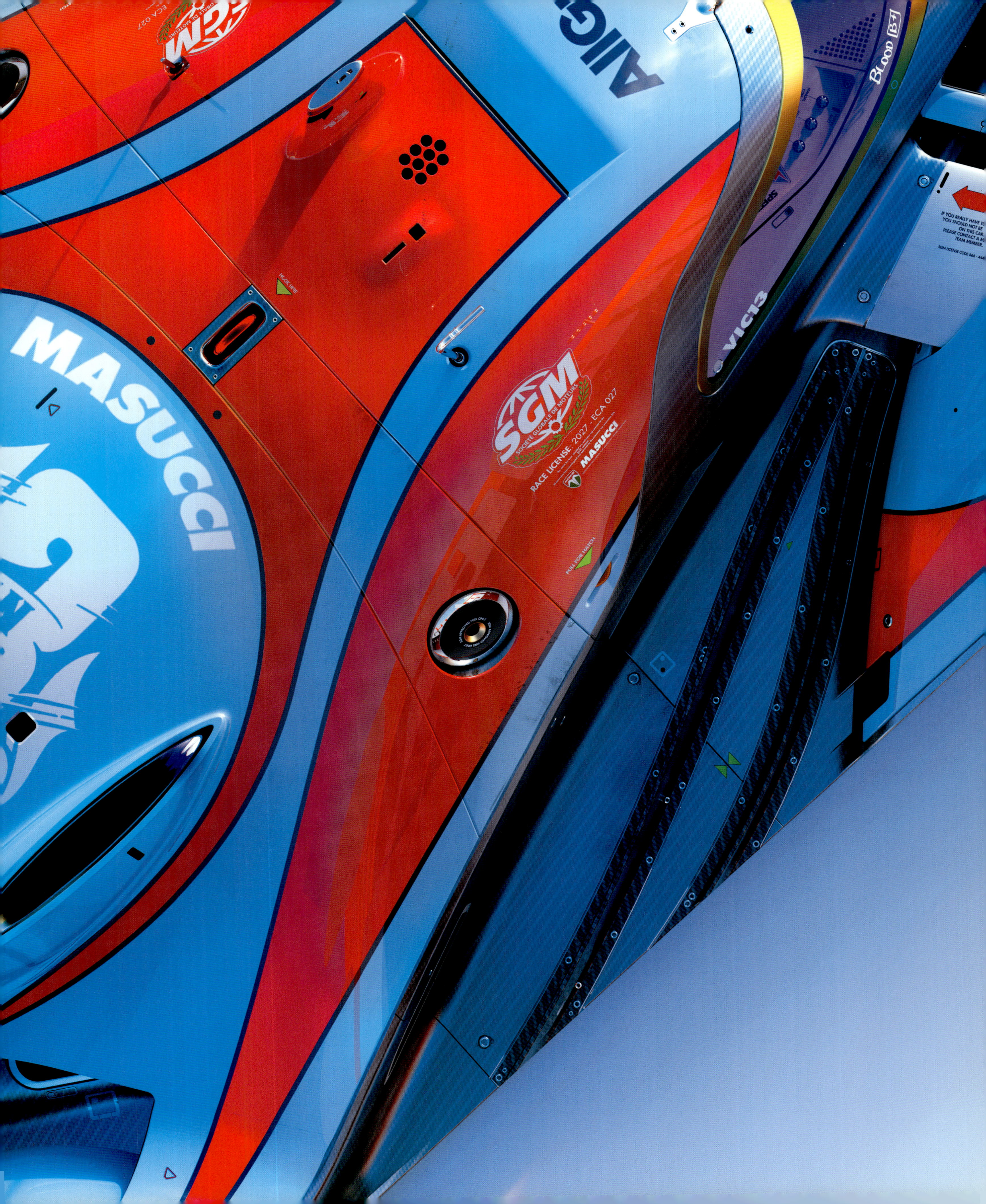

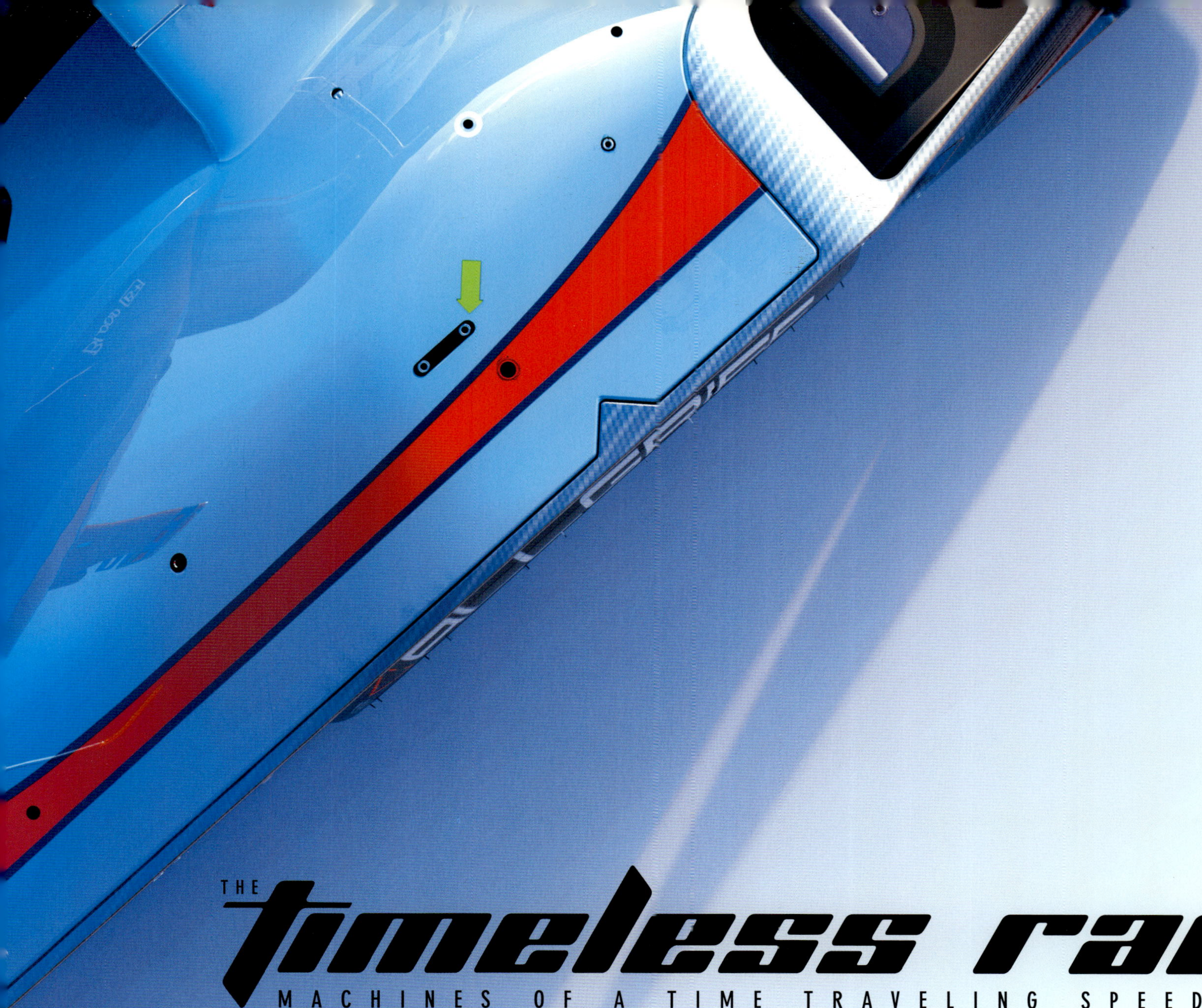

THE timeless racer®

MACHINES OF A TIME TRAVELING SPEED JUNKIE

designstudio PRESS

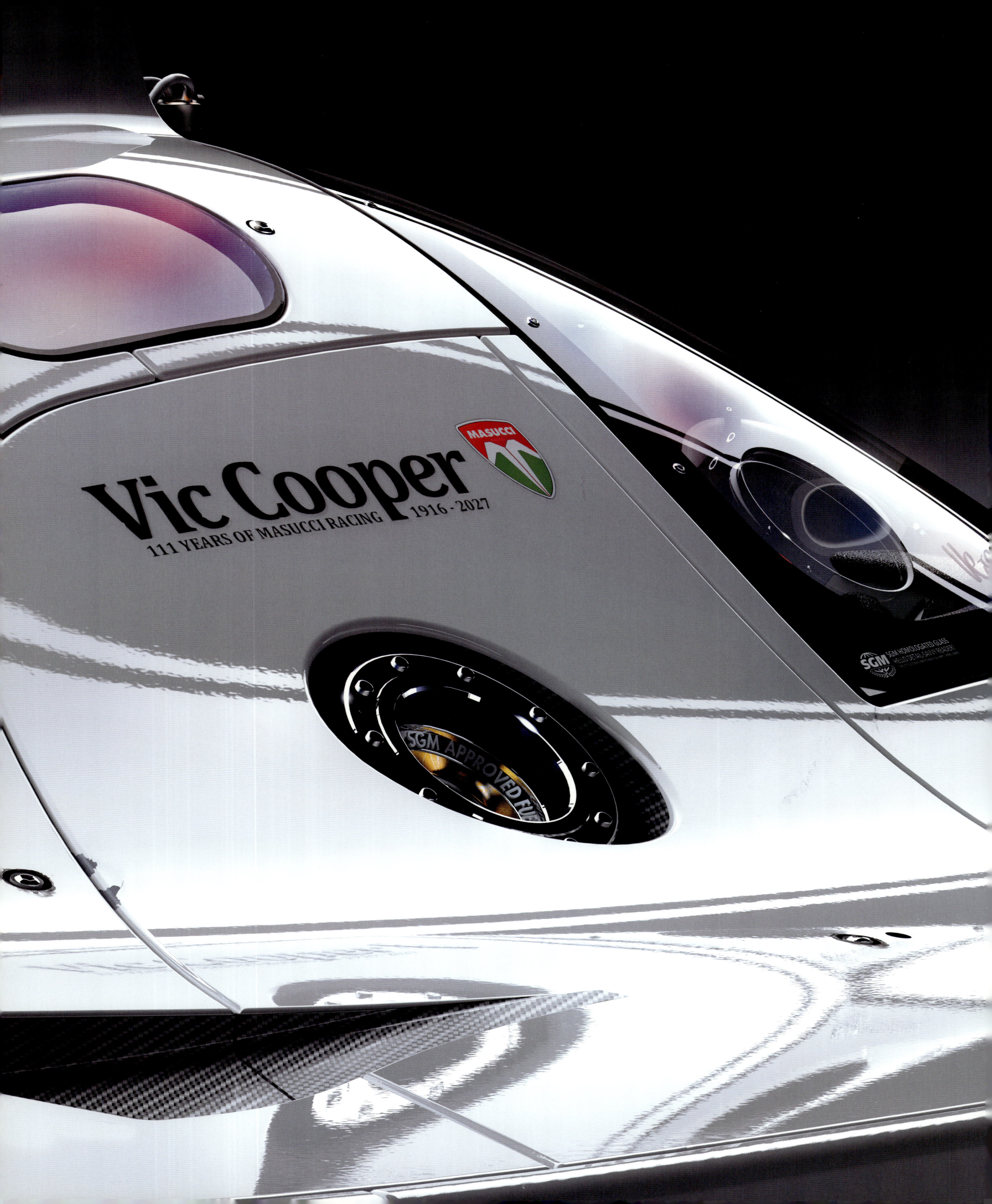

MASUCCI
Vic Cooper
111 YEARS OF MASUCCI RACING 1916 - 2027
SGM APPROVED FUE

CONTENTS

THE TIMELESS RACER: EPISODE 1

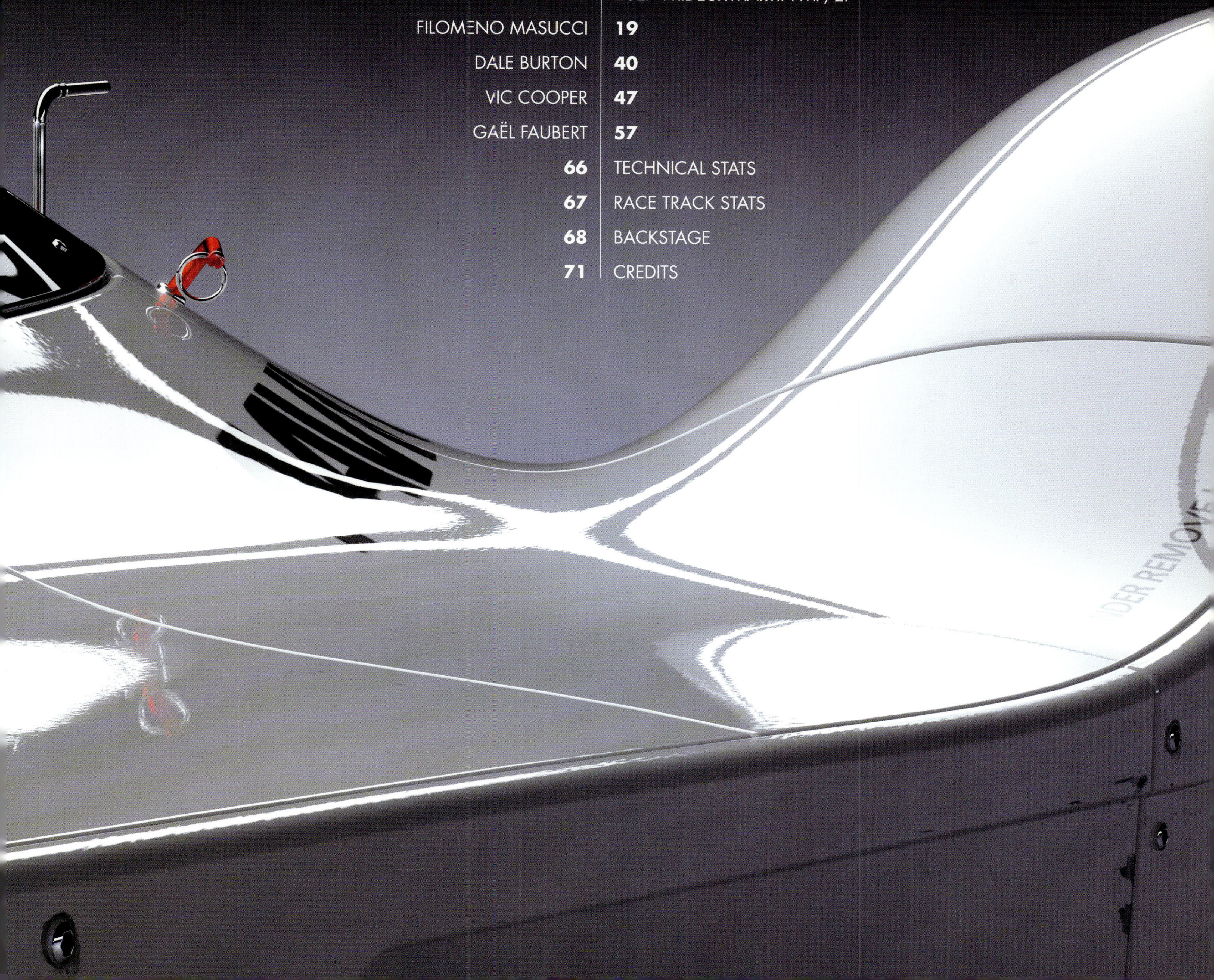

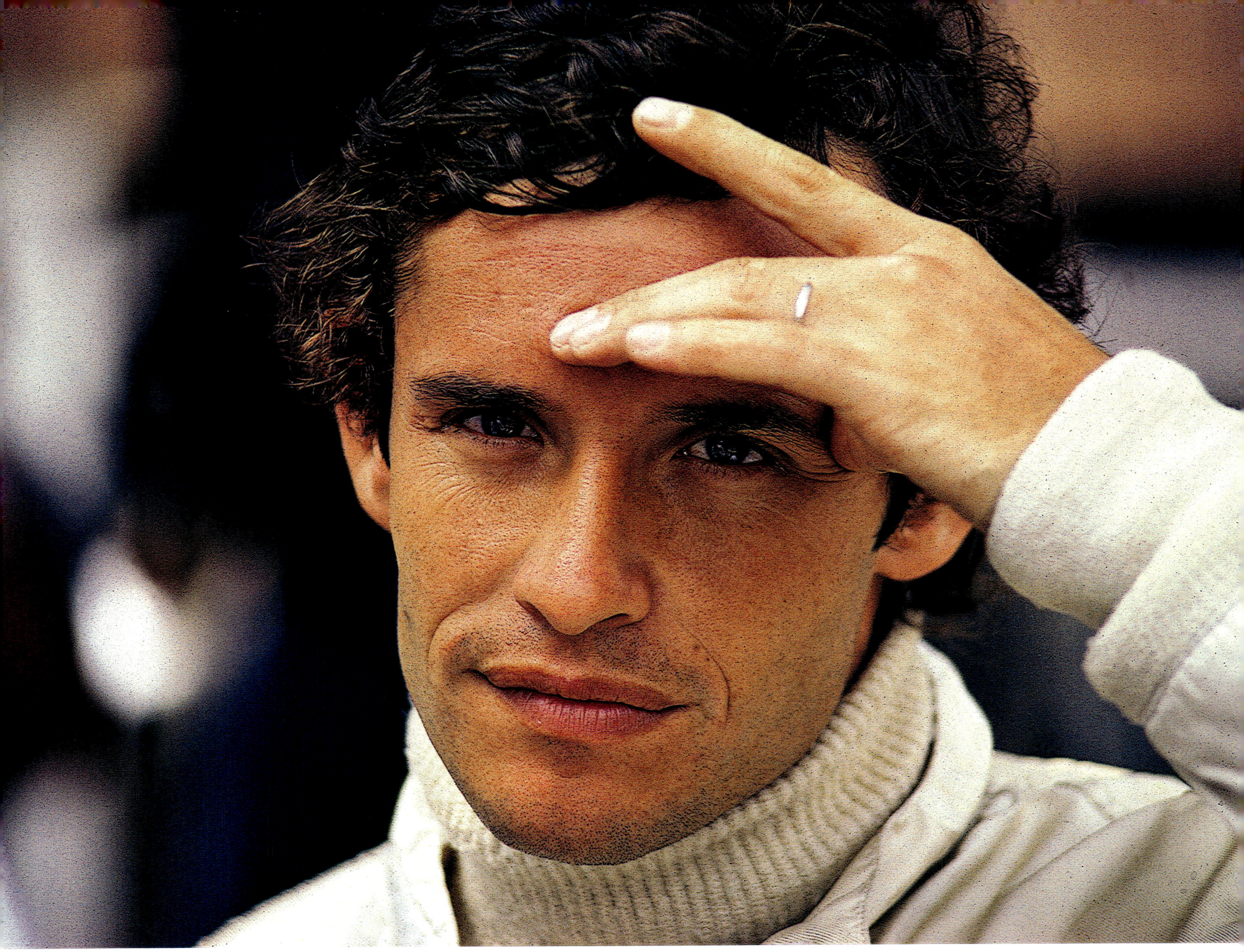

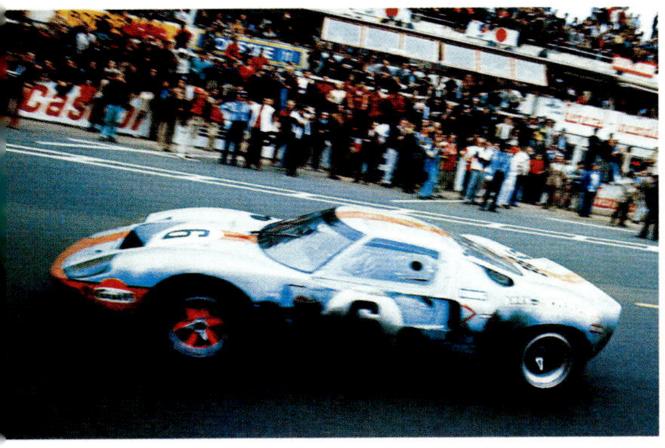

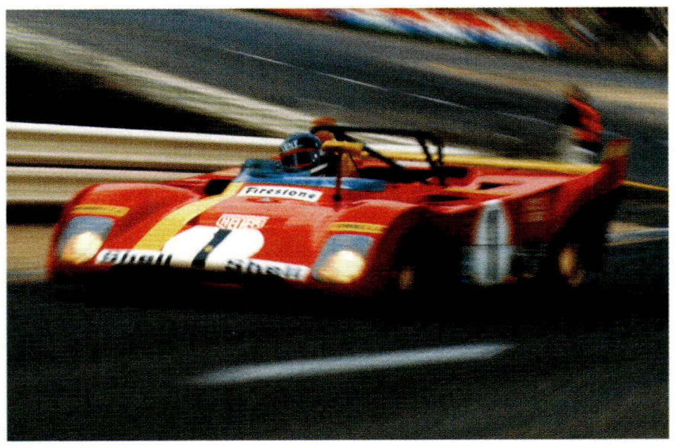

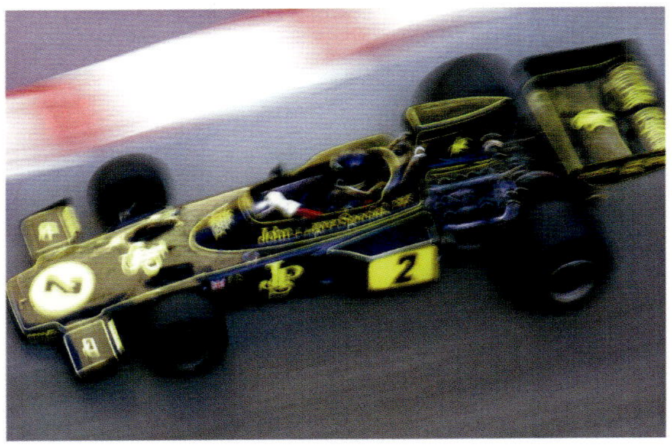

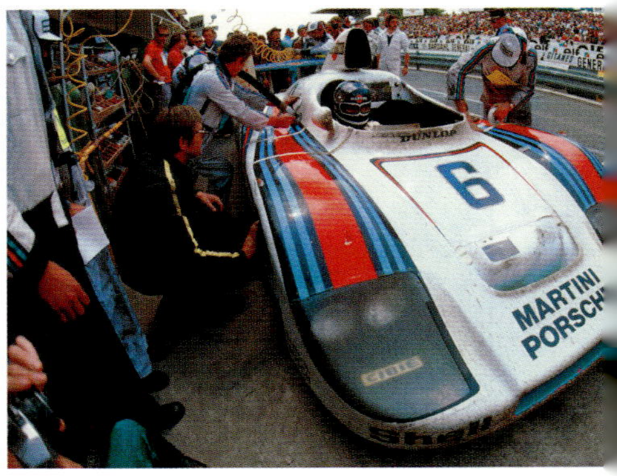

Top: *1976*. A great portrait of Jacky Ickx, during the F1 Monaco Grand Prix. Monte Carlo. May 30st ,1976. **Bottom row, from left to right: (1)** ***1969.*** Winner of the 24 Hours of Le Mans: Jacky Ickx and Jackie Oliver in the Ford GT 40 in Gulf colors, entered by the John Wyer Team. Le Mans, France. June 13th, 1969. **(2)** ***1972.*** Jacky Ickx in the Ferrari 312PB, flat out through the daring Eau Rouge corner during the 1000km of Spa. Spa-Francorchamps, Belgium. May 7th, 1972. **(3)** ***1974.*** Jacky Ickx racing Colin Chapman's iconic Lotus 72E-Cosworth through the legendary streets of Monaco during the F1 Grand Prix. Monte Carlo. May 26th, 1974. **(4)** ***1978.*** Jacky Ickx during a pit stop at the legendary 24 Hours of Le Mans in the Martini Porsche 936/78. Le Mans, France. June 10th, 1978. **Page 7:** ***1979***. Jacky Ickx with his iconic helmet at the 1979 German F1 Grand Prix, Hockenheim, driving the Ligier-Ford JS11. Hockenheim, Germany. July 29th,1979. All Photos by the wonderful Rainer W. Schlegelmilch / Getty Images.

Ci-dessus : *1976.* Un grand portrait de Jacky Ickx, lors du Grand Prix F1 de Monaco. Monte Carlo. 30 mai 1976. **Rang inférieur, de gauche à droite : (1)** ***1969.*** Vainqueurs des 24 Heures du Mans : Jacky Ickx et Jackie Oliver dans la Ford GT 40 aux couleurs Gulf de l'équipe John Wyer. Le Mans, France. 13 juin 1969. **(2)** ***1972.*** Jacky Ickx dans la Ferrari 312PB, à l'attaque du célèbre virage de l'Eau Rouge aux 1000km de Spa. Spa-Francorchamps, Belgique. 7 mai 1972. **(3)** ***1974.*** Jacky Ickx au volant de la mythique Lotus 72E-Cosworth de Colin Chapman dans les rues de Monaco lors du Grand Prix de F1. Monte Carlo. 26 mai 1974. **(4)** ***1978.*** Jacky Ickx lors d'un arrêt au stand aux 24 Heures du Mans au volant de la Porsche Martini 936/78. Le Mans, France. 10 juin 1978. **Page 7 :** ***1979.*** Jacky Ickx et son casque emblématique au volant de la Ligier-Ford JS11, lors du Grand Prix de F1 le 29 juillet 1979 à Hockenheim, Allemagne. Toutes les photos ont été prises par le talentueux Rainer W. Schlegelmilch / Getty Images.

Oben: *1976*. Jacky Ickx, während dem Großen Preis von Monaco. Monte Carlo; 30. Mai1976. **Unten, von links nach rechts: (1)** ***1969.*** Sieger bei den 24 Stunden von Le Mans: Jacky Ickx und Jackie Oliver im Gulf-farbenen Ford GT 40 des John Wyer Teams. Le Mans, Frankreich; 13.Juni 1969. **(2)** ***1972***. Jacky Ickx im Ferrari 312PB, mit Vollgas durch die berüchtigte Eau Rouge Kurve bei den 1000km von Spa. Spa-Francorchamps, Belgien; 7. Mai 1972. **(3)** ***1974***. Jacky Ickx in den legendären Gassen von Monaco, in Colin Chapmans Lotus 72E-Cosworth. Großer Preis von Monaco, Monte Carlo. 26. Mai 1974. **(4)** ***1978***. Jacky Ickx im Martini Porsche 936/78, während eines Boxenstopps bei den 24 Stunden von Le Mans. Le Mans, Frankreich; 10. Juni 1978. **Seite 7:** ***1979***. Jacky Ickx mit ikonischer Kriegsbemalung beim Großen Preis von Deutschland im Ligier-Ford JS11. Hockenheim, Deutschland; 29. Juli1979. Alle Fotos von Rainer W. Schlegelmilch / Getty Images.

FOREWORD BY JACKY ICKX

A REAL TIMELESS RACER

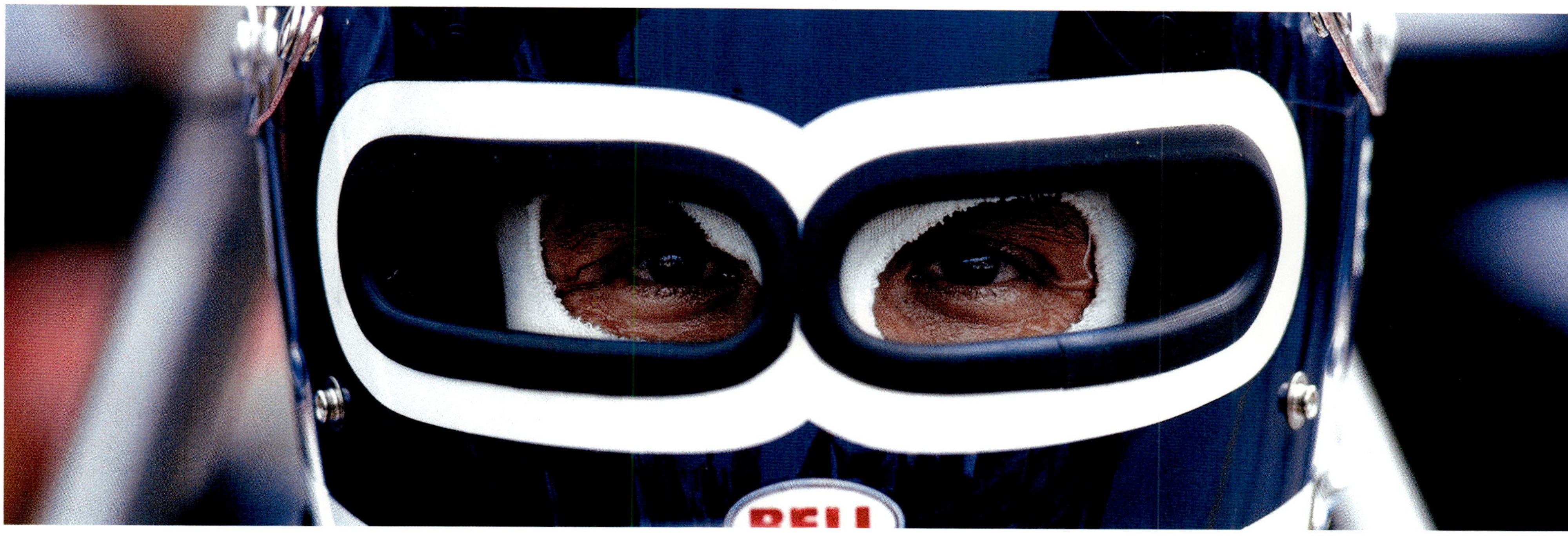

If I could travel back in time to one of my races, to experience it all over again, which one would it be? It is an impossible choice to make. I have many rich memories of my active years in motor racing—and what I remember the most are the people. There is no motorsports without their passion for racing and their hunger to win. People like Ken Tyrrell, who gave me a chance to race his single-seaters in 1965, alongside Jackie Stewart. Or Roy Salvadori—I drove his Cooper-Maserati in my first F1 Grand Prix in 1967, in the same team with the great Jochen Rindt. Racing was extremely dangerous back then, and the slightest mistake could have fatal consequences. But it was exciting, and I found something that I would be passionate about for the rest of my life. The teams traveled like families, fans could touch the cars in the paddocks, and photographers would stand with one foot on the track. And I went to work with iconic constructors like Enzo Ferrari and Porsche.

Endurance racing was a very different challenge. I vividly recall my first Le Mans win with Jackie Oliver in the Gulf GT40 in 1969, when we won by just a few meters, after a long 24 hours. The feeling of winning such an exhausting competition is difficult to describe. The Le Mans race would capture my passion fifteen more times, with the 1977 victory at Martini Racing being the most memorable one. I feel very fulfilled with a racing career that has spanned three different decades. I was lucky to have worked with people who supported me in winning Le Mans six times, twice being runner-up in the Formula One World Championship, winning the Can-Am title, and coming in first at the daring Paris–Dakar Rally in Africa.

With this in mind, I feel like I am living the time-travel dreams that this fictional book is about. Daniel's imagination is extraordinary, and it is joyful to see such a refreshing blend of visionary futurism with classic racing themes. Fortunately, racing has become much less dangerous, but if we believe in Daniel's vision, it will definitely not be less exciting. To the future!

S'il m'était donné de remonter le temps vers l'une de mes courses, laquelle choisir ? Le choix est impossible, tant j'ai de beaux et riches souvenirs de mes années dans le monde de la compétition automobile. Je me souviens surtout des gens, de notre passion commune, du désir partagé de victoire. Je me souviens de Ken Tyrrell m'offrant la chance de courir sur l'une de ses monoplaces en 1965, aux côtés de Jackie Stewart. Je me souviens de Roy Salvadori me confiant sa Cooper-Maserati à mon premier Grand Prix de F1 en 1967, dans l'équipe du grand Jochen Rindt. Et je revis les courses extrêmement dangereuses d'une époque où la moindre erreur pouvait être fatale. Mais la passion l'emportait, et persiste en moi. Je revois ces équipes voyageant comme des familles, ces fans pouvant toucher les voitures dans les paddocks, ces photographes un pied sur la piste… Ensuite, j'ai rejoint les plus prestigieuses écuries, celle d'Enzo Ferrari, et bien sûr Porsche.

La course d'endurance fut un tout autre défi. 1969 : je me vois encore à ma première victoire au Mans avec Jackie Oliver, gagnant de quelques mètres après 24 heures épuisantes au volant de la GT40 Gulf. Le sentiment de l'avoir emporté dans une telle compétition est indescriptible. Quinze participations au Mans, une véritable passion. Et que dire de ma victoire avec Martini Racing en 1977, la plus mémorable! Trois décennies de carrière m'ont comblé car j'ai eu la chance de travailler avec des gens remarquables. Avec eux j'ai acquis six victoires au Mans, été deux fois vice-champion du monde de Formule 1, gagné en Can-Am et au rallye Paris-Dakar.

Gardant ceci à l'esprit, j'ai l'impression de vivre des rêves de voyage dans le temps, objet de ce livre de science-fiction : le passé est là, non aboli, grâce à Daniel qui conjoint un futur visionnaire et les thèmes classiques du sport automobile. La course est heureusement devenue bien moins dangereuse, mais si nous en croyons la vision extraordinaire de Daniel elle ne sera pas moins passionnante. A l'avenir !

Wenn ich durch die Zeit zurück zu einem meiner Rennen reisen könnte – welches würde ich wählen? Ich kann es nicht sagen. Zu viele wunderbare Erinnerungen begleiten mich! Am liebsten denke ich an die Menschen. Ohne ihre Leidenschaft gäbe es keinen Motorsport. Menschen wie Ken Tyrrell, der mir 1965 ein Cockpit in seinem Formelwagen neben Jackie Stewart anbot. Oder Roy Salvadori – dessen Cooper-Maserati ich 1967 in meinem ersten Formel-1-Grand Prix fuhr, in einem Team mit dem unvergessenen Jochen Rindt. Später durfte ich dann mit Konstrukteurs-Ikonen wie Enzo Ferrari und Porsche arbeiten. Der Rennsport damals war extrem gefährlich, schon der kleinste Fehler konnte tödlich enden. Aber ich fand in dieser aufregenden Zeit, als Teams wie Familien reisten, Fans die Autos anfassen konnten und Fotografen mit einem Fuß auf der Rennstrecke standen, diese magische Motorsport-Faszination, die mich bis heute begleitet.

Eine besondere Erfahrung waren die Langstreckenrennen. Für mich heute immer noch ein Gefühl wie gestern: mein erster Sieg in Le Mans, 1969, mit Jackie Oliver im Gulf Ford GT40, als wir mit wenigen Metern Vorsprung gewannen – nach endlosen 24 Stunden. Das Gefühl, nach einer solchen Strapaze zu siegen, ist kaum zu beschreiben! Mein Leben ist nach einer Karriere über drei Rennsport-Jahrzehnte wirklich erfüllt. Und ich bin dankbar, mit Menschen gearbeitet haben zu dürfen, die es mir ermöglichten, sechsmal Le Mans zu gewinnen, zweimal Vize-Formel-1-Weltmeister zu werden, einen Can-Am-Titel zu erobern und bei der gefürchteten Rallye Paris-Dakar in Afrika zu siegen.

Manchmal fühle ich mich selbst wie ein zeitreisender Rennfahrer, um den es in diesem Buch geht. Daniels herausragende Vorstellungskraft lässt diesen erfrischenden Mix aus Futurismus und klassischem Motorsport zu einem großen Genuss werden. Zum Glück ist der Rennsport weniger gefährlich geworden. Aber wenn wir Daniels Vision vertrauen, wird er sicher nicht weniger aufregend. Auf die Zukunft!

JACKY ICKX | Monaco, 2013

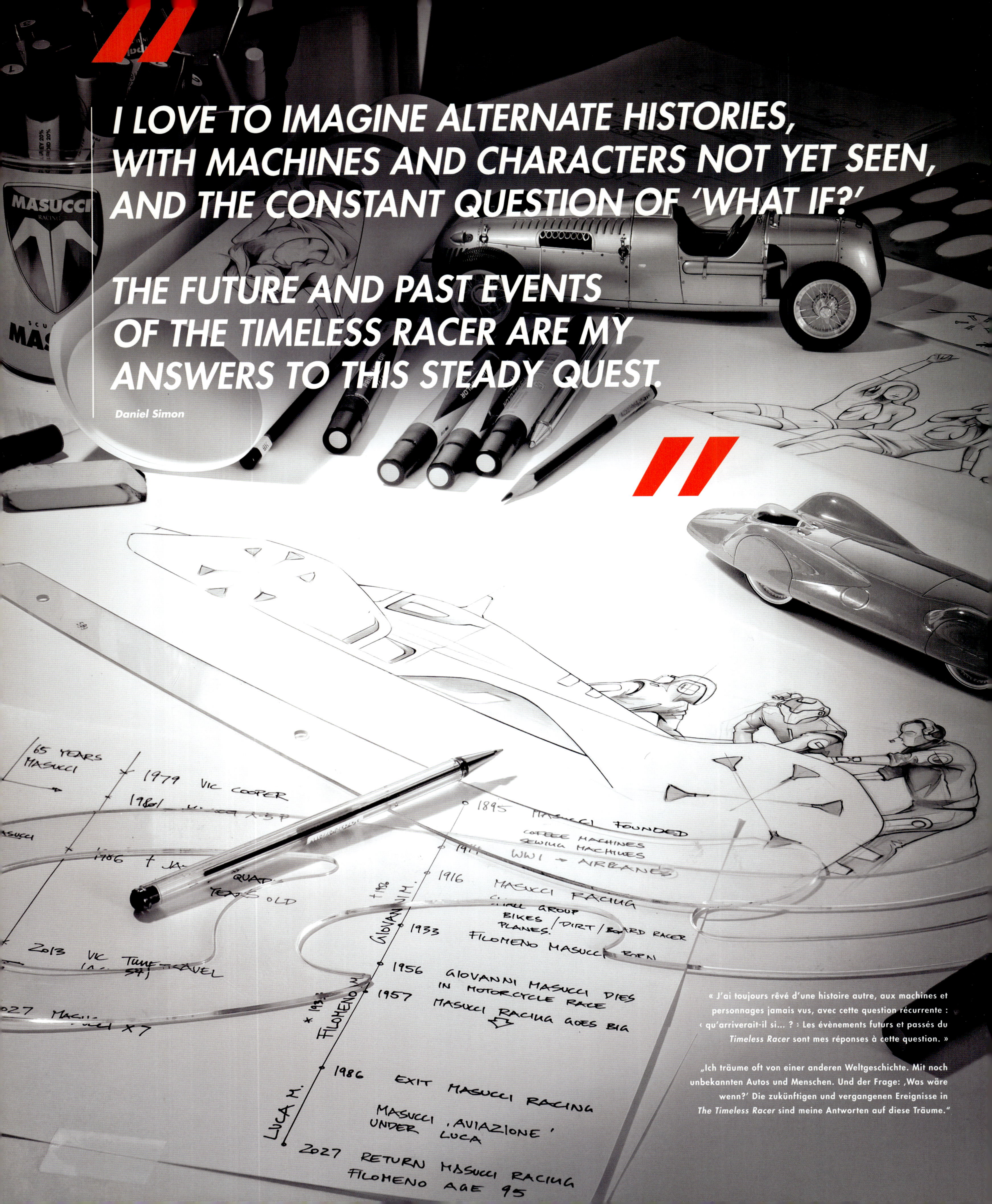

I LOVE TO IMAGINE ALTERNATE HISTORIES, WITH MACHINES AND CHARACTERS NOT YET SEEN, AND THE CONSTANT QUESTION OF 'WHAT IF?'

THE FUTURE AND PAST EVENTS OF THE TIMELESS RACER ARE MY ANSWERS TO THIS STEADY QUEST.

Daniel Simon

« J'ai toujours rêvé d'une histoire autre, aux machines et personnages jamais vus, avec cette question récurrente : ‹ qu'arriverait-il si… ? › Les évènements futurs et passés du *Timeless Racer* sont mes réponses à cette question. »

„Ich träume oft von einer anderen Weltgeschichte. Mit noch unbekannten Autos und Menschen. Und der Frage: ‚Was wäre wenn?' Die zukünftigen und vergangenen Ereignisse in *The Timeless Racer* sind meine Antworten auf diese Träume."

INTRODUCTION BY DANIEL SIMON
A JOURNEY THROUGH THE PAST AND FUTURE

A journey through the past and future. Time travel has sparked fantasies for generations and for car enthusiasts such as myself this scenario has much to offer. Time traveling to the 1920s to smell the air when Campbell and Segrave thundered down the beach of Daytona at over 230 mph when road cars still looked like horse carriages. To the '50s to smoke a cigar with moustachioed gentlemen racing superfast Formula One cars without seat belts. To the '90s to hear the crowd when Senna wins in Brazil. Or how about traveling the other way, to the future? Do modern race cars of 2100 even need drivers? Can a 2200 film fan still watch the Steve McQueen classic *Le Mans*? Does a collector in 2300 need a 288-year-old laptop to start Sebastian Vettel's F1 car? On which device will fans follow a transatlantic supersonic air race in 400 years' time? Will the winner still spray champagne? The past has answers I like to relive, the future has questions that fascinate me. I am ready to time travel both ways.

The Timeless Racer is your ticket those adventures. I invite you to time travel with me and racing driver Vic Cooper through an alternate history between 1916 and 2615, filled with machines, characters, and events never before seen. My inspiration comes from many places, but mostly from biographies, which only real life could have written. The grand Italian engineer Filomeno Masucci (a name so vibrant it can only be real; it is the name of my wonderful grandfather-in-law) is clearly inspired by the captivating careers of Colin Chapman and Enzo Ferrari. You may find hidden references to real racing history throughout the book; motorsports enthusiasts will spot them without footnotes. The form and design language in *The Timeless Racer* are driven by my never-ending obsession with automotive design in general and racing vehicle design in particular. Only in motorsports can you find the intriguing combination of aerodynamic sculpture, experimental engineering, and perfect attention to detail brought together in pursuit of a single goal: to cross the finish line before everybody else. It is an endless battle, fought by ingenious engineers on drawing boards, by mechanics in pit lanes, by rule makers in meeting rooms, and by racers on epic stages. Addictive stuff!

After the wonderful reception of *Cosmic Motors* and years of joyful work on some of Hollywood's biggest movies, I have returned to my drawing board and created what I truly love. Thank you to Scott Robertson of Design Studio Press, who remains an inspiring role model in my career and to Rainer W. Schlegelmilch for his timeless photography on page six and seven. A very special thank you to Jacky Ickx for contributing the foreword and letting me see that anything is possible. I feel very honored.

Welcome to *The Timeless Racer*.

Un voyage dans le passé et le futur. On connaît le vieux fantasme du voyage dans le temps. Et pour les amateurs de voitures, dont je suis, quel stimulus pour l'imaginaire ! Se téléporter dans les années 20, et humer l'ambiance de la plage de Daytona que Campbell et Segrave dévalaient à plus de 370 km/h, à une époque où les voitures ordinaires avaient encore la forme de calèches… Puis direction les années 50, pour fumer le cigare avec ces messieurs à moustache qui pilotaient des F1 dépourvues de ceinture de sécurité. Et dans les années 90, entendre les clameurs de la foule célébrant une victoire de Senna au Brésil. Mais voyageons dans l'autre sens, vers l'avenir. Les voitures qui courront en 2100 se passeront-elles de pilote ? Un cinéphile de 2200 admirera-t-il sur l'écran Steve McQueen dans le fameux film *Le Mans* ? Un collectionneur de 2300 aura-t-il besoin d'un ordinateur portable vieux de 288 ans pour faire démarrer la F1 de Sebastian Vettel ? Quel appareil permettra de suivre une transat aérienne supersonique dans 400 ans ? Le vainqueur débouchera-t-il encore un magnum de champagne ? J'aime revivre les réponses du passé, j'aime les questions posées à propos du futur, et c'est pourquoi je désire aller de l'un à l'autre.

The Timeless Racer vous propose de vivre ces aventures. Avec le pilote Vic Cooper, je vous invite à un voyage dans le temps entre les années 1916 et 2615. Mes sources d'inspirations proviennent essentiellement d'éléments biographiques : l'*ingeniere* Filomeno Masucci (le nom du père de ma belle-mère, à qui je veux rendre hommage) est inspiré par des personnalités telles que Colin Chapman et Enzo Ferrari. De nombreuses références à l'histoire de la compétition parsèment l'ouvrage, et les plus mordus les décrypteront sans peine. Le langage formel de ce livre est dicté par ma fascination pour les voitures de course. Il n'y a que là que l'on trouve cette combinaison de sculptures aérodynamiques, d'expérimentations en matière de design et de soin maniaque du détail, ceci dans un seul but : franchir la ligne d'arrivée avant les autres ! C'est une lutte sans fin, menée par des ingénieurs sur leur planche à dessin, des mécaniciens dans les stands, des spécialistes des règlements en tous genres et, bien sûr, des pilotes qui jouent leur vie sur la piste. Comment ne pas être passionné par tout ça ?

Après le merveilleux accueil de *Cosmic Motors*, suivi par des années de joyeux travail pour d'importantes productions hollywoodiennes, je suis retourné à ma planche à dessin pour créer ce que j'aime vraiment. Merci à Scott Robertson de Design Studio Press, modèle d'inspiration dans ma carrière, au grand Rainer W. Schlegelmilch pour ses photos intertemporelles publiées en pages 6 et 7. Et un merci tout particulier à Jacky Ickx, dont l'avant-propos me montre que tout est possible. J'en suis très honoré.

Bienvenue dans le monde du *Timeless Racer*.

Eine Reise durch Vergangenheit und Zukunft. Zeitreisen liefern uns seit Generationen Treibstoff für die großartigsten Fantasien. Bei Autoenthusiasten wie mir führen sie zuweilen zu wilden Träumen: Ich stehe in den 20er Jahren in Daytona und sehe Malcolm Campbell und Henry Segrave mit 370 km/h über den Strand donnern. In den 50ern treffe ich mich auf eine Zigarre mit den schnauzbärtigen Gentlemen, die Formel-1-Wagen ohne Gurt fahren, und in den 90ern bin ich bei Sennas Siegen in Brasilien dabei, die das ganze Land ausrasten lassen. Dann geht es in die Zukunft. Brauchen Rennwagen im Jahr 2100 Piloten? Kennt ein Cineast 2200 noch Steve McQueens *Le Mans*? Benötigt ein Sammler 2300 einen 288 Jahre alten Laptop um Sebastian Vettels Weltmeisterauto zu starten? Wie schaut man ein transatlantisches Überschall-Rennen in 400 Jahren? Und duscht dessen Sieger noch in Champagner? Die Antworten der Vergangenheit neu erleben, den faszinierenden Fragen der Zukunft auf der Spur. Die Zeitreise kann beginnen! Am besten in beide Richtungen gleichzeitig.

The Timeless Racer ist Ihr ganz persönliches Ticket zu diesen Abenteuern. Kommen Sie mit auf eine Reise in eine imaginäre Zeit zwischen 1916 und 2615 – voller fantastischer Maschinen, Rennen und Ereignisse. Die Inspiration für Charaktere kommt dabei oft von Geschichten, wie sie nur das wahre Leben schreiben kann. So ist der große italienische Konstrukteur Filomeno Masucci (dessen klangvoller Name übrigens von meinem tollen Schwiegergroßvater stammt) ganz bewusst eine Hommage an die echten und unverwechselbaren Teamchefs wie Colin Chapman und Enzo Ferrari. Dieses Buch ist voller versteckter Referenzen. Sie, liebe Motorsportkenner, werden sie ohne Fußnoten finden. In der Formensprache für *The Timeless Racer* lebe ich meine Leidenschaft für Design und Rennsport aus: automobile Skulpturen, in zweckoptimierter Symbiose mit technisch Denkbarem, mit einem einzigen Ziel im Visier – schneller zu sein als alle anderen. Rennsport ist ein ewiger Drahtseilakt zwischen Erlaubtem und Unerlaubtem, getrieben von der schlitzohrigen Kreativität genialer Ingenieure. Wenn das kein Stoff zum Träumen ist!

Nach den großartigen Erfahrungen mit meinem Buch *Cosmic Motors* und der Arbeit an einigen großen Hollywood-Filmen kehre ich mit *The Timeless Racer* in meine ganz persönliche Welt zurück. Ein großes Dankeschön geht an Scott Robertson von Design Studio Press, der mich immer wieder aufs Neue inspiriert, und an Rainer W. Schlegelmilch für seine Fotos auf den Seiten 6 und 7. Mein besonderer Dank für sein herzliches Vorwort gilt Jacky Ickx, dessen beispiellose Karriere mir zeigt, dass alles möglich ist – danke für diese Ehre.

Willkommen bei *The Timeless Racer*.

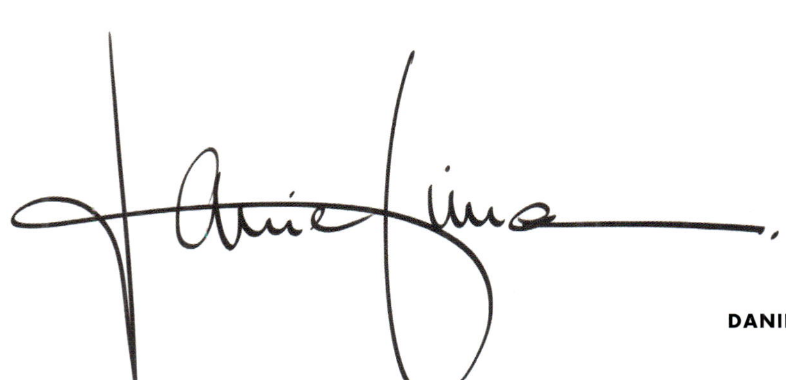

DANIEL SIMON | Los Angeles, 2013

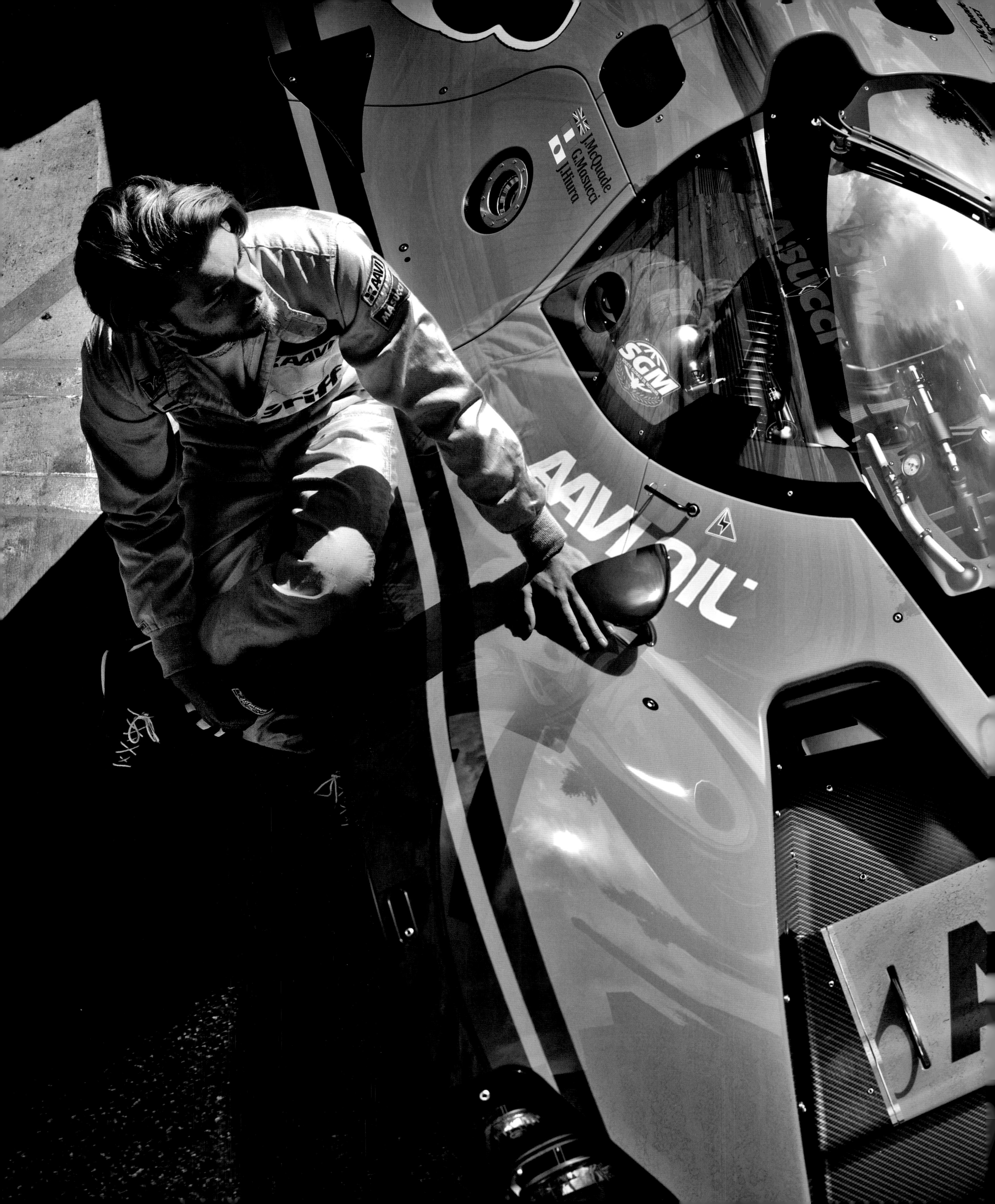

J.McQuade
G.Masucci
J.Hiura
AAVIOIL
SGM

THE**TIMELESSRACER**

DESTINATION MASUCCI

Destination Masucci. Vic Cooper is the Timeless Racer. He loves racing more than anything, and boy can he drive. No wonder: born in 1979, he is the son of British racing legend Jay McQuade, the first real superstar of motorsports. Starting in 1956, his father, McQuade was the star pilot of Masucci Racing, the most successful racing team in history—on land, water, and in the air. A charismatic gentleman and adventurer, Jay had a sixth sense for machines and speed and he gained more victories and fame than any other racer before him. The mastermind behind this unprecedented success was Filomeno Masucci who created daring cars, motorcycles, planes, and boats, sparking fantasies of an entire generation. Vic Cooper grew up surrounded by the all-consuming buzz of Masucci Racing, his father's fame, and the intimate warmth of the glamorous Italian racing dynasty.

But in 1986, it all tragically came to an end. McQuade lost control of his Masucci X-6 and was killed. The fatal accident of his star driver—and best friend—shattered Masucci's belief in motorsports, and Masucci Racing was closed forever. Throughout the years that followed, young Vic Cooper had only one dream: to become a successful racer just like his father, behind the wheel of a Masucci—the magical team that ceased to exist.

While Vic was dreaming, specialized agencies started offering simulated "alternate-history time travel" experiences called "spins." Although the spins were only a simulation, they were so indistinguishable from reality that "spinners," while hooked up to machines, would pay the ultimate price if they die within the spin: their mind would trigger real death. One policy that all time travel agencies share is that they require approval by the real-life counterparts to be programmed into such trips. Cooper persuaded the reluctant and worried Filomeno Masucci to clear him to experience the Masucci Team on a spin, despite the life-threatening realities of such an adventure.

Vic Cooper's time travels would exceed all his expectations. He re-united with the Italian uber-team not only to conquer the best racers of all times, but also to feel the addictive thrill of racing a Masucci—something his father always talked about. It felt so real! Everything seemed perfect. But alternate-history time travel has a trade off Vic could not anticipate . . .

The Timeless Racer celebrates the daring Masucci machines that Vic Cooper raced in alternative times between 1916 and 2615, and the machines of his strongest rivals. Episode 1 begins with the 2027 SGM Endurance Cup.

Godspeed, Vic Cooper.

Destination Masucci. Vic Cooper est le Timeless Racer. Il aime la course, et il a un excellent coup de volant. Né en 1979, il est le fils du légendaire pilote britannique Jay McQuade. Depuis 1956, celui-ci portait au firmament les couleurs de Masucci Racing, l'écurie la plus titrée de tous les temps sur terre, sur l'eau ou dans les airs. Mi-gentleman mi-aventurier, Jay jouissait d'un sixième sens pour tout ce qui concernait les machines de course et la vitesse, ce qui lui permit de remporter plus de victoires que quiconque avant lui. Le « cerveau » derrière ses succès s'appelait Filomeno Masucci. Celui-ci créa des voitures, motos, avions et bateaux qui firent rêver toute une génération. Vic Cooper grandit dans cette atmosphère, pris entre la gloire paternelle et celle d'une écurie mêlant glamour, chaleur familiale et réussite sportive.

Mais en 1986, tout prit fin. McQuade mourut après avoir perdu le contrôle de sa Masucci X-6. Filomeno fut terriblement affecté par cet accident, car il perdait ainsi le seul véritable ami qu'il eut jamais parmi les pilotes. Il décida alors de cesser l'aventure Masucci Racing. Malgré cela, dans les années qui suivirent, le jeune Vic ne nourrit qu'une ambition : devenir champion comme son père, au volant d'une Masucci.

Dans le même temps, des sociétés mirent au point des « voyages dans le temps alternant avec l'histoire ». Il s'agissait d'expériences de simulation tellement puissantes qu'elles en devenaient bien réelles. Reliés à des machines, les cobayes étaient projetés dans un futur si tangible que, si leurs avatars mouraient pendant l'expérience, eux-mêmes n'en réchapperaient pas ! Pour y participer, Cooper dut commencer par lever les réticences de Filomeno Masucci. En effet, son approbation était requise pour lancer le processus. Malgré les risques encourus par Vic et par son écurie, il donna son accord.

Les résultats de ces voyages dans le temps allaient dépasser toutes les espérances de Vic. Il gagna des courses, comme si tout était vrai ! Il retrouva la grande écurie italienne et put enfin ressentir l'immense satisfaction, si souvent évoquée par son père, qu'il y avait à courir et gagner avec une Masucci. Tout semblait donc parfait. Mais le voyage intertemporel allait avoir des conséquences que Vic n'aurait pu anticiper…

The Timeless Racer célèbre les audacieuses Masucci victorieuses de 1916 à 2615 avec Vic Cooper, ainsi que les machines de ses meilleurs rivaux. L'épisode 1 commence avec la Coupe d'Endurance SGM 2027.

Godspeed, Vic Cooper.

Heimkehr zu Masucci. Vic Cooper ist der „Timeless Racer", rennverrückt und fahrerisch hoch begabt. Kein Wunder: 1979 geboren, ist er der Sohn des Briten Jay McQuade, des ersten echten Motorsport-Superstars. Seit 1956 war McQuade der Starpilot bei Masucci Racing, dem erfolgreichsten Rennstall der Welt – zu Lande, zu Wasser und in der Luft. Abseits der Rennstrecke stilvoller Gentleman und Abenteurer, war er vor allem für seinen sechsten Sinn für Motoren und Speed bekannt. Niemand fuhr mehr Siege ein als er. Hinter all diesen Erfolgen stand der tollkühne Konstrukteur Filomeno Masucci. Seine extraordinären Autos, Motorräder, Flugzeuge und Boote brachten Rennsportfans weltweit zum Träumen. Einen Jungen, der wie Vic in dieser Atmosphäre aus Gefahr und Glamour aufgewachsen war, prägt dies ein ganzes Leben.

1986 änderte sich plötzlich alles. McQuade verunglückte in seinem Masucci X-6 tödlich. Der Verlust seines besten Freundes erschütterte Filomeno Masuccis Glauben an den Sport so tief, dass er Masucci Racing für immer aus dem Rennsport zurückzog. Doch während der folgenden Jahre hatte der junge Vic Cooper nur einen Traum: Wie sein Vater ein international erfolgreicher Rennfahrer zu sein, am Steuer eines Masucci – der magischen Marke, die es nun nicht mehr gab.

Während Vic träumte, begannen kommerzielle Agenturen, Zeitreise-Erlebnisse anzubieten. An Maschinen angeschlossen, konnten Wagemutige programmierbare Traumwelten erleben – von der Realität nicht zu unterscheiden und wie im wahren Leben im Extremfall tödlich. Dieses Riskio konnte Vic nicht abschrecken. Um das Rennteam für seine Zeitreisen originalgetreu simulieren lassen zu können, fehlte nur noch Filomeno Masuccis Segen. Hin- und hergerissen zwischen den realen Gefahren, die Vic erwarten würden, und dem Verständnis für einen Sohn auf den Spuren seines Vaters, gab der geniale Konstrukteur nach.

Die Zeitreisen übertrafen Vics kühnste Vorstellungen. Nicht nur, dass er endlich wieder Teil des italienischen Über-Teams war, diesmal saß er selbst am Steuer! Erst jetzt verstand Vic wirklich, wovon sein Vater immer geschwärmte hatte. Und es war so real! Alles schien perfekt. Bis sich zeigte, dass diese Art von Vergnügen einen unerwarteten Nachteil hatte …

The Timeless Racer präsentiert die extraordinären Masucci-Boliden, die von Vic Cooper zwischen 1916 und 2615 pilotiert wurden, und die Maschinen seiner stärksten Gegner. Episode 1 beginnt mit dem SGM Endurance Cup der Saison 2027.

Gute Reise, Vic Cooper.

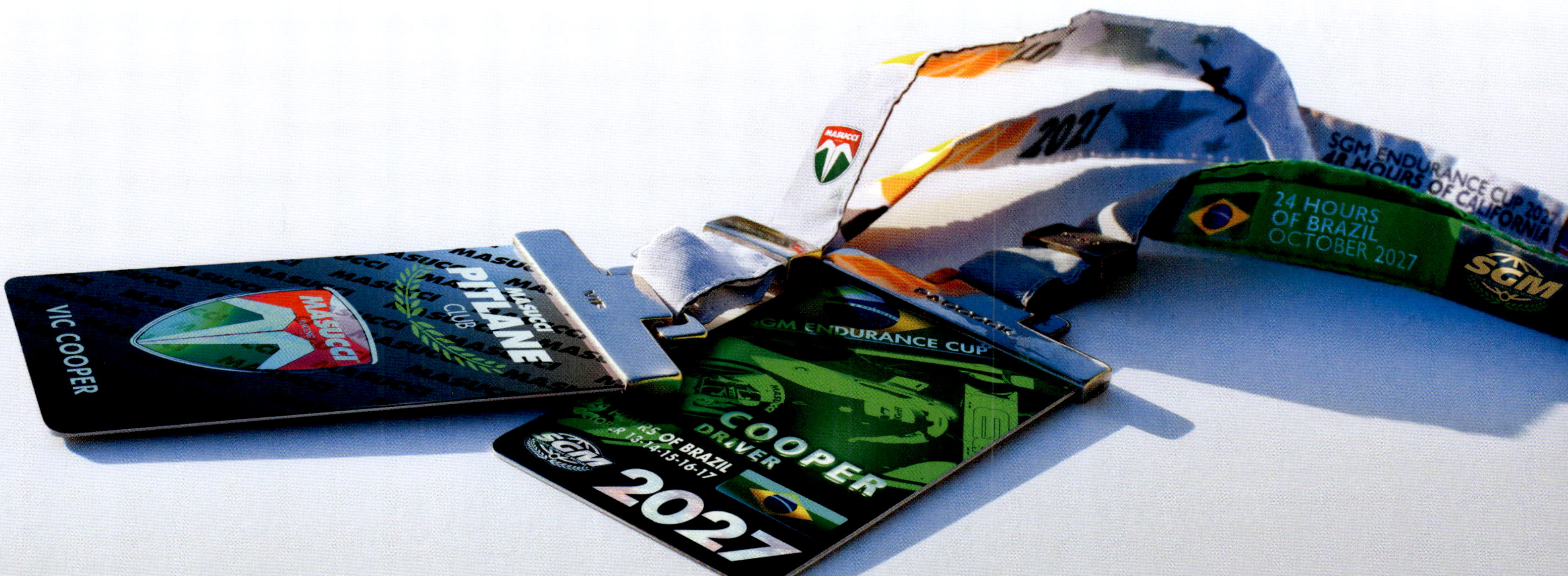

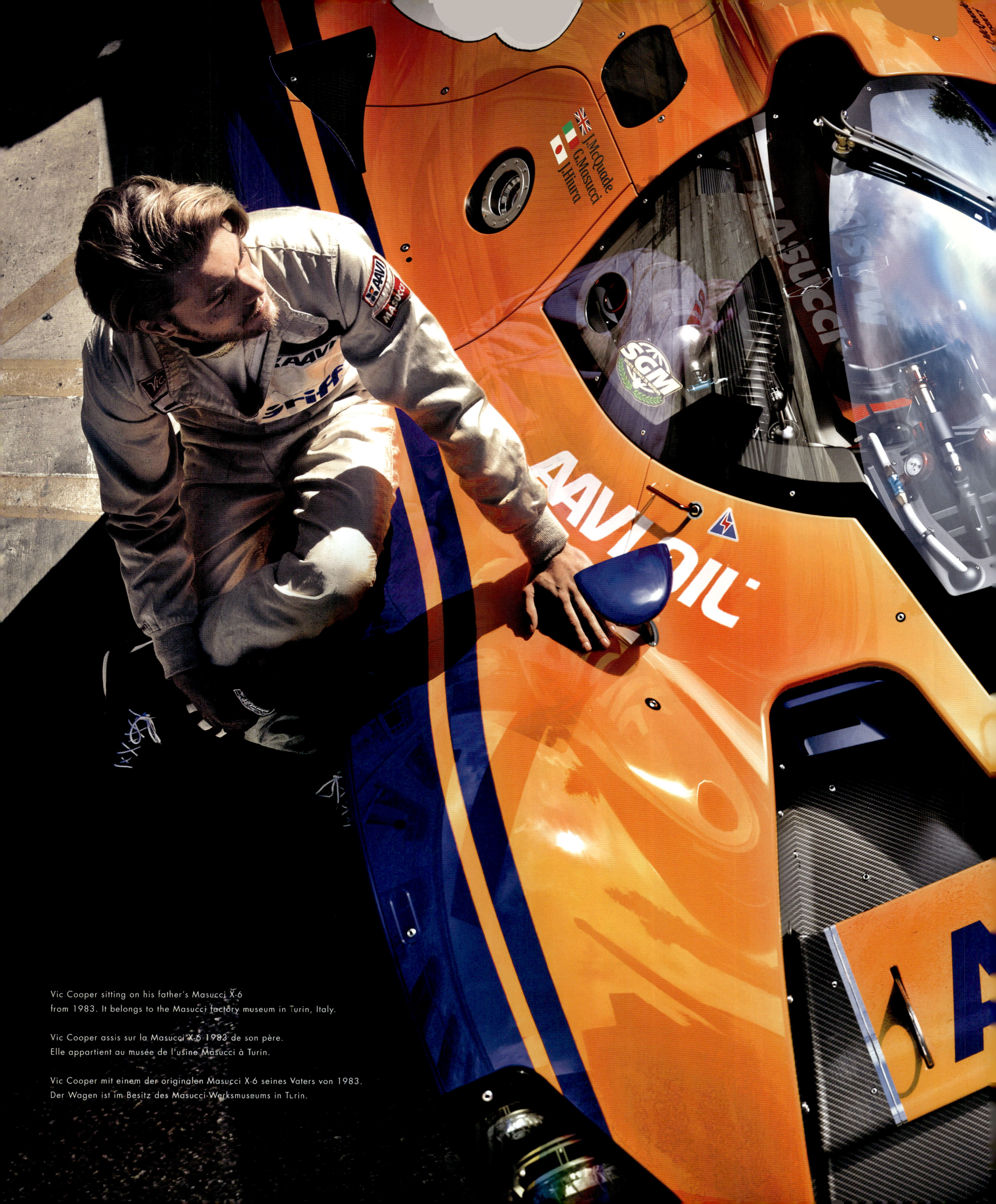

Vic Cooper sitting on his father's Masucci X-6
from 1983. It belongs to the Masucci factory museum in Turin, Italy.

Vic Cooper assis sur la Masucci X-6 1983 de son père.
Elle appartient au musée de l'usine Masucci à Turin.

Vic Cooper mit einem der originalen Masucci X-6 seines Vaters von 1983.
Der Wagen ist im Besitz des Masucci-Werksmuseums in Turin.

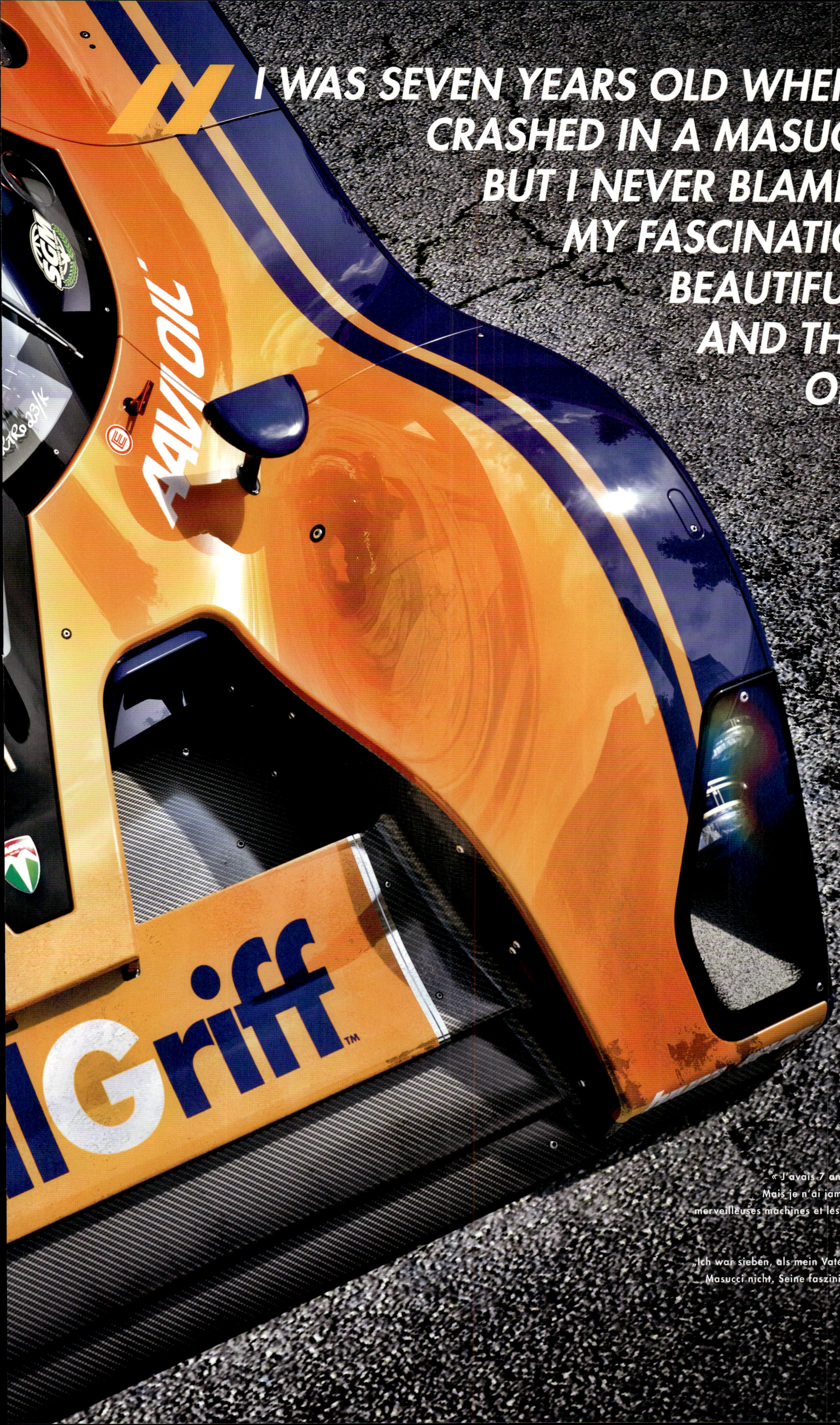

"I WAS SEVEN YEARS OLD WHEN MY FATHER CRASHED IN A MASUCCI, IN 1986. BUT I NEVER BLAMED MASUCCI. MY FASCINATION WITH HIS BEAUTIFUL MACHINES AND THE MEMORIES OF MY DAD AT THE RACES KEEP ME ALIVE."

Vic Cooper
THE TIMELESS RACER

« J'avais 7 ans en 1986 quand mon père s'est tué dans une Masucci. Mais je n'ai jamais blâmé Masucci pour cela. Ma fascination pour ses merveilleuses machines et les souvenirs de mon père en course me gardent en vie. »
Vic Cooper | **COUREUR INTERTEMPOREL**

„Ich war sieben, als mein Vater 1986 im Masucci verunglückte. Aber ich beschuldige Masucci nicht. Seine faszinierenden Konstruktionen und die Erinnerung an meinen Vater inspirieren mich."
Vic Cooper | **ZEITREISENDER RENNFAHRER**

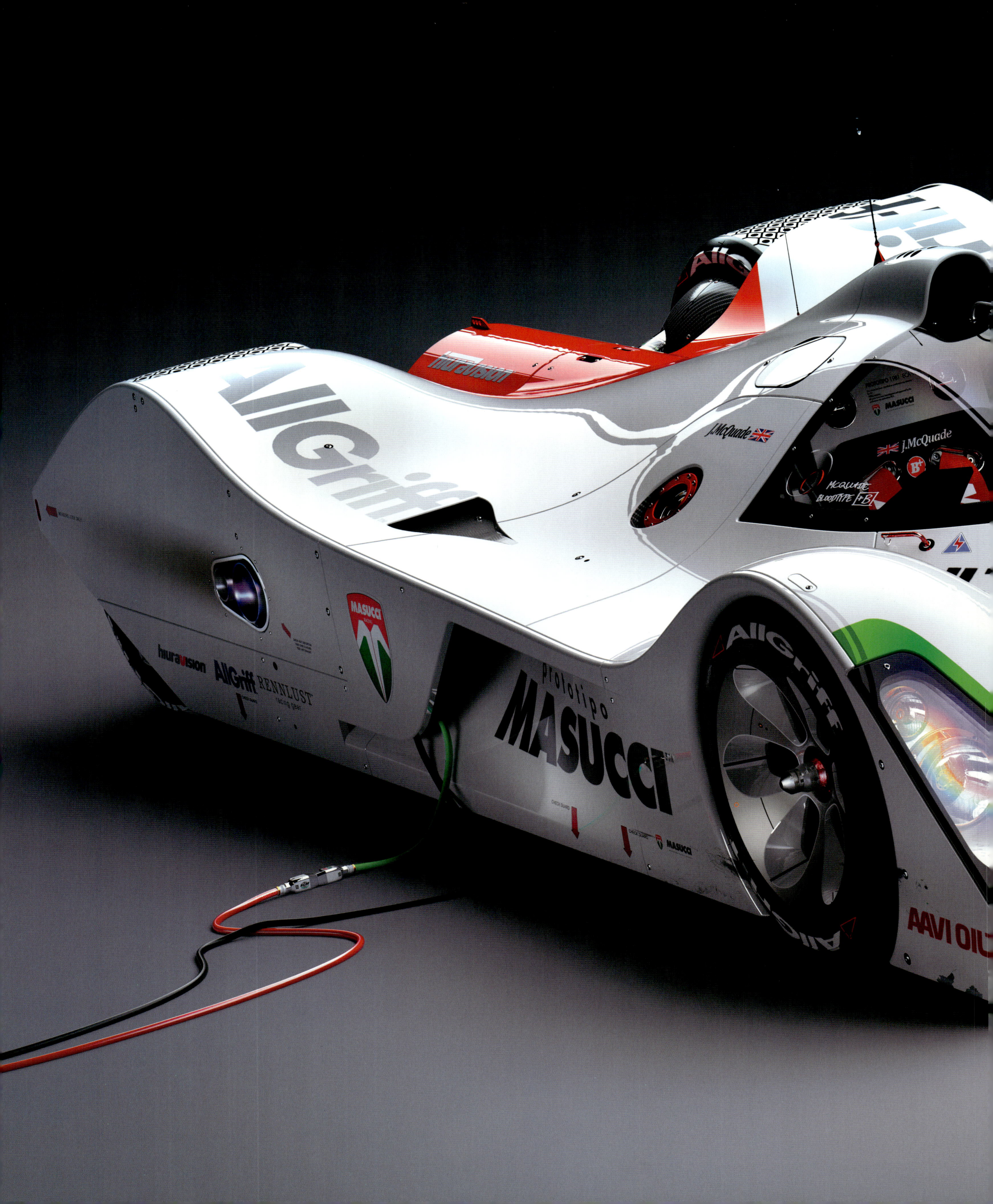
AllGriff
J.McQuade
prototipo
MASUCCI
hiuravision
AllGriff RENNLUST
racing gear
MASUCCI

MASUCCI X5/X6

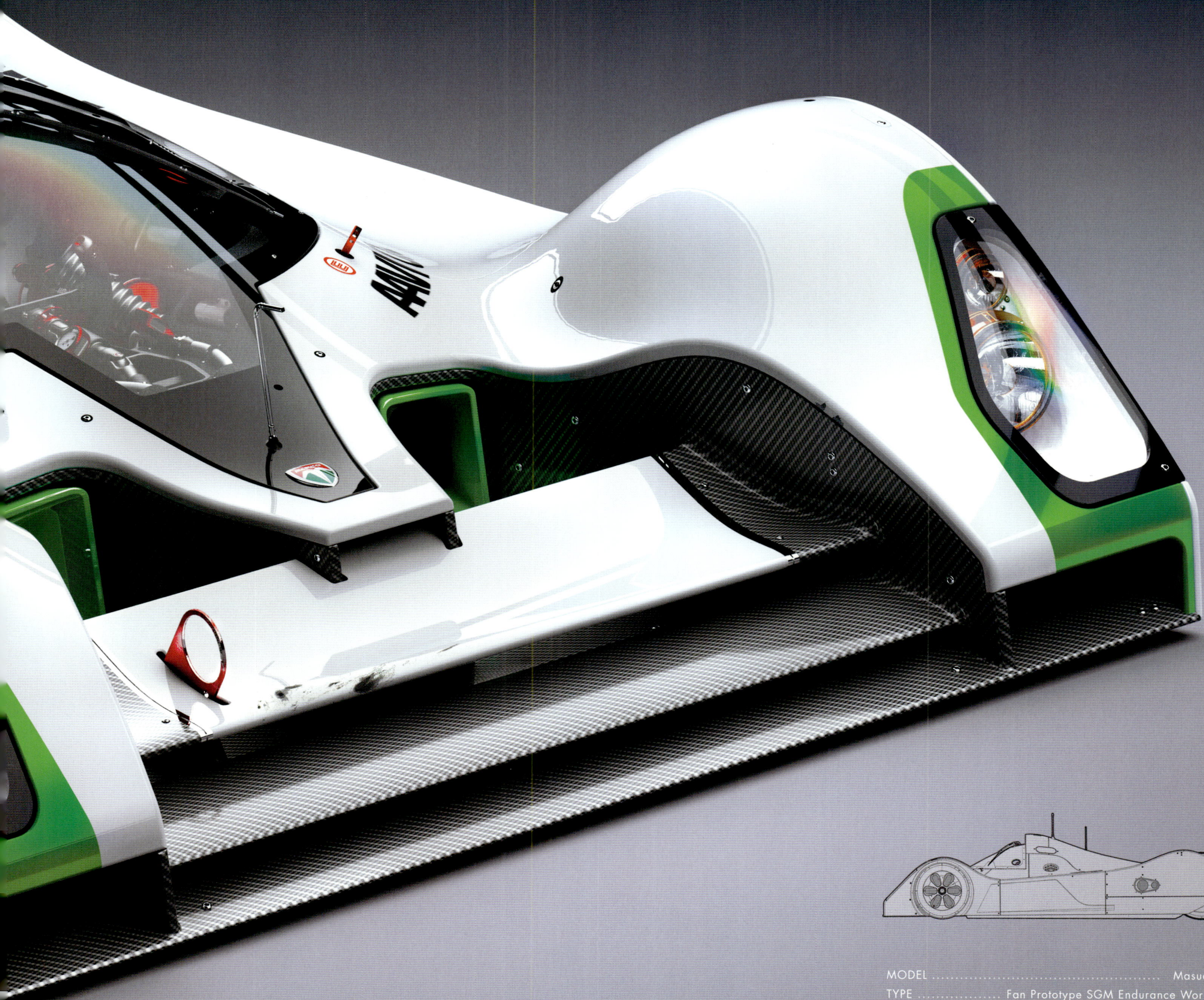

MODEL	Masucci X-5
TYPE	Fan Prototype SGM Endurance World Cup
YEAR	1981
DESIGNER	Filomeno Masucci
ENGINE	Masucci V12 5998cc
POWER OUTPUT	886 hp
TOP SPEED	448 km/h / 278 mph
PINCIPLE DRIVER	Pia Saravese / Jay McQuade
L / W / H	4146mm / 2000mm / 957mm
WHEELBASE	2970mm

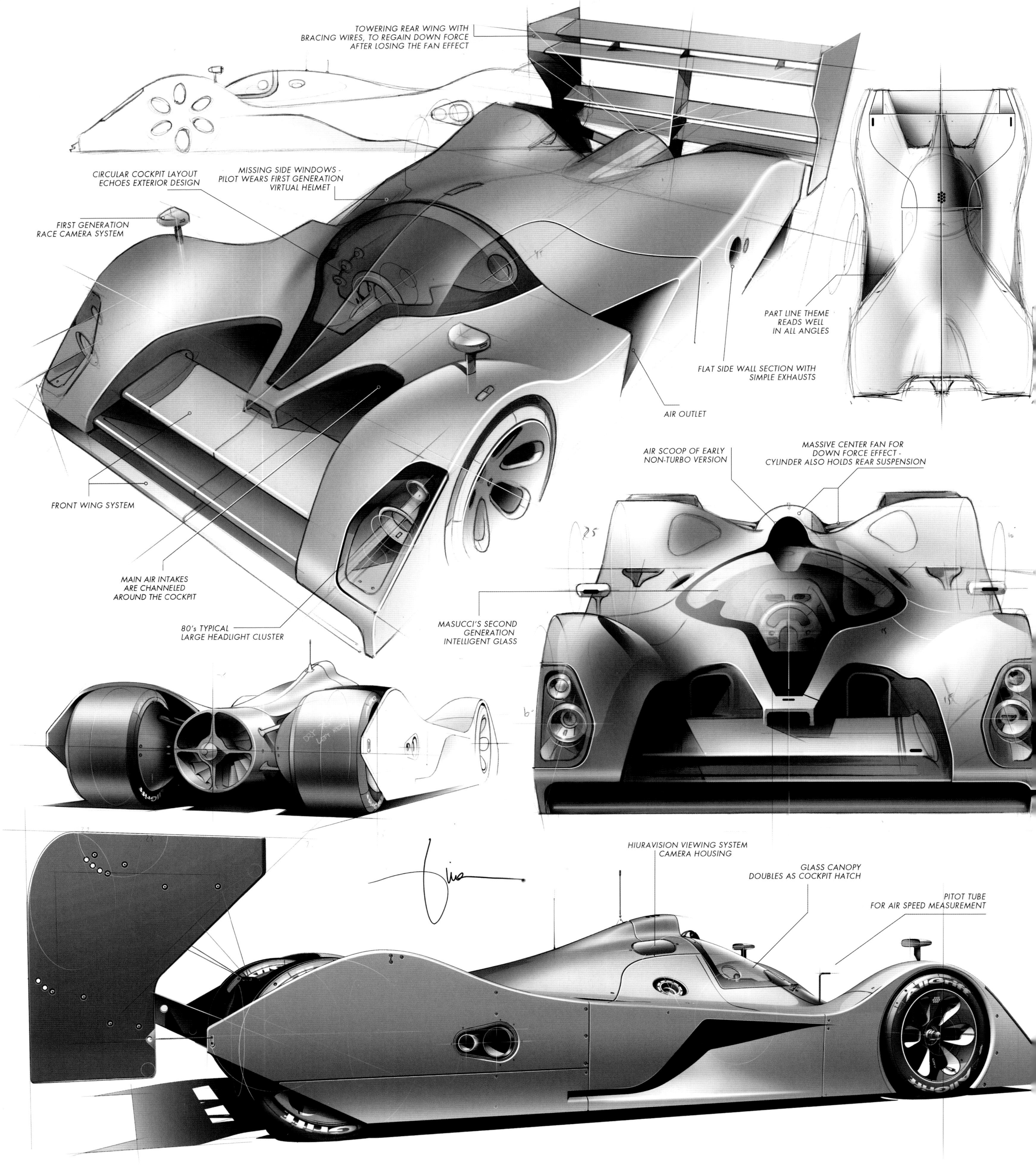
TOWERING REAR WING WITH
BRACING WIRES, TO REGAIN DOWN FORCE
AFTER LOSING THE FAN EFFECT
CIRCULAR COCKPIT LAYOUT
ECHOES EXTERIOR DESIGN
MISSING SIDE WINDOWS -
PILOT WEARS FIRST GENERATION
VIRTUAL HELMET
FIRST GENERATION
RACE CAMERA SYSTEM
PART LINE THEME
READS WELL
IN ALL ANGLES
FLAT SIDE WALL SECTION WITH
SIMPLE EXHAUSTS
AIR OUTLET
FRONT WING SYSTEM
AIR SCOOP OF EARLY
NON-TURBO VERSION
MASSIVE CENTER FAN FOR
DOWN FORCE EFFECT -
CYLINDER ALSO HOLDS REAR SUSPENSION
MAIN AIR INTAKES
ARE CHANNELED
AROUND THE COCKPIT
80's TYPICAL
LARGE HEADLIGHT CLUSTER
MASUCCI'S SECOND
GENERATION
INTELLIGENT GLASS
HIURAVISION VIEWING SYSTEM
CAMERA HOUSING
GLASS CANOPY
DOUBLES AS COCKPIT HATCH
PITOT TUBE
FOR AIR SPEED MEASUREMENT

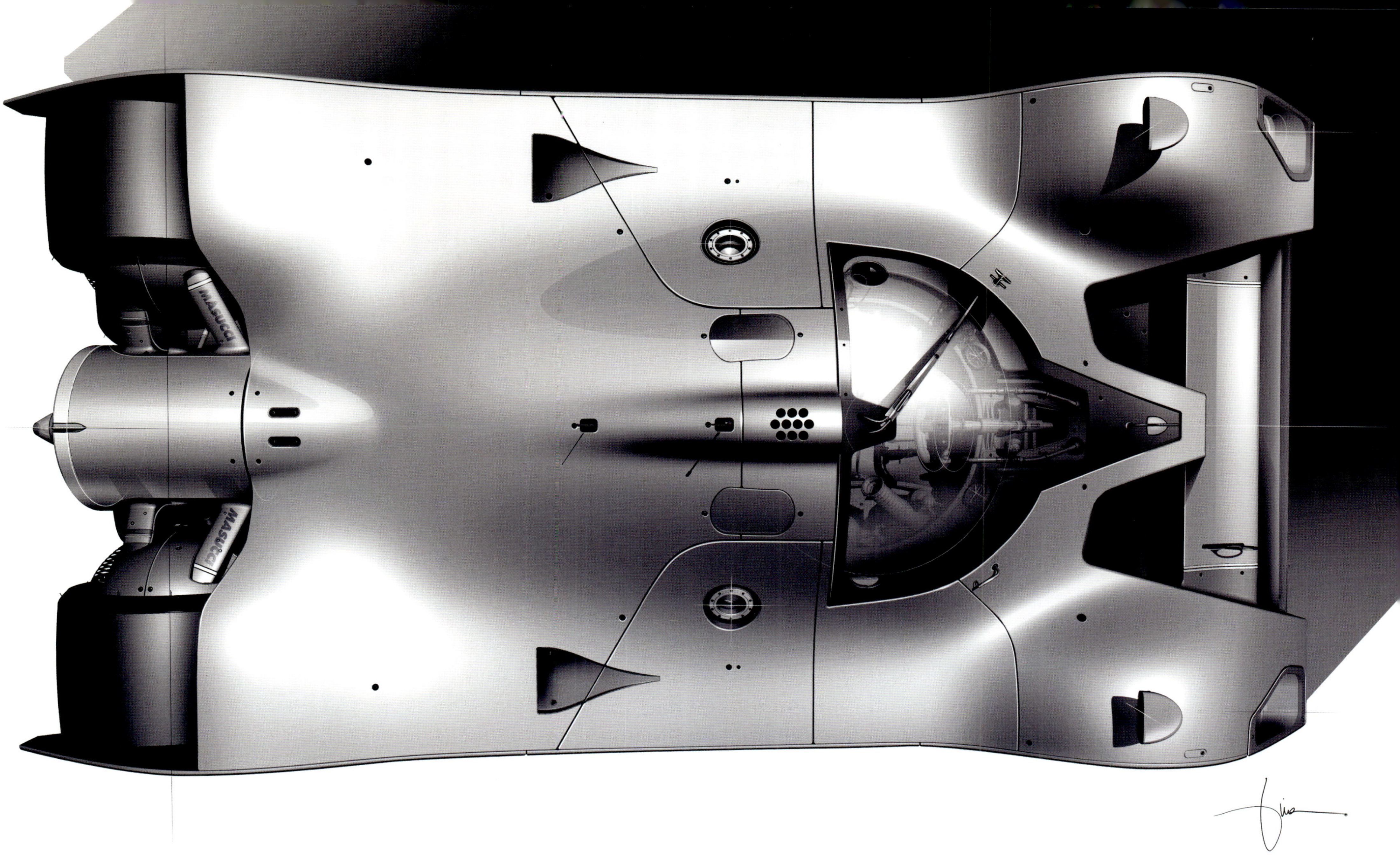

DESIGN PHASE MASUCCI X5
A MONSTER OF THE '80s

A monster of the '80s. Design is solving current or future problems. Designing a fictitious car from the past is therefore an unusual design task, specific to the world of fantasy and storytelling. The X-5 tells the story of Italian constructor extraordinaire Don Filomeno Masucci, motor racing icon, known to push the limits at times too far.

The original design of the Masucci X-5 Prototype is first and foremost a fan car concept—a configuration in which a large fan sucks air from the sealed underside of the car to glue it on the road. In the real world, the concept reached fame with the unforgettable Chaparral 2J and was even briefly tried in F1, with Gordon Murray's 1978 Brabham BT46. The X-5 plays an advanced '80s car in this story, hence its inspiration from that exciting period of racing. The list includes the mighty Porsche 956, the Sauber Mercedes C9, and the elegant XJR-14 from Jaguar. The nose of the X-5 vaguely brings to mind the stunning Peugeot 905 Evo 2, a French marvel developed under the auspices of Jean Todt not long before he joined Scuderia Ferrari.

Modern racing, even in this fantasy setting, has rules. The Endurance Cup is governed by the Société Globale de Moteurs (SGM). It is this organization that declared the groundbreaking vacuum fan of the Masucci X-5 illegal immediately after its presentation, even though it fit into a loophole in the rule books. It took Masucci years to adjust the great X-5 chassis to winged downforce and it would finally win many races as the X-6 Turbo.

Un monstre des années 80. Le design résoud les problèmes actuels ou futurs. Concevoir une voiture fictive du passé implique des audaces propres à l'univers du conte fantastique. L'histoire de la X-5 est celle d'une extraordinaire icône de la course automobile, Don Filomeno Masucci, connu pour repousser toutes les limites parfois trop loin.

Le concept de la X-5 « Prototipo » est avant tout celui d'une voiture à effet de sol. Une turbine aspire l'air sous la voiture et la « colle » ainsi à la piste. Concept devenu célèbre avec l'inoubliable Chaparral 2J, et même brièvement essayé en F1 avec la Brabham BT46 développée par Gordon Murray en 1978. La X-5 tient un grand rôle dans cette histoire. Voiture de pointe des années 80, elle illustre cette période qui est celle de la redoutable Porsche 956, des Sauber-Mercedes C9 et de l'élégante Jaguar XJR-14. Le nez de la X-5 évoque celui de l'époustouflante Peugeot 905 Evo 2, merveille française conçue sous les auspices de Jean Todt, peu avant qu'il ne rejoigne la Scuderia Ferrari.

La compétition doit répondre à des règles, et celles qui régissent la Coupe d'Endurance sont édictées par la Société Globale de Moteurs. C'est la SGM qui déclara illégal le système d'aspiration de la X-5 juste après sa présentation, alors que celui-ci repondait simplement à une faille du règlement. Par la suite, Masucci adapta le châssis de la X-5 à celui d'un schéma aérodynamique plus classique, à ailerons. Le résultat donna la phénoménale X-6 Turbo.

Ein Monster der Achtziger. Design soll aktuelle und zukünftige Probleme lösen. Den Masucci X-5 zu entwerfen, der in der Vergangenheit tatsächlich hätte existieren können, war daher eine ungewöhnliche Aufgabe. Zusätzlich sollte sich in dem Wagen die Geschichte des umtriebigen italienischen Konstrukteurs Don Filomeno Masucci widerspiegeln – eine Ikone des Motorsports, die stets im roten Bereich des Machbaren operierte.

Das Design des Masucci X-5 Prototyps basiert auf dem Unterdruckprinzip. Ein am Heck platziertes Gebläse saugt Luft vom versiegelten Unterboden ab, um den Wagen brutal auf die Straße zu pressen. Tatsächlich berühmt geworden ist das Konzept im unvergessenen Chaparral 2J; im Brabham BT46 wurde es sogar in der Formel 1 eingesetzt. In meinen fiktiven 80er Jahren war der X-5 der revolutionäre Sportwagen schlechthin. Beim Zeichnen inspirierten mich dementsprechend der legendäre Porsche 956, der fortschrittliche Sauber-Mercedes C9 und der elegante Jaguar XJR-14. Die offene Front des X-5 erinnert an den Peugeot 905 Evo 2, der seinerzeit unter Jean Todt entwickelt wurde.

Das hier verwendete Reglement stammt von der Société Globale de Moteurs (SGM), der Rennorganisation, die ich für dieses Buch eigens erfunden habe. Und es war die SGM, die das Gebläse des X-5 nach dessen Vorstellung kurzerhand verbot, obwohl eine schwammige Formulierung im Regelwerk dieses durchaus erlaubt hätte. Es dauerte Jahre, bis das gute X-5 Chassis auf Flügel abgestimmt war und als X-6 Turbo endlich um Siege fuhr.

AFTER 1986 I FOUND TIME FOR MY FAMILY, BUT I CAN'T STOP THINKING ABOUT RACING.

Filomeno Masucci | **MOST SUCCESSFUL CONSTRUCTOR IN RACING HISTORY, SEEN HERE IN 2027 AT THE AGE OF 95**

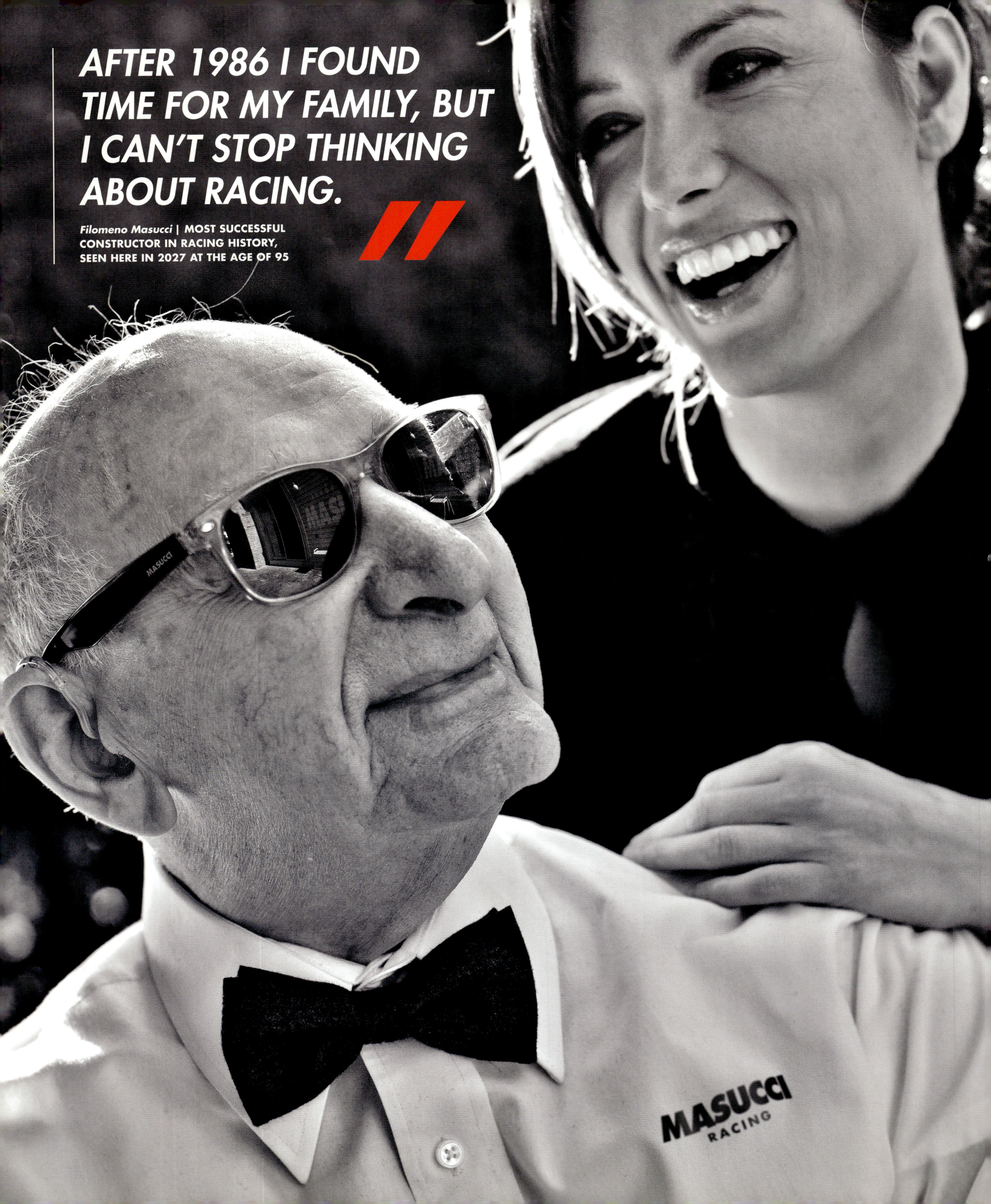

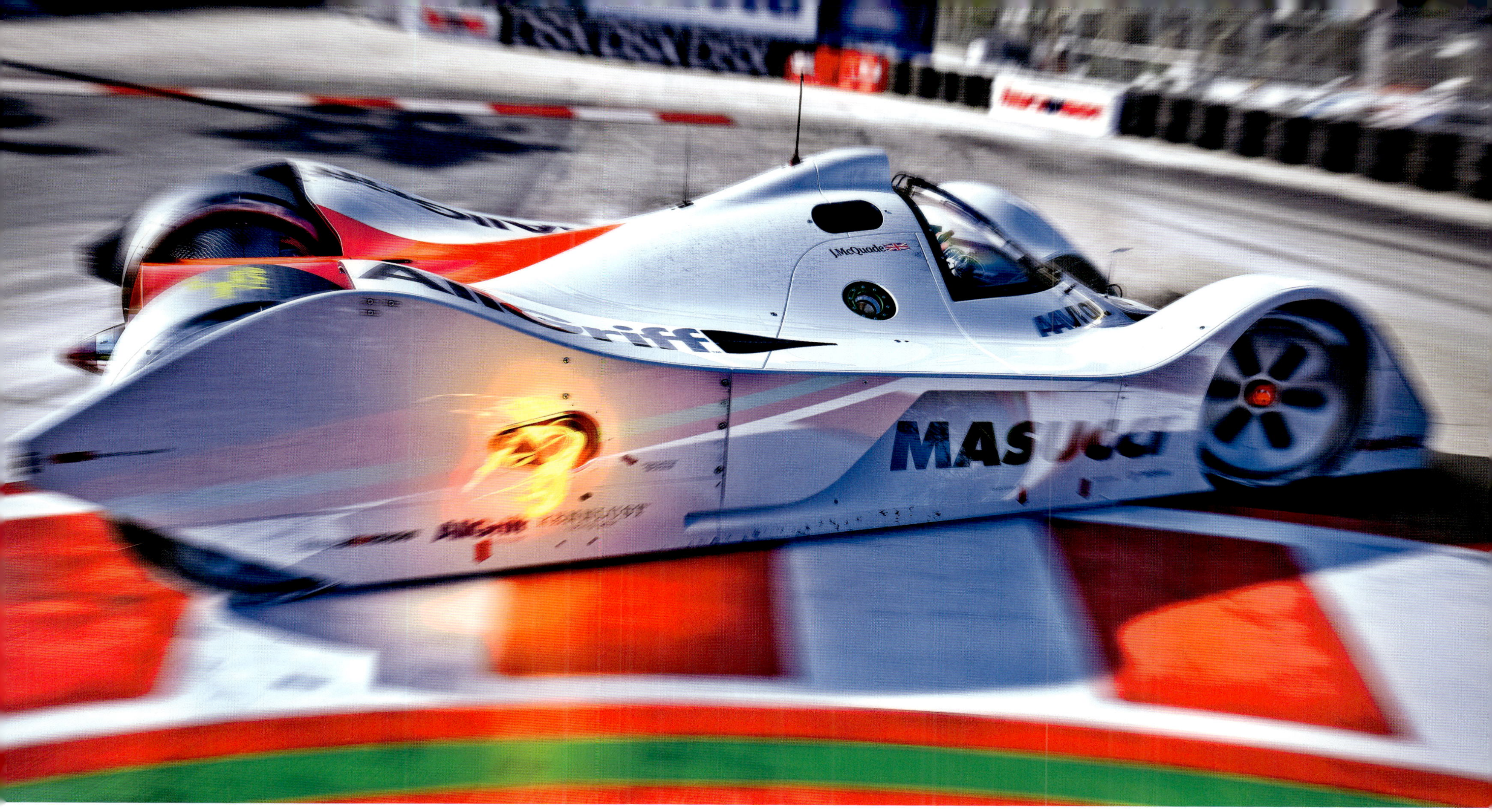

DON**FILOMENO**MASUCCI
THE MASTERMIND OF RACING MACHINES

The mastermind of racing machines. Filomeno "Filo" Masucci (born 1933 in Turin) is a renowned Italian designer, engineer, and entrepreneur who brought the once small Masucci Racing Team of his father to world fame. Starting in 1916, Filo's father, Giovanni Masucci (1893–1953), was the head of Industria Masucci. Originally known for high-end sewing and coffee machines, during World War I they became known for innovative aircraft. Giovanni was a petrolhead and ran a small but successful racing team on the side. Even through World War II, he kept experimenting with all kinds of racing designs. He died in 1953 while setting a new world speed record in a Masucci speed plane.

Filo shared his father's passion for racing and expanded the small Masucci Racing operation into the largest and most successful racing group of all time. His trademarks between 1956 and 1986 were unusual concepts, extremely lightweight construction, and uncompromised engineering. People said he admired fine machines more than fine pilots, but the many drivers who became champions with him admired Filo Masucci as a pioneer in technology and design. The controversial X-5/X-6 project, however, was infamous for being too dangerous. After the fatal crash of his only driver friend, Jay McQuade, in the Masucci X-6 Turbo in 1986, Filo closed down Masucci Racing and retired. Only in 2027, with the appearance of Vic Cooper, did Masucci Racing return to the paddock. Filo's son Luca Masucci would run all racing efforts under the eyes of his now 95-year-old father, who can be seen here with one of his six granddaughters, Deanna, in 2027. "After 1986 I found more time for my family," Filo said. "But I can't stop thinking about racing."

Le cerveau des machines de course. Filomeno « Filo » Masucci, né en 1933 à Turin, est à la fois entrepreneur, ingénieur et designer. A force de travail, c'est lui qui a hissé la modeste écurie Masucci Racing au sommet. Son père Giovanni Masucci (1893-1953) dirigeait depuis 1916 Industria Masucci, qui concevait initialement des moulins à café et des machines à coudre, et se diversifia avec des avions durant la Première Guerre mondiale. Parallèlement à ces activités, Giovanni, véritable passionné d'engins motorisés, mit en place une petite équipe de compétition, qui connut quelques succès avec des créations toujours à la pointe de l'innovation. Même pendant la Seconde Guerre mondiale, l'équipe continua de travailler. Giovanni mourut en 1953, sur le point d'établir un record de vitesse en avion.

Filo partageait avec son père la passion de la course et la volonté de réussite pour Masucci Racing. Entre 1956 et 1986, il s'illustra par son sens de l'innovation : concepts inédits, constructions ultra-légères, et ingénierie sans compromis. Il avait la réputation de préférer les machines aux pilotes, mais ceux qui devinrent champions avec lui admiraient le pionnier en matière de technologie et de design. Le projet X-5/X-6 était controversé car très dangereux. Après l'accident fatal de Jay McQuade en 1986, Filo mit fin aux activités de Masucci Racing. Ce n'est qu'en 2027, avec l'arrivée de Vic Cooper, que l'écurie réapparut sur les circuits. Luca Masucci la dirigeait, sous l'observation de son père âgé de 95 ans. Le « cerveau » pose ici avec l'une de ses six petites-filles, Deanna, en 2027 : « Après 1986 j'ai consacré plus de temps à ma famille. Mais la course occupait encore toutes mes pensées. »

Der Virtuose der Rennmaschinen. Filomeno „Filo" Masucci (geb. 1933 in Turin) ist ein renommierter italienischer Designer, Ingenieur und Unternehmer. Er brachte den kleinen Rennstall seines Vaters, Masucci Racing, zu Weltruhm. Filos Vater Giovanni Masucci (1893-1953) führte seit 1916 die Firma Industria Masucci, die ursprünglich für hochwertige Kaffee- und Nähmaschinen und seit dem Ersten Weltkrieg auch für innovative Flugzeuge bekannt war. Giovanni hatte Benzin im Blut und unterhielt ein kleines Rennteam. Selbst während des Zweiten Weltkriegs versuchte er, seine verwegenen Rennmaschinen weiterzuentwickeln. 1953 kam er bei einem Masucci-Flugrekordversuch ums Leben.

Sohn Filo, von der Rennfaszination des Vaters längst angesteckt, übernahm die Geschäfte und machte Masucci Racing zum grössten und erfolgreichsten Rennstall aller Zeiten. Seine Markenzeichen zwischen 1956 und 1986: extremer Leichtbau und kompromisslose Ingenieurskunst. Es hieß, Filo würde seine Technologie immer über die Piloten stellen. Wer aber die Chance bekam, auf einem Masucci zu gewinnen, nahm das hin und bewunderte den Konstrukteur als besessenen Designpionier. Das X-5/X-6 Projekt allerdings war von Anfang an höchst umstritten. Der tragischer Tod seines einzigen Fahrerfreundes Jay McQuade in einem Masucci X-6 Turbo veranlasste Filo 1986, das Team aus dem Motorsport zurückzuziehen. Es sollte bis zum Jahr 2027 dauern, bis Masucci Racing mit Vic Cooper als Fahrer in den Rennsport zurückkehren würde. Die Geschäfte führte Filomenos Sohn Luca, unter den Augen des nun 95-jährigen Vaters Filo. Links ist Filo 2027 zu sehen (mit Deanna, einer seiner sechs Enkeltöchter): „Seit 1986 habe ich endlich Zeit für meine Familie gefunden. Aber ich muss ständig an den Rennsport denken."

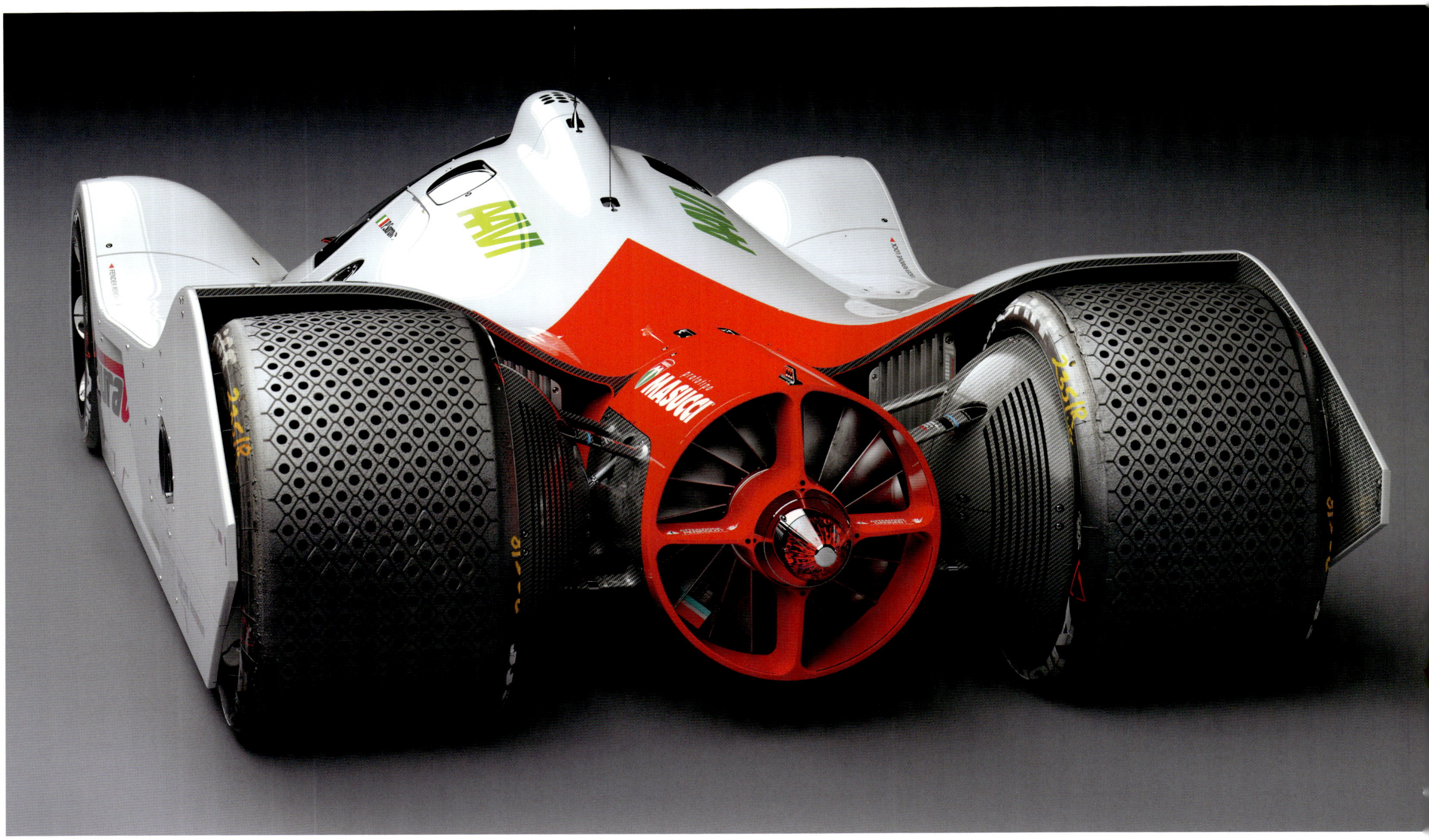

1981 MASUCCI PROTOTIPO X5

THE WHITE VACUUM CLEANER

The white vacuum cleaner. In 1981, Masucci celebrated 65 years of successful motor racing, and one of their most controversial machines was born: the X-5. It later came as a shock that the pinnacle of Filomeno Masucci's mechanical genius would trigger the end of Masucci Racing for many years.

The revolutionary X-5 fan car was developed in cooperation with Hiuravison, a Japanese technology empire. The project was a huge financial risk. In its opening season, 1982, the SGM Endurance Cup promised prestige and global brand recognition. At the same time, its rules offered many interesting possibilities. The X-5 was designed for the SGM Endurance Cup Super Class, and exploited a loophole in the regulations to use a fan concept. A large fan in the rear of the car sucked air from underneath the mostly sealed-off vehicle to create tremendous downforce. This concept had been on Masucci's mind for a few years, but now the moment had come to stun the world. Without adding drag from aerodynamic wings, the X-5 could achieve enormous cornering speeds. Masucci's chief test driver, Pia Saravese, even confirmed vision problems after a maximum lateral G-force test in this brutally fast monster. The virtual helmet viewing system by Hiuravision was another manifestation of Masucci's avantegarde thinking: troublesome but promising, it made side windows on the car obsolete, resulting in an even stiffer chassis. The suspension units were entirely made of light and hyper-strong carbon-fiber, also a first in this racing class. Three white prototypes were built and two still exist today.

L'aspirateur blanc. En 1981, l'année où elle célébrait 65 ans de succès en compétition, l'écurie Masucci Racing présenta sa machine la plus controversée, la X-5. Paradoxalement, cette création représentant la quintessence du génie de Filomeno Masucci était aussi celle qui allait précipiter la disparition de son écurie.

La X-5 à effet de sol, engin révolutionnaire, avait été développée à grand risque financier avec Hiuravison, conglomérat high-tech japonais. Les nouvelles règles de la Coupe d'Endurance offraient d'intéressantes opportunités techniques pour la saison d'ouverture de 1982, ouvrant ainsi le champ du prestige et de la notoriété mondiale. La X-5 avait été conçu pour la Super Class de la Coupe d'Endurance SGM. Une faille dans la réglementation permit d'utiliser un nouveau concept, en l'occurrence une turbine installée à l'arrière et aspirant l'air sous le véhicule, créant ainsi un effet de sol qui générait une adhérence considérable. En s'épargnant la traînée aérodynamique des ailerons, la X-5 pouvait passer les virages à des vitesses phénoménales. Pia Saravese, pilote chargé des essais chez Masucci, eut même des problèmes de vue après un test de force G latérale aux commandes de la X-5 ! Très caractéristique des créations Masucci était le système de vision par casque virtuel mis au point par Hiuravision. Encore sujet à défaillances mais très prometteur, il rendait obsolètes les vitres latérales sur la voiture. Trois prototypes blancs furent construits et deux existent encore aujourd'hui. Notez la suspension arrière en fibre de carbone.

Der weiße Staubsauger. 1981 feierte Masucci Racing sein 65-jähriges Jubiläum. Anlass, ein ganz besonderes Fahrzeug zu entwickeln: den X-5. Dass ausgerechnet diese beeindruckende Vorführung Filo Masuccis technischer Genialität das spätere Aus seines Rennstalls begründen würde, ist eine tragische Episode der Motorsportgeschichte.

Der revolutionäre X-5 wurde unter hohem finanziellen Risiko zusammen mit dem japanischen Technologiekonzern Hiuravision entwickelt. Eine erfolgreiche Teilnahme am SGM Endurance Cup versprach viel Prestige, und das Reglement für die erste Saison 1982 bot zahlreiche interessante, technische Schlupflöcher. Der X-5 war für die SGM Endurance Cup Super Class konstruiert und der Einsatz seiner Unterdruck-Technologie war nur durch eine Lücke im Regelwerk möglich. Eine riesiges Gebläse am Heck saugt Luft unter dem versiegelten Unterboden ab und erzeugt dadurch einen gigantischen Anpressdruck. Mit dem Wagen wurden deshalb extrem hohe Kurvengeschwindigkeiten möglich, ohne Spoiler und Flügel anbauen zu müssen. Masuccis Testfahrerin Pia Saravese berichtete sogar von Sehstörungen, ausgelöst durch die extremen Querbeschleunigungen. Eine weitere Neuheit am X-5, allerdings noch fehleranfällig, war ein virtuelles Helmkamerasystem, das Seitenscheiben überflüssig werden ließ. Außerdem besaß der Jubiläums-Masucci erstmals eine leichte, aber hochstabile Kohlefaseraufhängung. Vom X-5 wurden insgesamt drei Prototypen hergestellt, von denen zwei noch heute existieren.

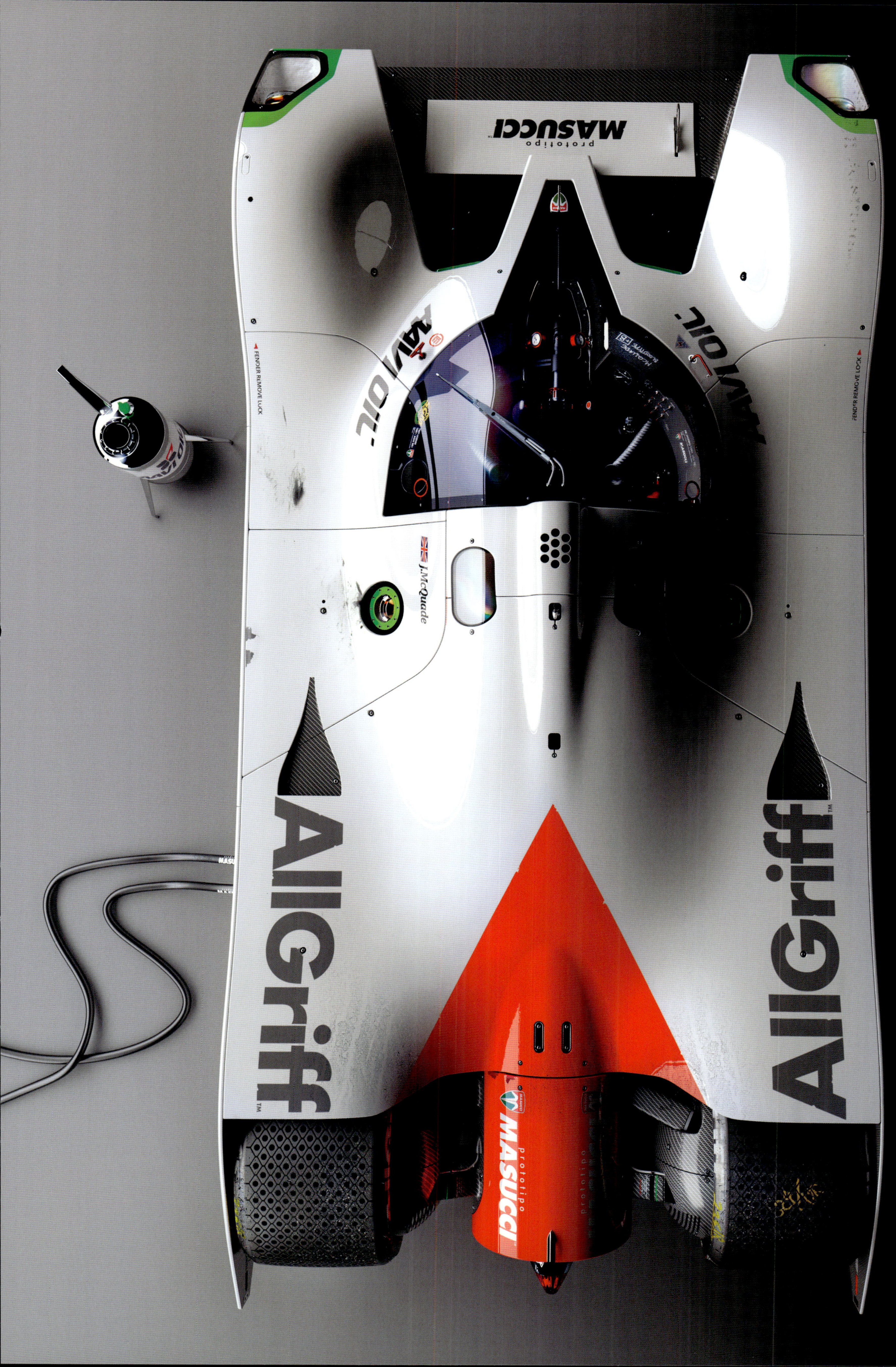
AllGriff
AllGriff
prototipo MASUCCI
MAVI OIL
MAVI OIL
J.McQuade
FENDER REMOVE LOCK
FENDER REMOVE LOCK

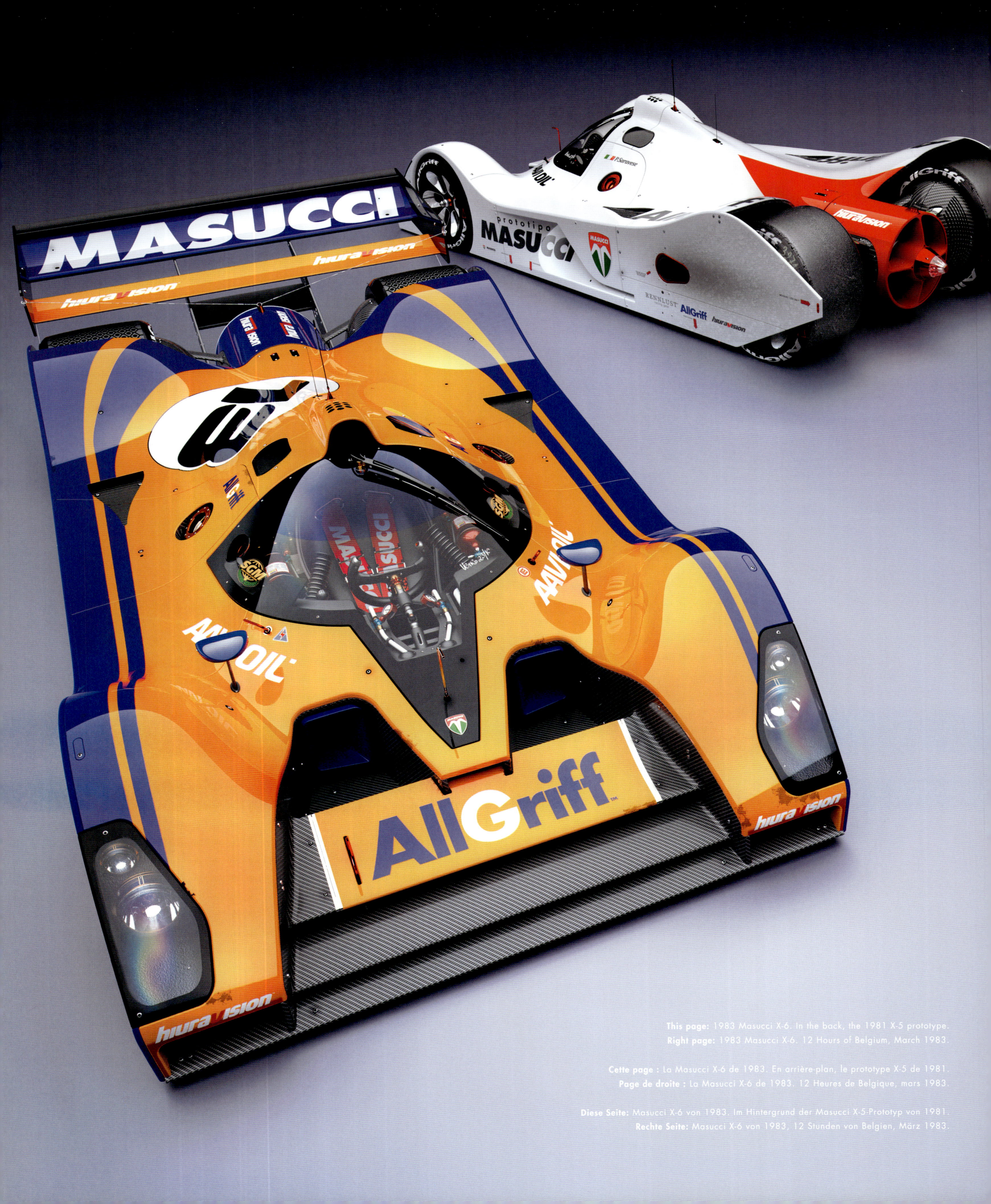

This page: 1983 Masucci X-6. In the back, the 1981 X-5 prototype.
Right page: 1983 Masucci X-6. 12 Hours of Belgium, March 1983.

Cette page : La Masucci X-6 de 1983. En arrière-plan, le prototype X-5 de 1981.
Page de droite : La Masucci X-6 de 1983. 12 Heures de Belgique, mars 1983.

Diese Seite: Masucci X-6 von 1983. Im Hintergrund der Masucci X-5-Prototyp von 1981.
Rechte Seite: Masucci X-6 von 1983, 12 Stunden von Belgien, März 1983.

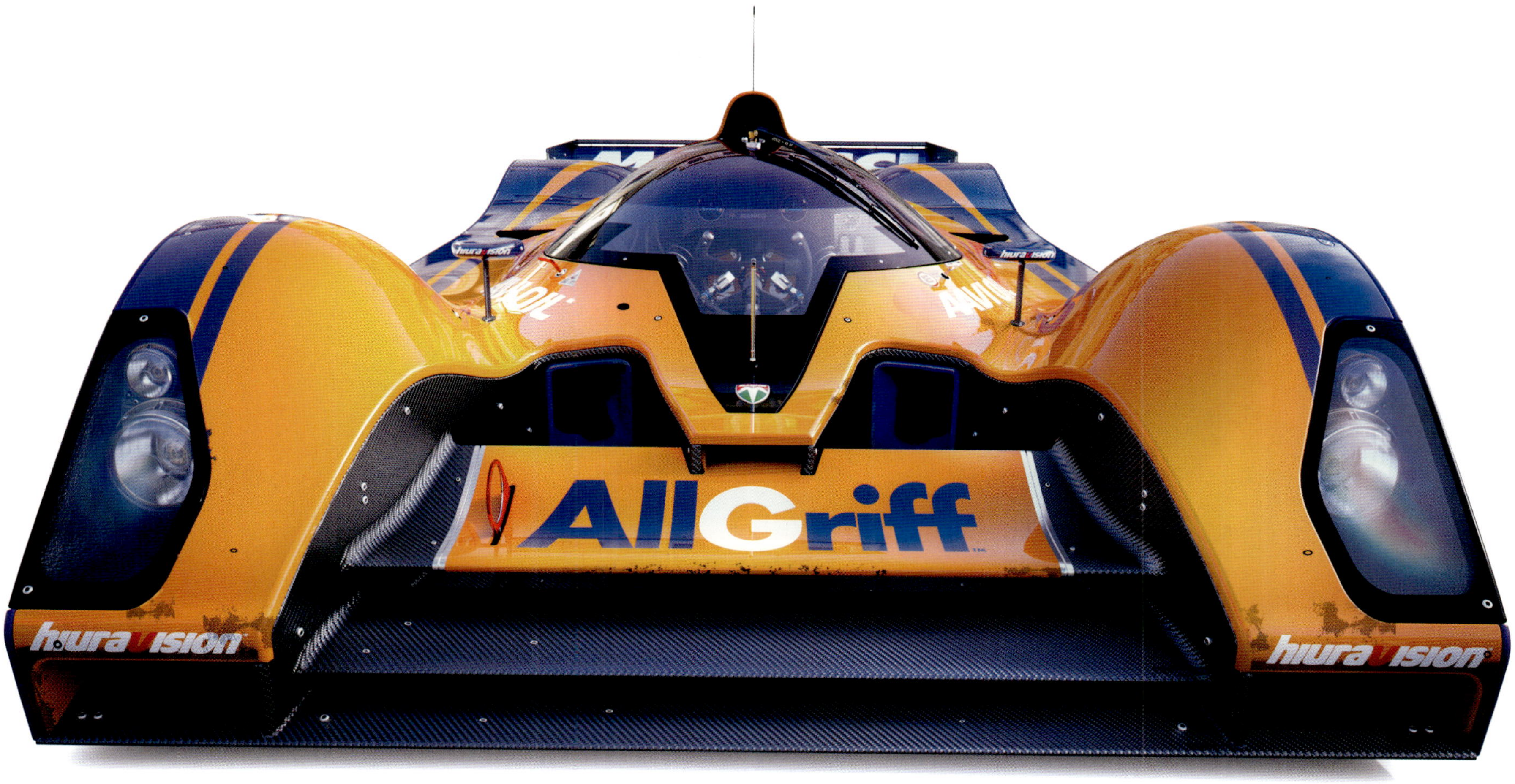

1982-86 MASUCCI X6
THE ORANGE DEMON

The Orange Demon. The Masucci X-6 was the unplanned successor of the ingenious X-5, and raced for five consecutive seasons in the SGM Endurance Cup. The X-6 marks the tragic turning point in Masucci's incredible career.

When the clever X-5 was presented in 1981, SGM clearly saw its potential to win every single race. They used their power to declare it illegal, and Filo Masucci had no choice but to scrap the brilliant fan concept and start again, but not quite from scratch. He kept the extremely costly X-5 chassis and started to adjust the car to aerodynamic downforce with huge wings and a new underbody. The gigantic fan housing in the rear part of the structure was now used for engine cooling. The X-6 showed good pace, but by 1984 had won only one race. The naturally aspired V12 was too unreliable over long distances! That changed in 1985, when turbocharged engines were allowed and Masucci had the right card up his sleeve: the new massive 6998cc V12 engine was durable and with four turbos and electronic management it delivered up to 1620 hp. Combined with the now well-tested X-6 chassis, it was a winner. Known as the "Orange Demon," the X-6 Turbo could be easily recognized by the missing roof air scoop. It won McQuade the 1985 championship (see page 26). By 1986, the competition had copied most of Masucci's ideas. Under intense pressure, McQuade won the first two races by mere seconds. On June 12, 1986, he lost control of his X-6 Turbo, crashed and died. The causes of this fatal crash were never fully determined. Filomeno Masucci could not overcome the loss of McQuade, his only driver friend and retired immediately.

Le Démon orange. La Masucci X-6, qui succéda à la X-5 alors même que son existence n'était pas prévue au départ, disputa cinq saisons de la Coupe d'endurance SGM. Elle marqua aussi un tournant tragique dans le parcours de Masucci.

Quand la X-5 fut présentée en 1981, la SGM en mesura immédiatement tout le potentiel. Elle pesa alors de tout son poids pour l'interdire, et Filo Masucci dut abandonner son projet pour repartir d'une page blanche… ou presque ! Il conserva en effet le châssis de la X-5 et travailla l'aérodynamisme à l'aide d'imposants ailerons et de nouveaux soubassements. Quant au grand « ventilateur » arrière, il servait maintenant à refroidir le moteur. Bien que très rapide, la X-6 ne gagna qu'une seule course jusqu'en 1984, le V12 atmosphérique multipliant les défaillances sur longues distances. L'autorisation du turbo, en 1985, changea les choses : le nouveau V12 de 6998 cm³ s'avérait fiable, tandis que la greffe de quatre turbos lui permettait de développer 1620 ch. La combinaison de ce moteur et d'un châssis éprouvé firent de la X-6 Turbo la voiture à battre. Au volant du « Démon orange », que l'on reconnaissait à sa prise d'air manquante sur le toit, McQuade remporta le championnat 1985 (voir p.26). Pour la saison 1986, la concurrence reprit à son compte la plupart des idées de Masucci. Soumis à une intense pression, McQuade ne gagna les deux premières courses que d'une poignée de secondes. Mais le 12 juin, il perdit le contrôle de sa X-6 Turbo dans des circonstances qui restent obscures. Filomeno mit un terme immédiat à ses activités. Il ne se remit jamais de la perte de McQuade, le seul véritable ami qu'il eut jamais parmi les pilotes.

Der Orange Teufel. Der Masucci X-6 gilt als verhängnisvoller Wendepunkt in Masuccis einmaliger Konstrukteurslaufbahn. Der Wagen ist ein erzwungener Abkömmling des genialen X-5 und wurde fünf Jahre in Folge im Endurance Cup eingesetzt.

Nachdem das raffinierte Unterdruckgebläse des weißen X-5 durch die SGM kurzerhand verboten worden war – zu überlegen würde der Wagen nach dem Geschmack der SGM gewinnen – musste Masucci schnell ein Lösung finden. Er hielt an dem mit großem Aufwand entwickelten Chassis des X-5 fest und begann, den Wagen aerodynamisch auf riesige Heckflügel umzustellen. Das auffallende Gebläsegehäuse am Heck blieb als tragendes Element erhalten, wurde jetzt jedoch nur zur Motorkühlung verwendet. Der orange X-6 war schnell, gewann aber bis Ende 1984 nur ein einziges Rennen … Der Sechs-Liter-V12 Sauger war einfach nicht standhaft genug! Das änderte sich 1985, als im Endurance Cup Turbos erlaubt wurden. Masucci zog sein Ass aus dem Ärmel: ein neues, extrem zuverlässiges Sieben-Liter-V12-Aggregat mit vier Turbos und elektronischem Motormanagement. Mit gigantischen 1620 PS, in einem mittlerweile perfekt abgestimmten Chassis, gewann McQuade auf dem „Orangen Teufel" 1985 die Endurance-Meisterschaft (siehe Seite 26). 1986 hatte die Konkurrenz viele von Masuccis Ideen kopiert und McQuade konnte die ersten zwei Rennen nur knapp behaupten. Am 12. Juni 1986 verunglückte er im Masucci X-6 Turbo tödlich. Die Umstände des Unfalls wurden nie vollständig aufgeklärt. Filomeno Masucci konnte den Verlust von McQuade, seines einzigen Freundes unter den Fahrern, nicht verkraften und zog das Team aus dem Rennsport zurück.

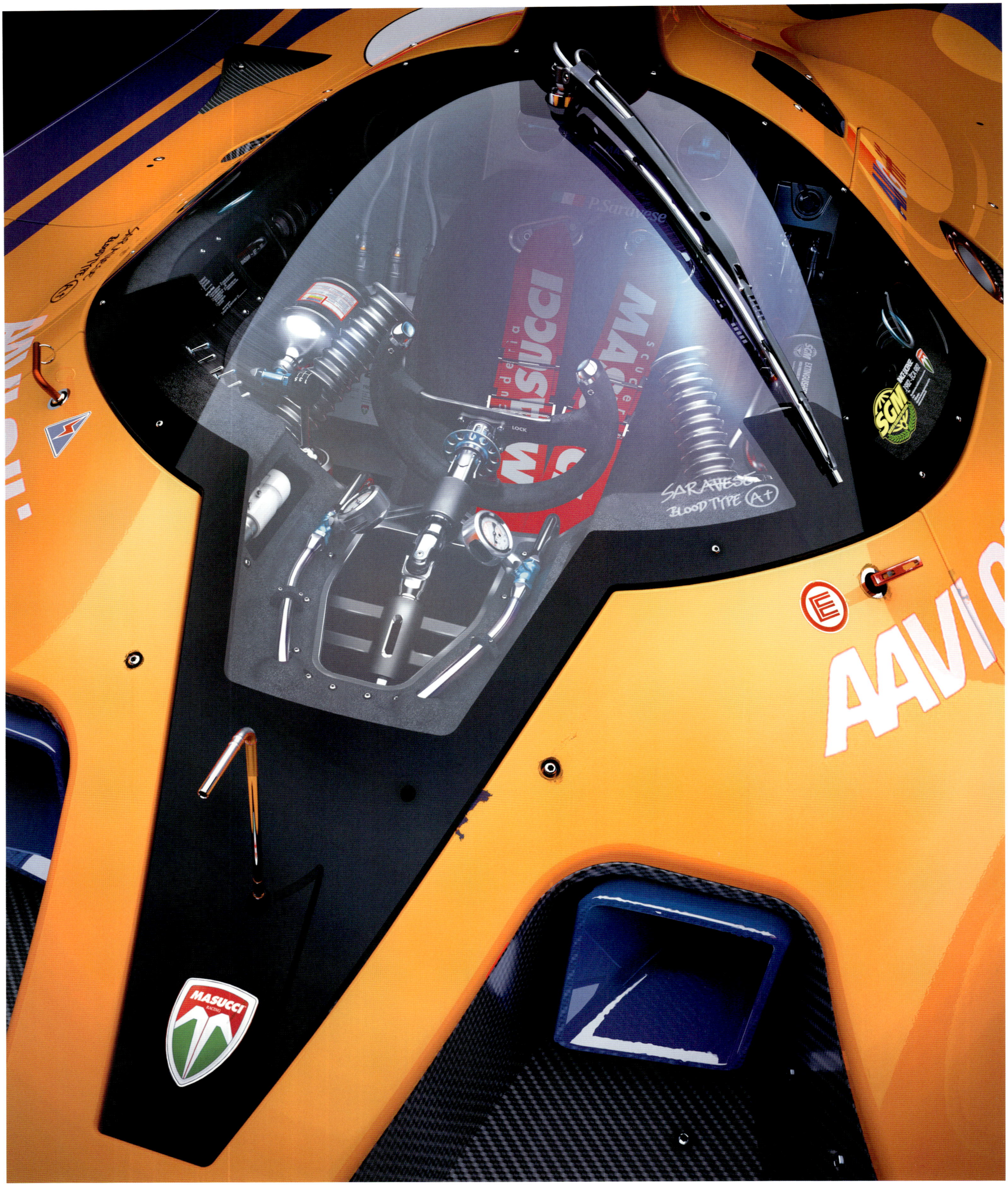
MASUCCI
P.Saravese
LOCK
SARAVESE
BLOOD TYPE A+
SGM
MASUCCI
RACING

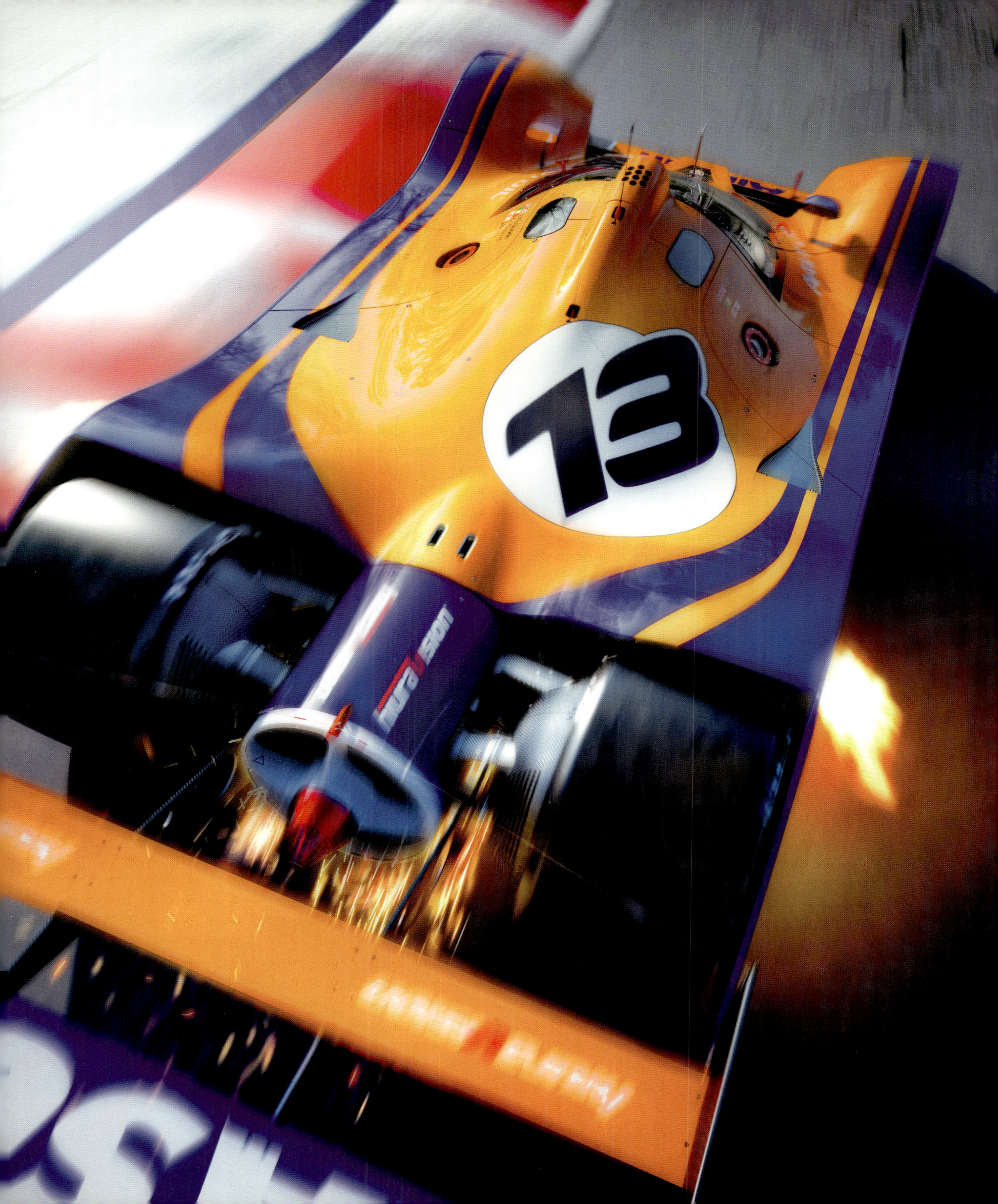
13

The 1985 X-6 Turbo, which won McQuade a championship. Note the missing air scoop on top.

La X-6 Turbo 1985. Notez l'absence de prise d'air sur le toit.

Der 1985 X-6 Turbo, mit dem McQuade zum Titel raste. Zu erkennen am fehlenden Lufteinlass auf dem Dach.

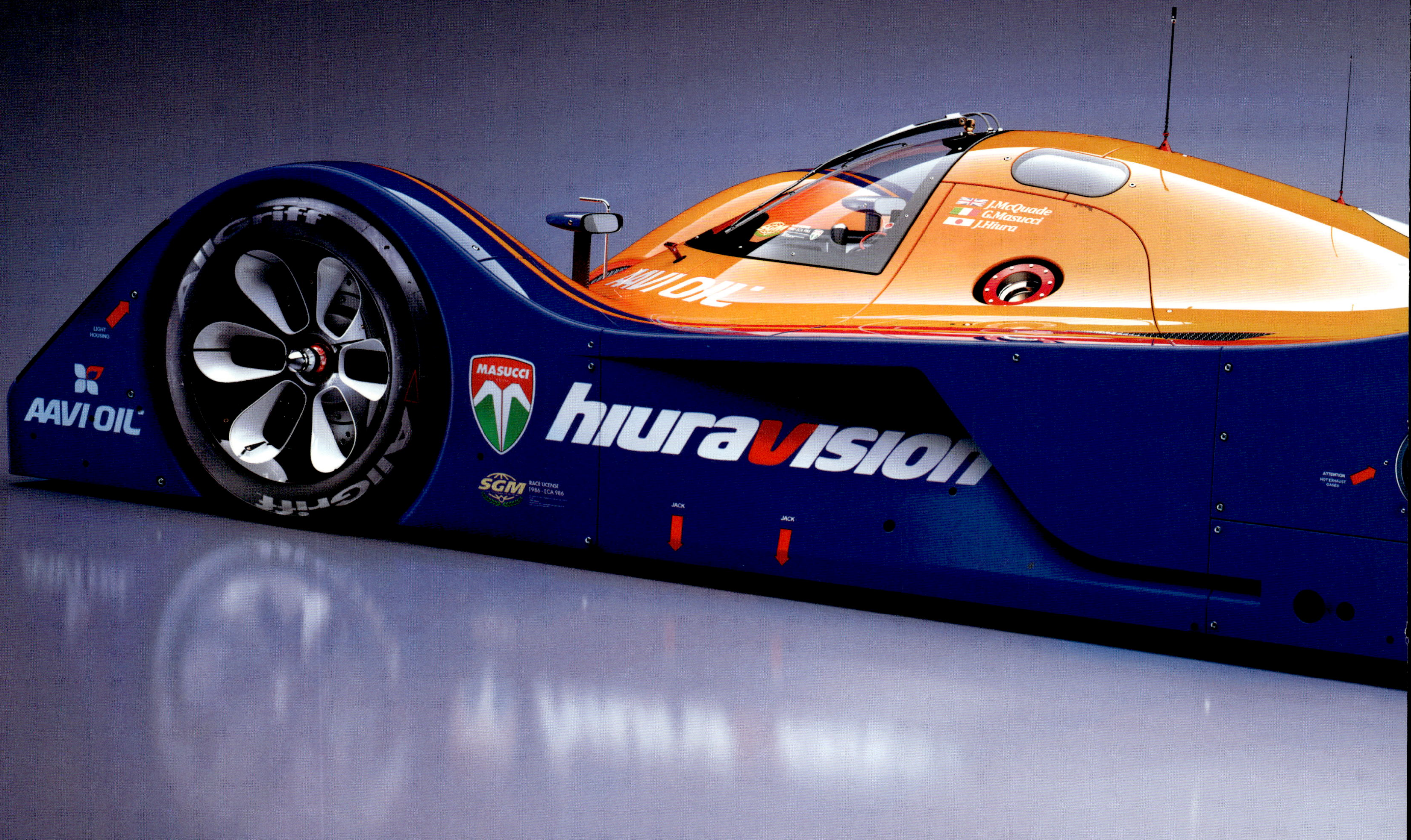

At the 1982 season opening in Pescara, Italy, the Masucci X-6 stunned the crowd with enormous rear wings in various shapes and sizes. This was the clearly visible attempt at getting downforce back into the X-5 concept after the SGM outlawed its vacuum fan. The fan itself was still in place as a structural component and to cool the V12, but had no more effect on aerodynamics. The side skirts, controlling the pressure under the car, were also gone. There was so little time to test the car with a new floor and wing setup that the crowd could witness Masucci testing different configurations during the practice session in Pescara, a situation Filomeno felt extremely uncomfortable with. The race license and starting number 13—the number that McQuade had used since the '50s—were approved just moments before the practice session started. The X-6 in the hands of Masucci veteran driver Jay McQuade showed promising speeds. It was obvious that the car had some potential even without its innovative ground effect, but was still far away from Pia Saravese's record-shattering performances in winter testing with the fan running.

The rest is history, the X-6 Turbo won the 1985 championship and later killed Masucci's favorite driver, Jay McQuade, in 1986. All Masucci could say was, "I hereby announce the withdrawal of Scuderia Masucci from all racing activities. The personal loss is too painful." It would not be until 2027 that the name Masucci returned to racing. Enter Vic Cooper.

En 1982, à l'ouverture de la saison à Pescara, en Italie, la Masucci X-6 créa la surprise avec ses spectaculaires appendices à l'arrière, censés améliorer la déportance après la mise à l'index de la turbine par la SGM. Celle-ci restait toutefois en place, à la fois en tant que composante structurelle et pour refroidir le V12, mais sans effet sur l'aérodynamisme. Les bas de caisse, permettant de contrôler la pression sous la voiture avaient quant à eux disparu. L'écurie Masucci avait eu très peu de temps pour tester la voiture dans cette nouvelle configuration. Elle dut mettre à profit les essais précédant la course pour en finaliser la mise au point, devant la foule. Filomeno se sentait très mal à l'aise. La licence de course et le numéro de départ – le 13, utilisé par Jay McQuade depuis les années 50 – furent validés peu avant le début de la séance. Entre les mains du vétéran McQuade, la X-6 atteignit des vitesses prometteuses. Même sans son brillant concept de turbine, le potentiel était évident. Mais on était encore loin des performances obtenues par Pia Saravese pendant d'hiver.

Le reste appartient à l'histoire. La X-6 Turbo remporta le championnat 1985 et, en 1986, causa la mort de Jay McQuade, pilote préféré de Masucci. Celui-ci trouva seulement la force de déclarer : « Je vous annonce le retrait de la Scuderia Masucci de toutes les activités de compétition. La perte personnelle est trop douloureuse. » Et le nom de Masucci resta éloigné des circuits jusqu'en 2027. Arriva alors un certain Vic Cooper.

Beim Eröffnungslauf 1982 in Pescara schockierte der Masucci X-6 mit seinen mächtigen Heckflügeln die Fans. Da die SGM das Ansauggebläse des X-5 kurzerhand als regelwidrig eingestuft hatte, versuchte Masucci Racing, mit riesigem Flügelwerk dem Wagen als X-6 Version den nötigen Anpressdruck zurückzugeben. Auch die seitlichen Schürzen waren verschwunden. Das Gebläse selbst blieb vorerst installiert, um den V12 zu kühlen, besaß aber keine aerodynamische Funktion mehr. Allerdings hatte das Masucci-Team zu Hause in Turin kaum Zeit, den Wagen zu testen. So musste das offizielle Training in Pescara genutzt werden – sehr zum Unmut des Teamchefs und Perfektionisten Filomeno. Selbst die Rennlizenz für den X-6 und die Startnummer 13 – McQuades Glücksbringer seit den 50er Jahren – wurden erst kurz vor Trainingsbeginn freigegeben. Im ersten Rennen konnte der X-6 mit Jay McQuade am Steuer nur im Mittelfeld mithalten. Doch er zeigte selbst ohne die nun illegale Ansaugtechnik ein hohes Potenzial.

Der Rest ist Geschichte. Der X-6 Turbo brachte 1985 die Meisterschaft, 1986 verlor Jay McQuade in ihm sein Leben. Filomeno Masuccis kurzes Statement sollte seine letzte öffentliche Äußerung für 41 Jahre werden: „Mit Bedauern gebe ich den sofortigen Ausstieg der Scuderia Masucci aus allen Rennaktivitäten bekannt. Der persönliche Verlust ist zu schmerzhaft." Erst 2027 kehrte der Name Masucci an die Rennstrecken zurück. Es gab wieder einen Grund: Vic Cooper.

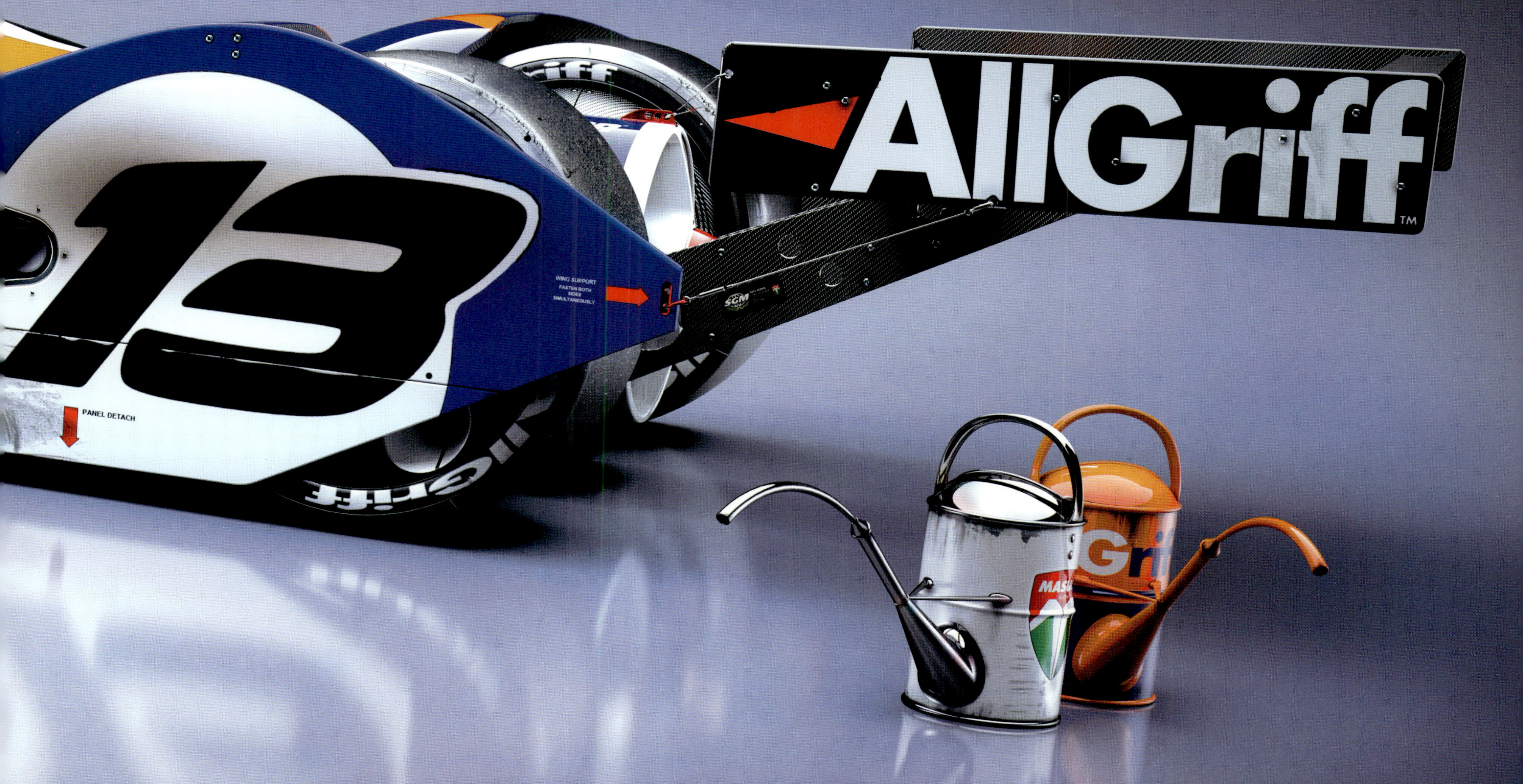

I HEREBY ANNOUNCE THE WITHDRAWAL OF SCUDERIA MASUCCI FROM ALL RACING ACTIVITIES. THE PERSONAL LOSS IS TOO PAINFUL.

Filomeno Masucci 1986 | AFTER THE FATAL ACCIDENT OF JAY MCQUADE, FATHER OF VIC COOPER

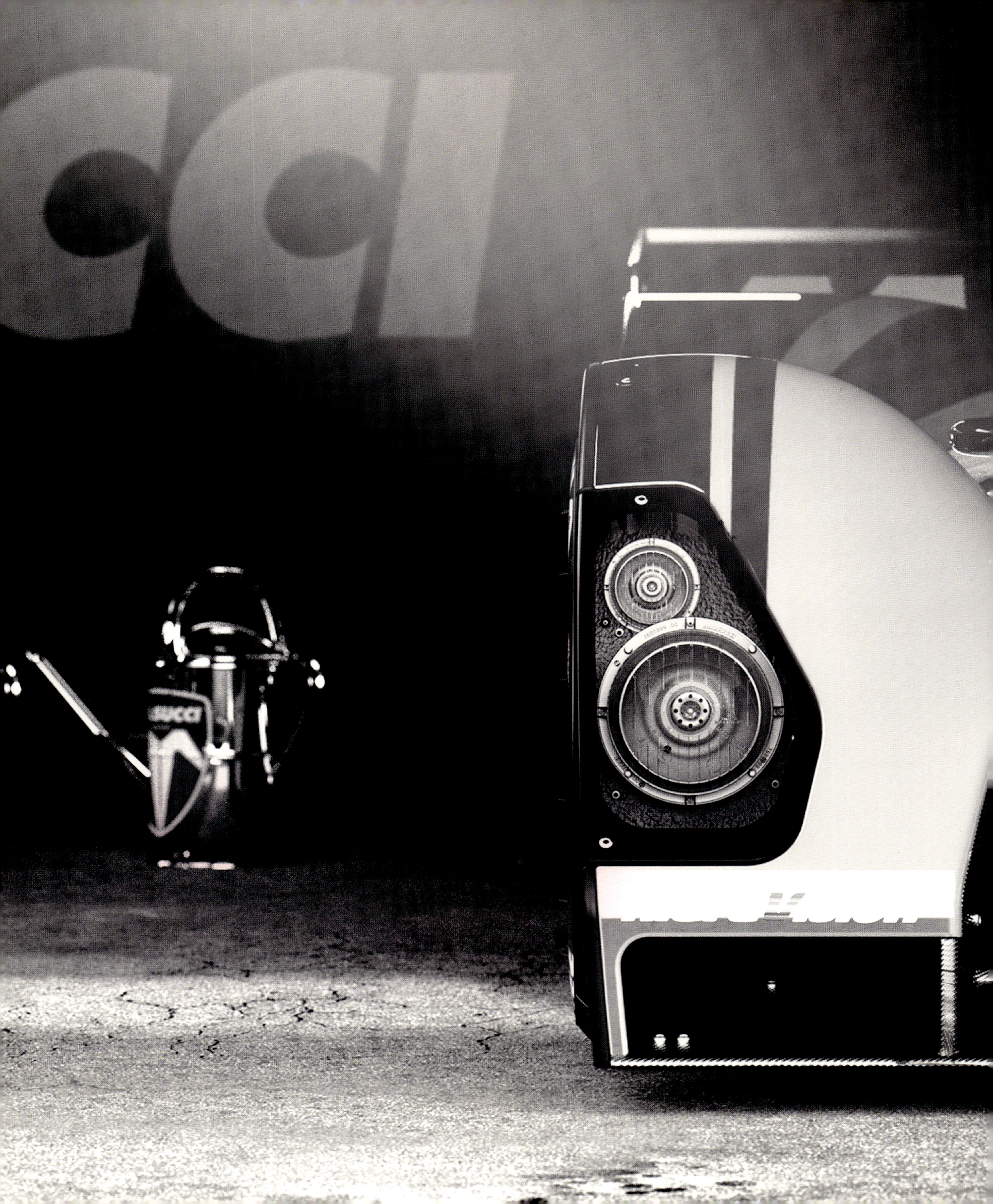

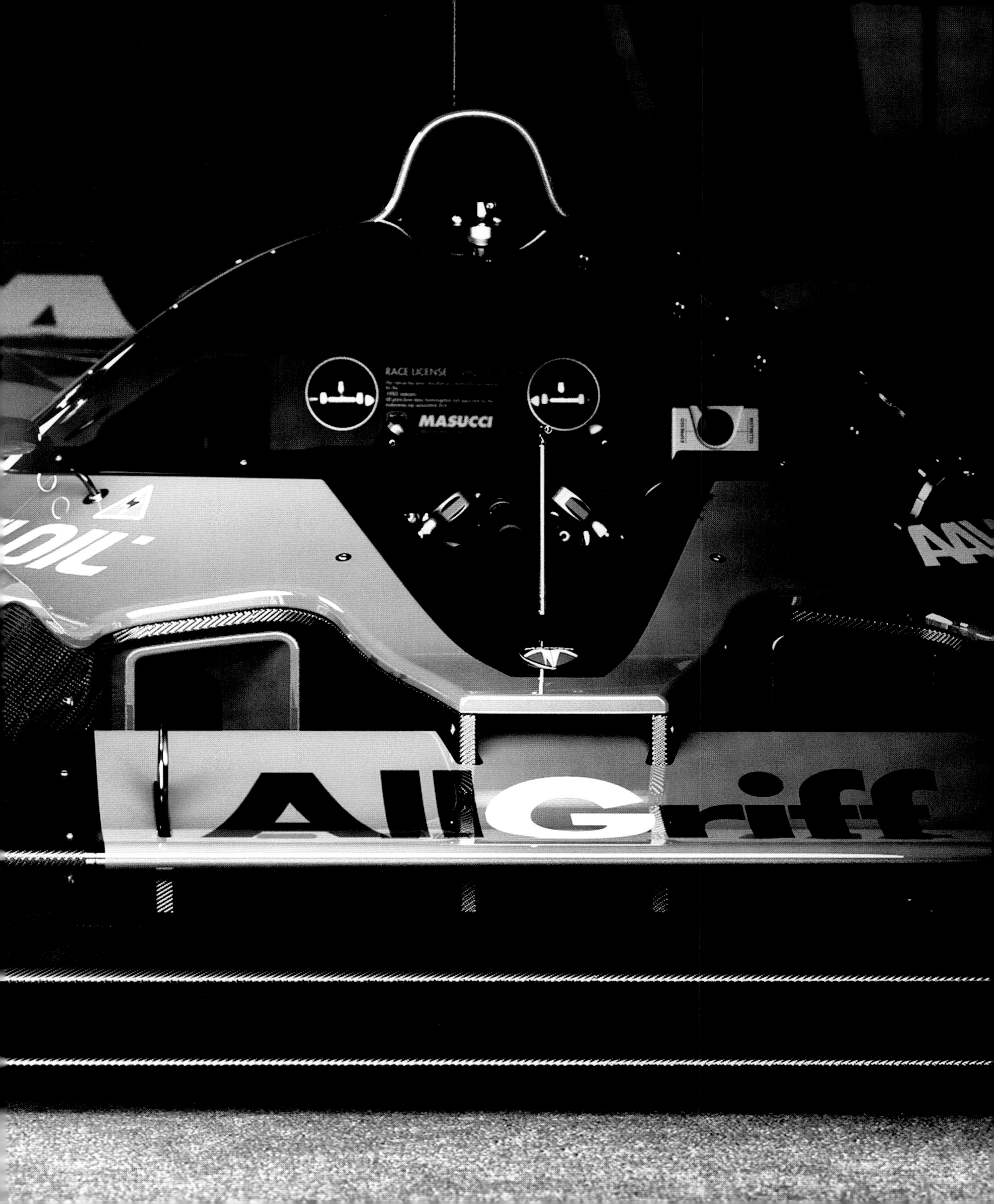
RACE LICENSE
MASUCCI
ESPRESSO
RISTRETTO
AllGriff

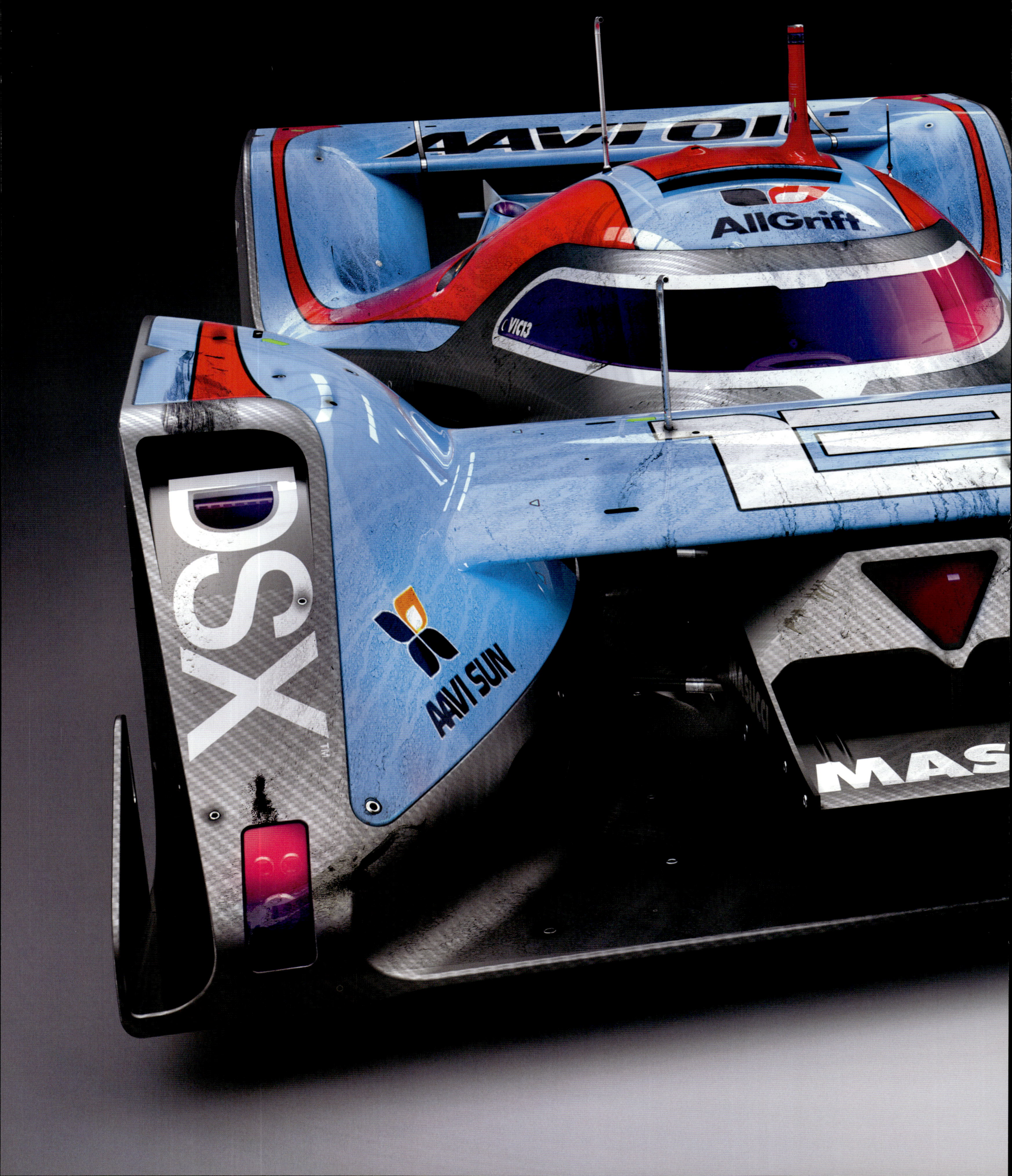
AllGrift
DSX
AAVI SUN

WELCOME TO THE YEAR 2027

MASUCCI X7

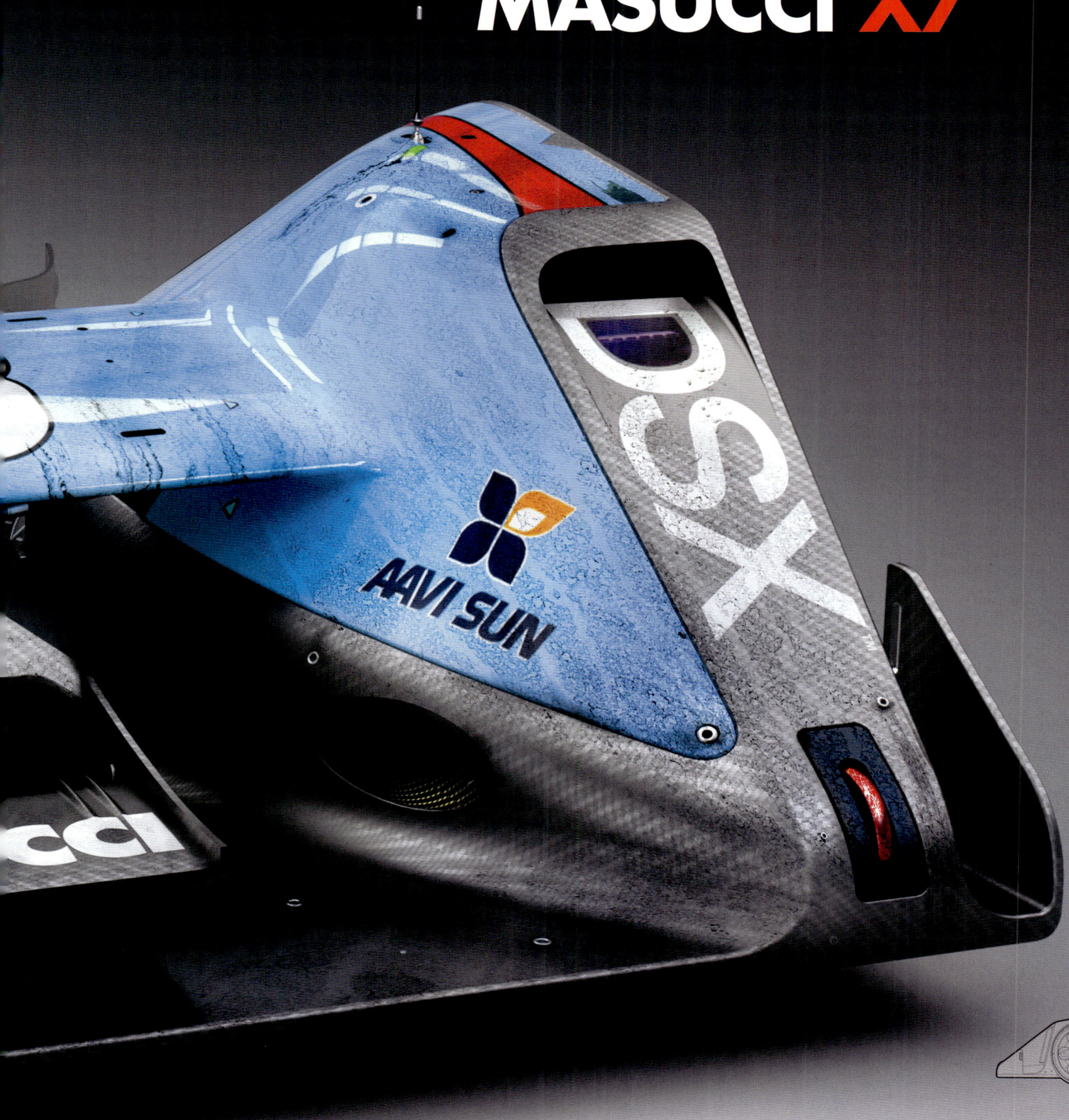

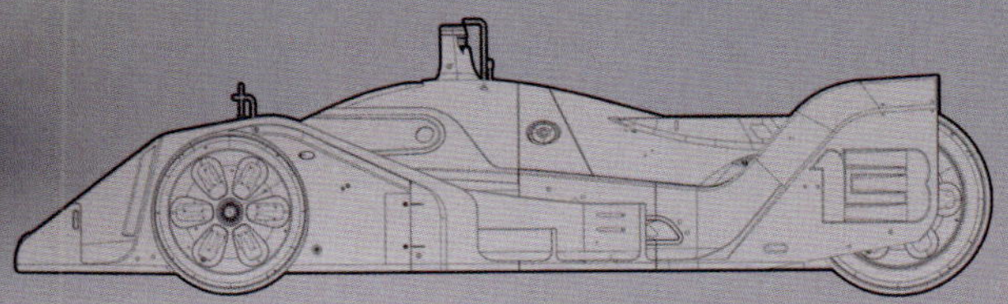

MODEL	Masucci X-7S
TYPE	SGM Endurance World Cup
YEAR	2027
DESIGNER	Luca Masucci / Dale Burton
ENGINE	Masucci Gas Turbine 'Ciri' 4998cc / electric
POWER OUTPUT	835 hp
TOP SPEED	435 km/h / 270 mph
PINCIPLE DRIVER	Vic Cooper
L / W / H	4445mm / 2200mm / 1180mm
WHEELBASE	3056mm

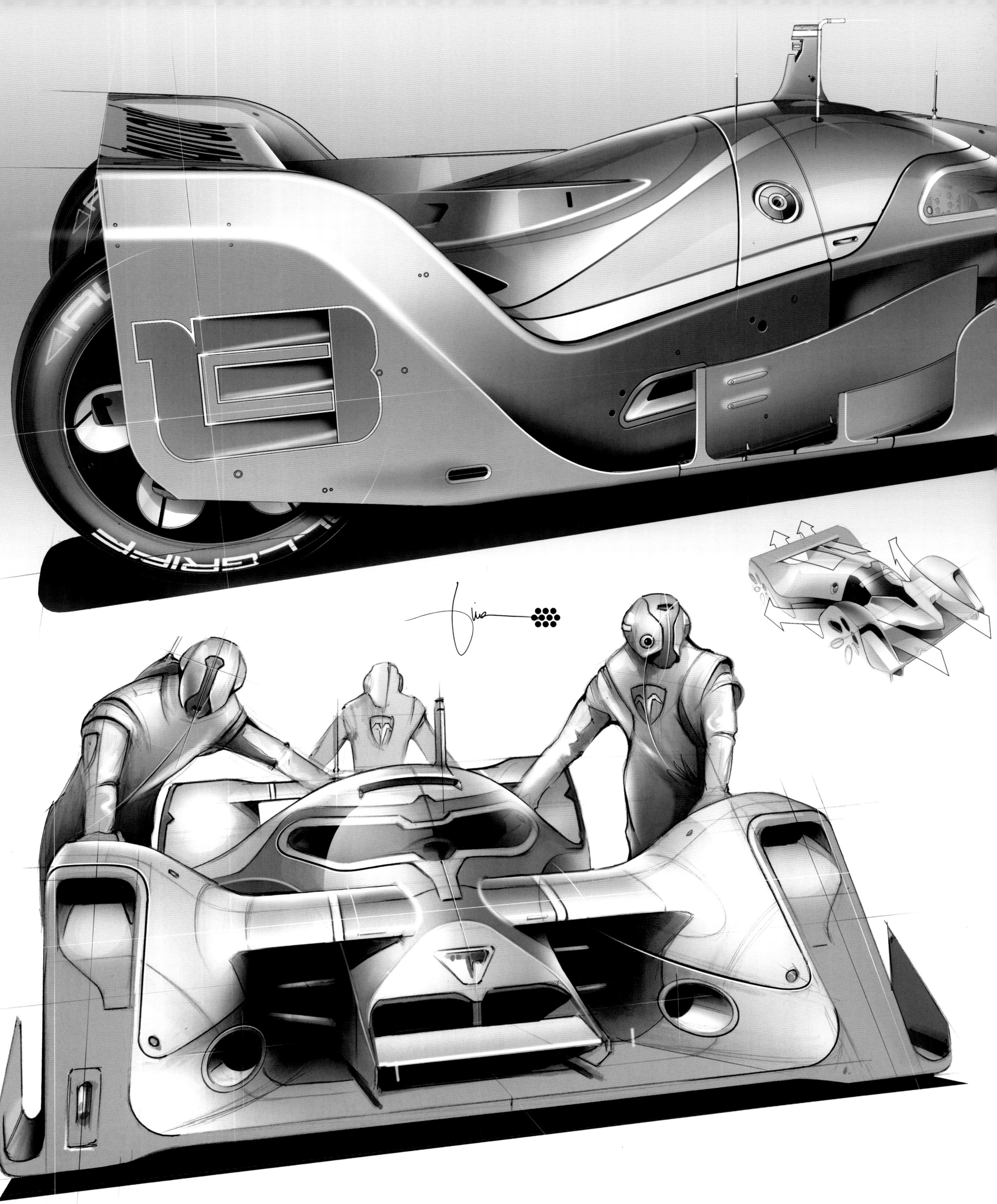

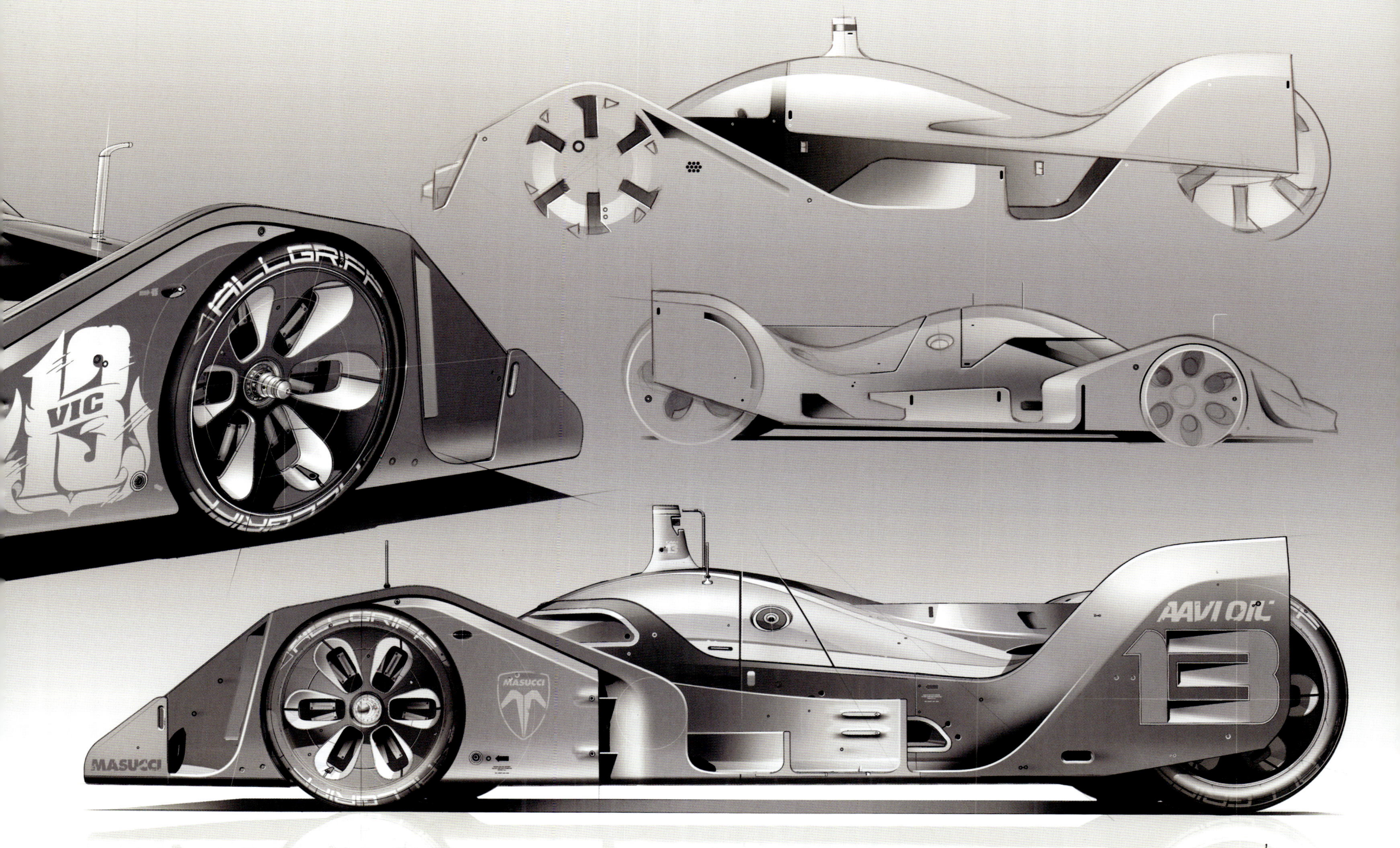

DESIGNPHASE**MASUCCIX7**

CREATING MASUCCI'S REVIVAL

Creating Masucci's revival. Designing the car in which hero Vic Cooper would win the 2027 Endurance Cup race was pure joy. I had dreamed for a long time of creating a fantasy racer inspired by the ultra-iconic Porsche 917 and this project was my call to action.

The influence of the 917 can be seen in the soft cockpit treatment, the round window graphics, and the full rear fenders. Also notable are my color schemes, a playful homage to the legendary liveries of the wild '70s, yet with different hues and applications. Despite these strong influences, I put a lot of effort into making the X-7 an innovative and unique design statement.

The simple design philosophy behind this concept was to carve organic and fluent shapes into a rectangular form, without touching the planar side surfaces. This is done both for aesthetic reasons, since I love the contrast of flat and curved shapes, and in light of the sports car regulations of the Société Globale de Moteurs, which required the imaginary Masucci designers to maintain a square plan view. An emphasis was put on the plan view of the X-7 and it clearly illustrates the controlled airflow over the car: air is forced past the front wheel arches, guided by a set of variable blades nestled between the monocoque and the fenders. I also created a variety of different nose cones for different down force configurations.

Renaissance de Masucci. Imaginer la voiture avec laquelle Vic Cooper devait remporter la dernière manche de la Coupe d'Endurance 2027 aura été une pure joie. En effet, je rêvais depuis longtemps de créer un modèle inspiré de la mythique Porsche 917.

Son influence, bien qu'abstraite, se retrouve notamment dans la forme douce du cockpit, les graphismes partant de la zone du pare-brise, ainsi que l'aileron arrière prolongeant la carrosserie. A noter également, la livrée au style très « années 70 », mais avec des teintes et applications différentes. Toutefois, malgré ces puissantes influences, j'ai voulu faire de la Masucci X-7 un manifeste artistique à part entière.

La philosophie de ce concept est de tailler des formes organiques fluides dans un cube statique, sans toucher aux surfaces latérales planes. Cela obéit à des considérations esthétiques – j'aime le contraste des formes planes et courbes –, mais aussi aux règlements imaginaires de la Société Globale de Moteurs, obligeant à maintenir une vue en plan carré. J'ai mis l'accent sur l'architecture de visualisation du plan, guidant le flux d'air en douceur des roues avant vers l'arrière, avec notamment ces ailerons de tailles variable nichés sur les flancs. J'ai également conçu des « nez » différents, qui permettent d'adapter la voiture à différentes exigences aérodynamiques.

Masuccis Neuanfang – der Entwurf. Das Auto zu entwerfen, mit dem Vic Cooper das finale Endurance Cup-Rennen der Saison 2027 gewinnen sollte, war ein Genuss. Schon lange wollte ich einen Wagen zeichnen, der von den zeitlosen Formen des Porsche 917 inspiriert ist. Die Fantasiewelt in *The Timeless Racer* bot dafür endlich den perfekten Rahmen.

Die Porsche-inspirierten Elemente entdeckt jeder 917-Kenner: die weichen Linien des Cockpits, die runde Fenstergrafik und die vollen Hinterradhäuser. Auch die Lackierungen sind eine verspielte Hommage an die absolut legendären Grafiken der wilden 70er. Trotz dieser intensiven Einflüsse habe ich viel Wert auf die Eigenständigkeit und Originalität des Designs gelegt.

Die Designphilosophie hinter dem X-7 ist sehr skulptural. Fließende Formen wurden aus einem Block herausgeschnitten, ohne dabei die Seitenflächen zu verändern. Einerseits aus ästhetischen Gründen, weil mich Kontraste zwischen flachen und gewölbten Flächen faszinieren. Andererseits zwang das Sportwagenreglement der Société Globale de Moteurs (SGM) die imaginären Masucci-Designer, die eckige Grundfläche des Autos zu erhalten. Ein weiterer Fokus lag auf der aerodynamischen Architektur. Der Fahrtwind wird innenseitig an den vorderen Radhäuser vorbeigeleitet, wo variable Leitbleche den Luftstrom gezielt kontrollieren.

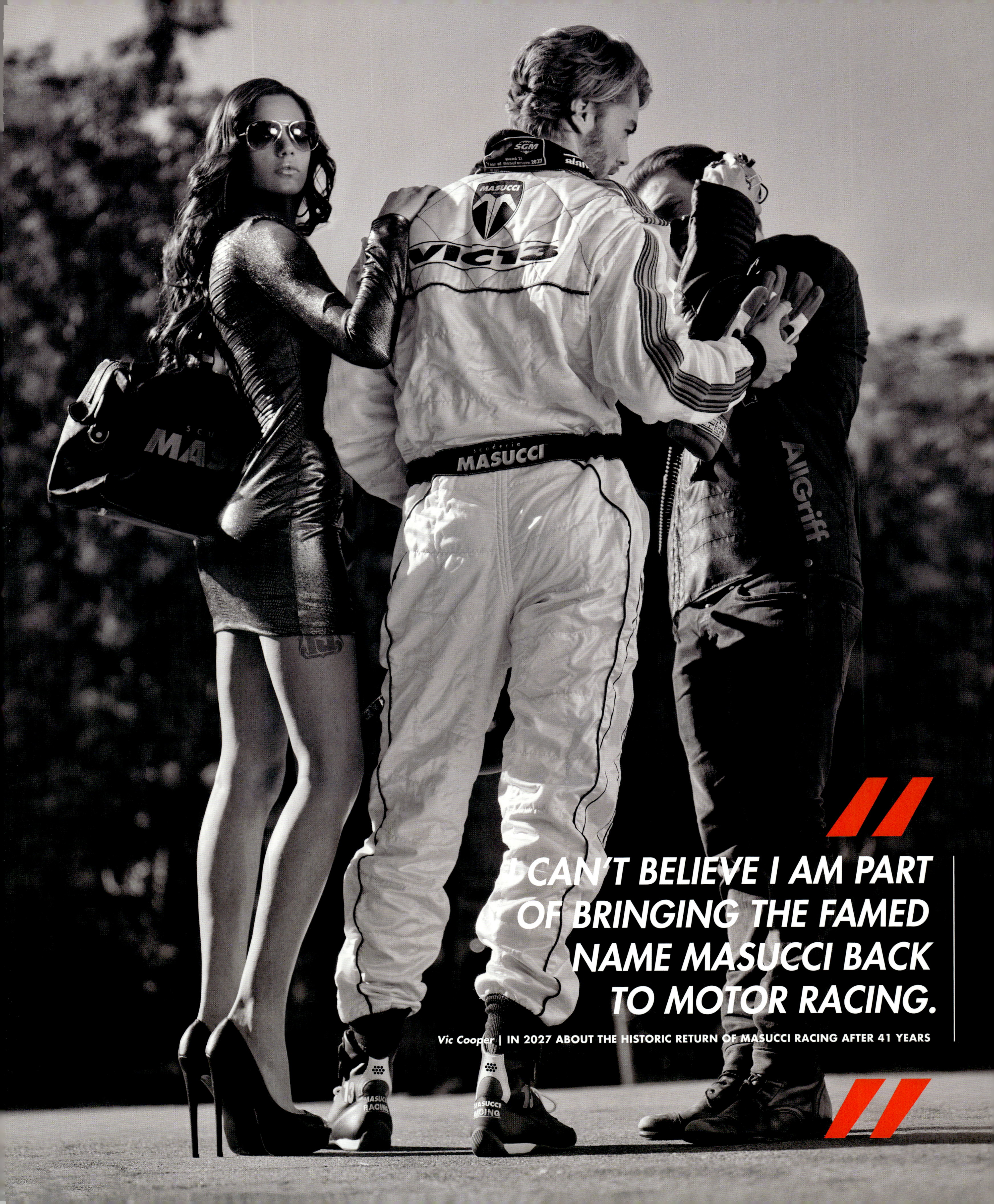
VIC13
scuderia
MASUCCI
AllGriff
CAN'T BELIEVE I AM PART
OF BRINGING THE FAMED
NAME MASUCCI BACK
TO MOTOR RACING.
Vic Cooper | IN 2027 ABOUT THE HISTORIC RETURN OF MASUCCI RACING AFTER 41 YEARS

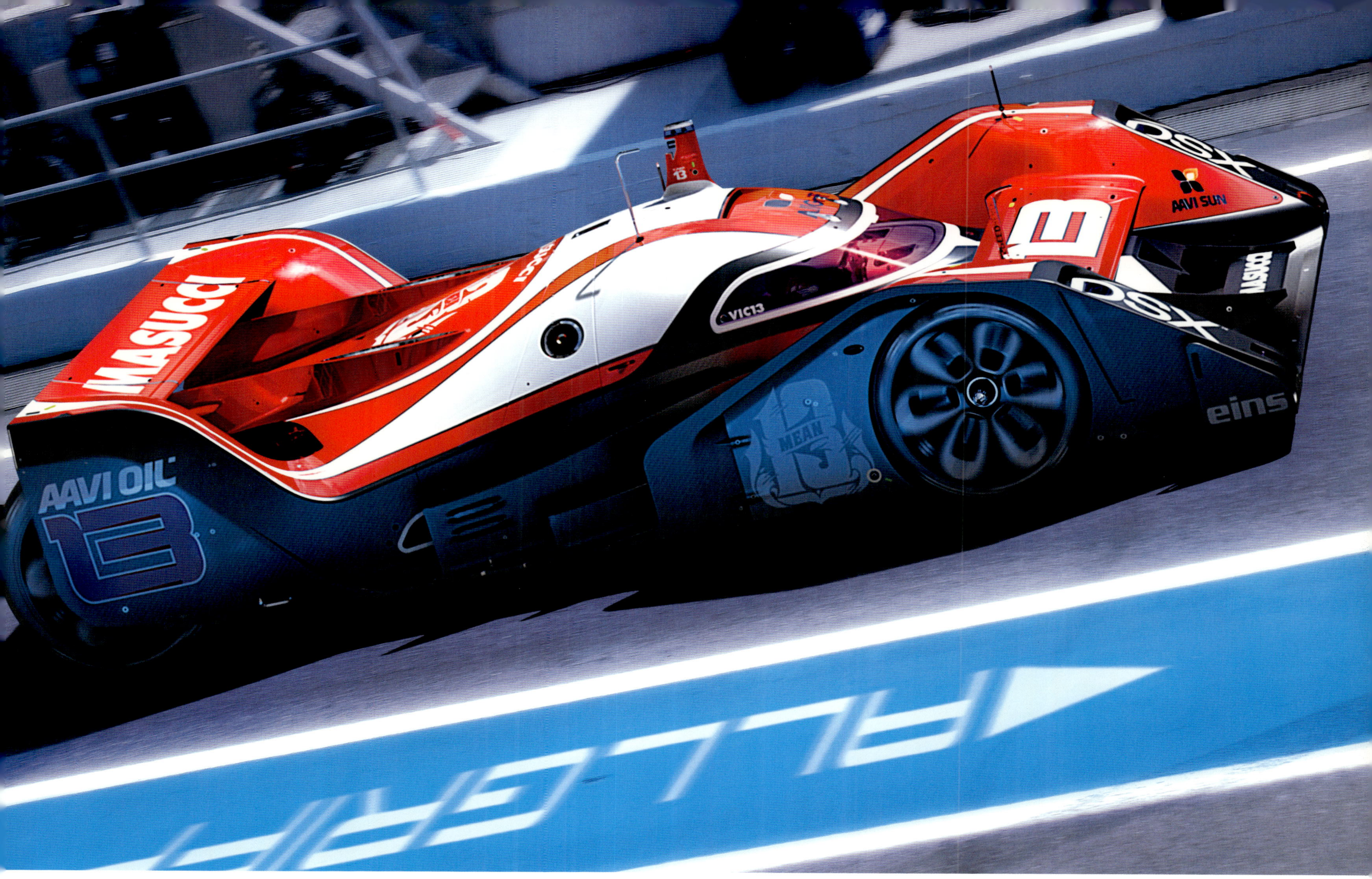

2027MASUCCI**PROTOTIPOX7-A**

A DIFFICULT BEAST WITH POTENTIAL

A difficult beast with potential. The Masucci X-7 development was a troublesome undertaking. Industria Masucci, Vic Cooper's only ticket to win a 2027 Endurance Cup race, had been out of motor racing for many years and doing business in suborbital space flights and advance drive research. They had just launched a global campaign for their high tech gas turbines. When CEO Luca Masucci gave in to the pressure of his father Filomeno and agreed to develop a winning race car for Cooper, Luca insisted on promoting his advanced-aircraft business with a turbine car—at first a disastrous decision. Two prototypes went up in flames and injured Cooper lightly—reminders of the doomed year 1986. Transmission issues, acceleration lags, and bad handling had the X-7A barely qualify for the two opening races in Tokyo and Southampton. Regardless of those mishaps, the ambitious project caught the attention of Dale Burton, the charismatic CEO of Aavi Oil and as a racing addict the biggest sponsor motor racing ever saw. "I was inspired by the potential of the unusual X-7 concept and bored with the—deserved—dominance of the French Prideux-Martins," said Burton later, explaining his secret funding of the project. Only at the fourth race, the 12 Hours of South Africa, was Burton's deal revealed, when Cooper's X-7B qualified in corporate Aavi colors blue and red. "I can't believe I am part of bringing the famed name Masucci back to motor racing," added an excited Cooper.

Une bête difficile à fort potentiel. Délicate genèse pour la Masucci X-7. Industria Masucci représentait la seule chance de victoire pour Vic Cooper dans la Coupe d'Endurance 2027. Seulement voilà, l'entreprise se consacrait depuis longtemps à d'autres activités, comme les vols spatiaux suborbitaux, et venait de lancer une campagne mondiale sur ses turbines à gaz. Le PDG Luca Masucci céda pourtant à la pression de son père Filomeno. Ils conçurent un modèle pour Cooper, Luca y voyant la possibilité de promouvoir ses affaires en y adaptant une de ses turbines. Mais deux prototypes prirent feu, blessant légèrement Cooper, ce qui rappela la maudite année 1986. Du fait de problèmes de transmission, d'accélérations chaotiques et d'une tenue de cap erratique, la X-7A se qualifia à grand peine pour les courses d'ouverture à Tokyo et Southampton. Pourtant, l'ambitieux projet attira l'attention de Dale Burton, patron de la société pétrolière Aavi, plus grand sponsor jamais connu du sport automobile. « J'ai été inspiré par le potentiel de la X-7, en même temps qu'ennuyé par la domination – certes méritée – des Prideux-Martin, les voitures françaises », déclara Burton pour expliquer son financement occulte du projet. Ce n'est que lors de la 4ème course, les 12 Heures d'Afrique du Sud, où la X-7B de Cooper se qualifia sous les couleurs d'Aavi, que le « deal » avec Burton fut révélé. « Je peine encore à croire que je participe au retour de Masucci dans l'univers de la compétition », ajouta Cooper enthousiaste.

Ein stures Biest mit Potenzial. Der Masucci X-7 war von Problemen geplagt. Industria Masucci, Vic Coopers einzige Hoffnung auf einen Sieg, hatte sein Racing Team 1986 aufgelöst und sich in den letzten Jahren auf experimentelle Luftfahrttechnik spezialisiert. Als Luca Masucci der Rückkehr in den Motorsport zustimmte, stellte er eine Bedingung: das Auto für Cooper müsse als Turbinenwagen konstruiert werden. Industria Masucci hatte gerade eine weltweite Kampagne für ihre Hightech-Gasturbinen gestartet – da würde ein solcher Bolide zur Firmenstrategie passen. Eine Entscheidung mit Folgen. Zunächst gingen zwei Prototypen in Flammen auf, wobei Cooper leicht verletzt wurde und Erinnerungen an das schicksalhafte Jahr 1986 wach wurden. Außerdem ließen Getriebeprobleme, Beschleunigungslöcher und das unausgereifte Fahrverhalten die Qualifikation des X-7A für die beiden Eröffnungsrennen fast scheitern. Trotz allem wurde Dale Burton – Chef von Aavi Oil und größter Motorsport-Sponsor aller Zeiten – auf das Team aufmerksam. „Das Potenzial des X-7-Konzepts hat mich ziemlich beeindruckt", sagte Burton später. „Außerdem war ich von der – verdienten – Dominanz des Prideux-Teams gelangweilt." Das zunächst geheime Sponsoring wurde beim vierten Rennen verkündet, den 12-Stunden von Südafrika. Dort lief Coopers X-7B erstmals in den Aavi-Farben Blau und Rot auf. „Es ist ein unbeschreibliches Gefühl, bei der Rückkehr Masuccis in den Rennsport dabei zu sein", fügt Cooper hinzu.

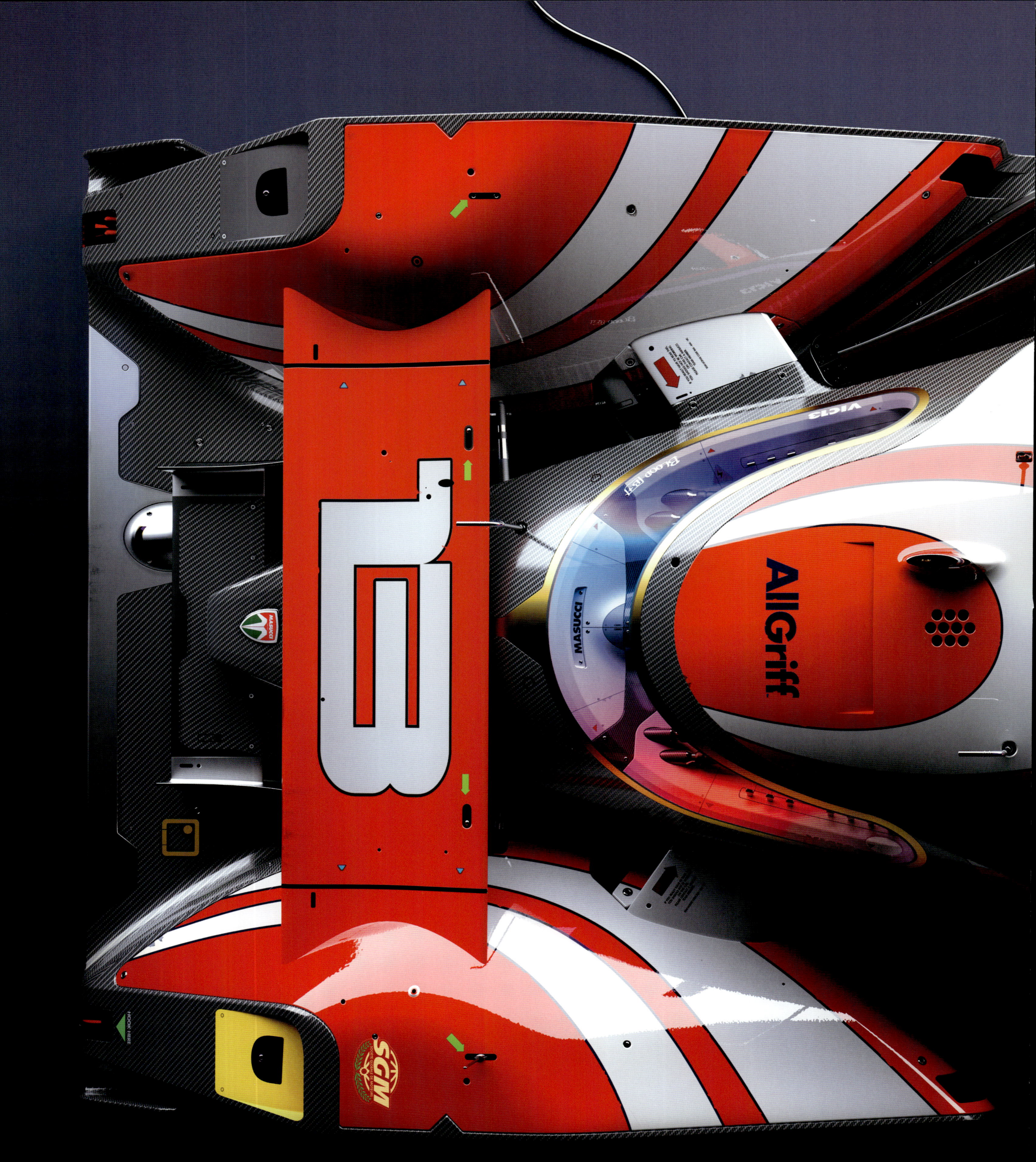
AllGriff
13
MASUCCI
SGM

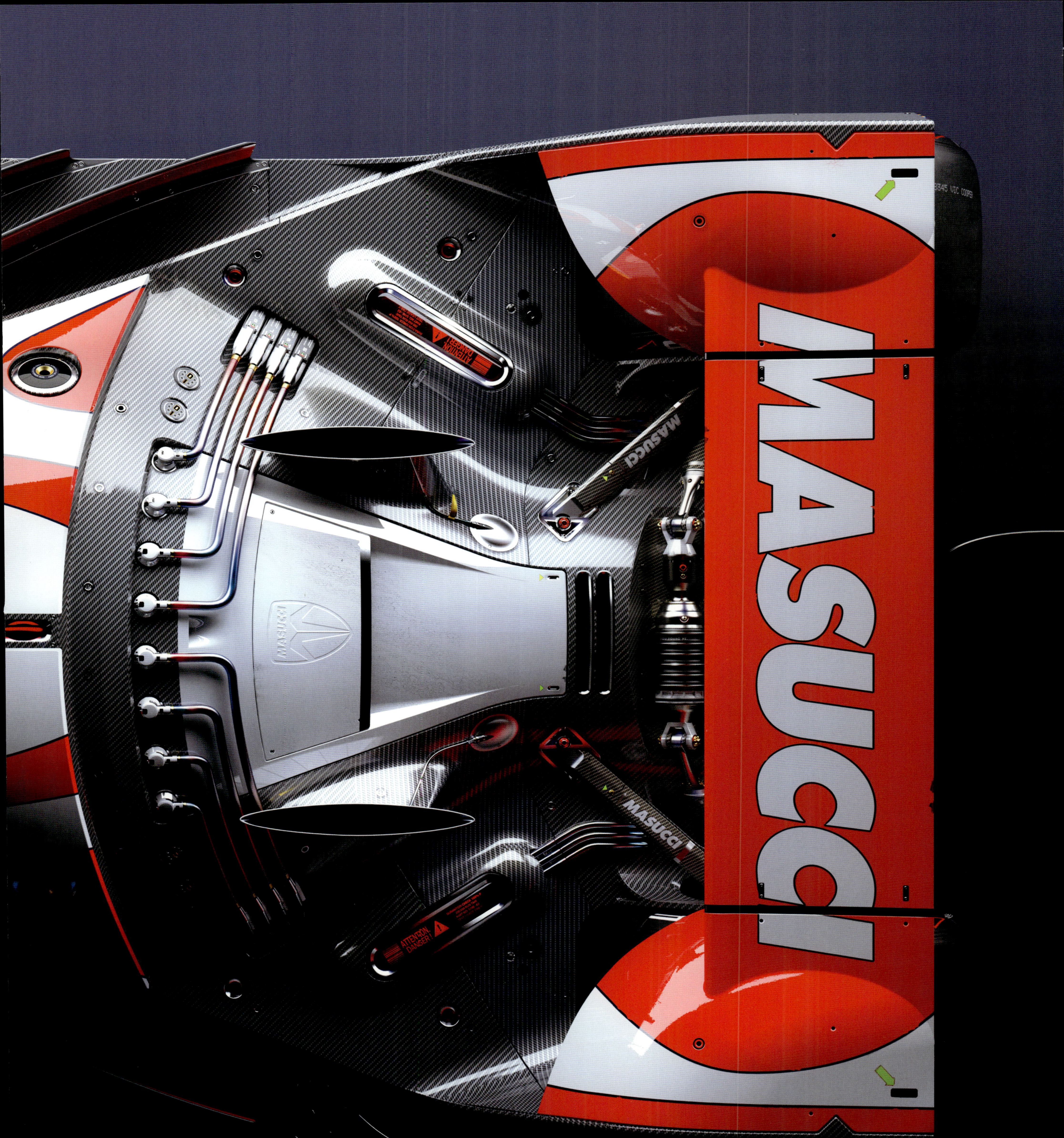
MASUCCI

The gas turbine electric hybrid in the X-7 was far from competitive when the 2027 season opened, and it was only five months since the first drawings were done in Turin. The car looked stunning in Masucci's house colors, red and white, during the first qualifying session in Tokyo (page 35). But that did not help the performance. "The power lag after turns is frustrating. We are fast on the straights, but that is no magic. We need speed out of turns," said Vic Cooper. Cooper barely qualified within the 110% rule during the first race in Japan. On racing day he gained five positions before the first turn, but had to retire after two hours' racing due to turbine failures. At least the car did not go up in flames like in testing!

Le moteur hybride à turbine à gaz et électrique de la X-7 était encore loin d'être compétitif au début de la saison 2027, cinq mois seulement après les premiers dessins. A la première séance de qualification à Tokyo (page 35), la voiture était superbe sous les couleurs rouge et blanc Masucci. Mais les performances ne suivaient pas. « Le décalage de puissance après quelques tours est frustrant. Nous sommes rapides en ligne droite, mais pas assez dans les courbes », déclara Vic Cooper. Il se qualifia toutefois de justesse grâce à la règle des 110%. En course, il gagna 5 places avant le premier virage, mais se retira deux heures après sur défaillance de la turbine. Au moins, la voiture n'avait pas pris feu comme aux essais !

Zu Beginn der Rennsaison 2027 zeigte sich der X-7 mit seinem komplexen Hybridsystem aus Gasturbine und Elektromotoren alles andere als wettbewerbsfähig. Allerdings war er auch erst vor kaum fünf Monaten im Turiner Masucci-Designbüro entstanden. Als der Wagen in Tokio zum ersten Mal aus der Boxengasse rollte, sah er in der Masucci-typischen rot-weißen Lackierung bereits phänomenal aus (siehe Seite 35). Allein was fehlte, war Leistung. „Auf der Geraden sind wir schnell, aber aus Kurven fehlt uns der Speed", befand Vic Cooper. Trotzdem machte er beim Start sofort fünf Positionen gut, fiel aber nach zwei Stunden mit Turbinenschaden aus. Einziger Fortschritt: Der X-7 brannte nicht wie bei den Testfahrten ab!

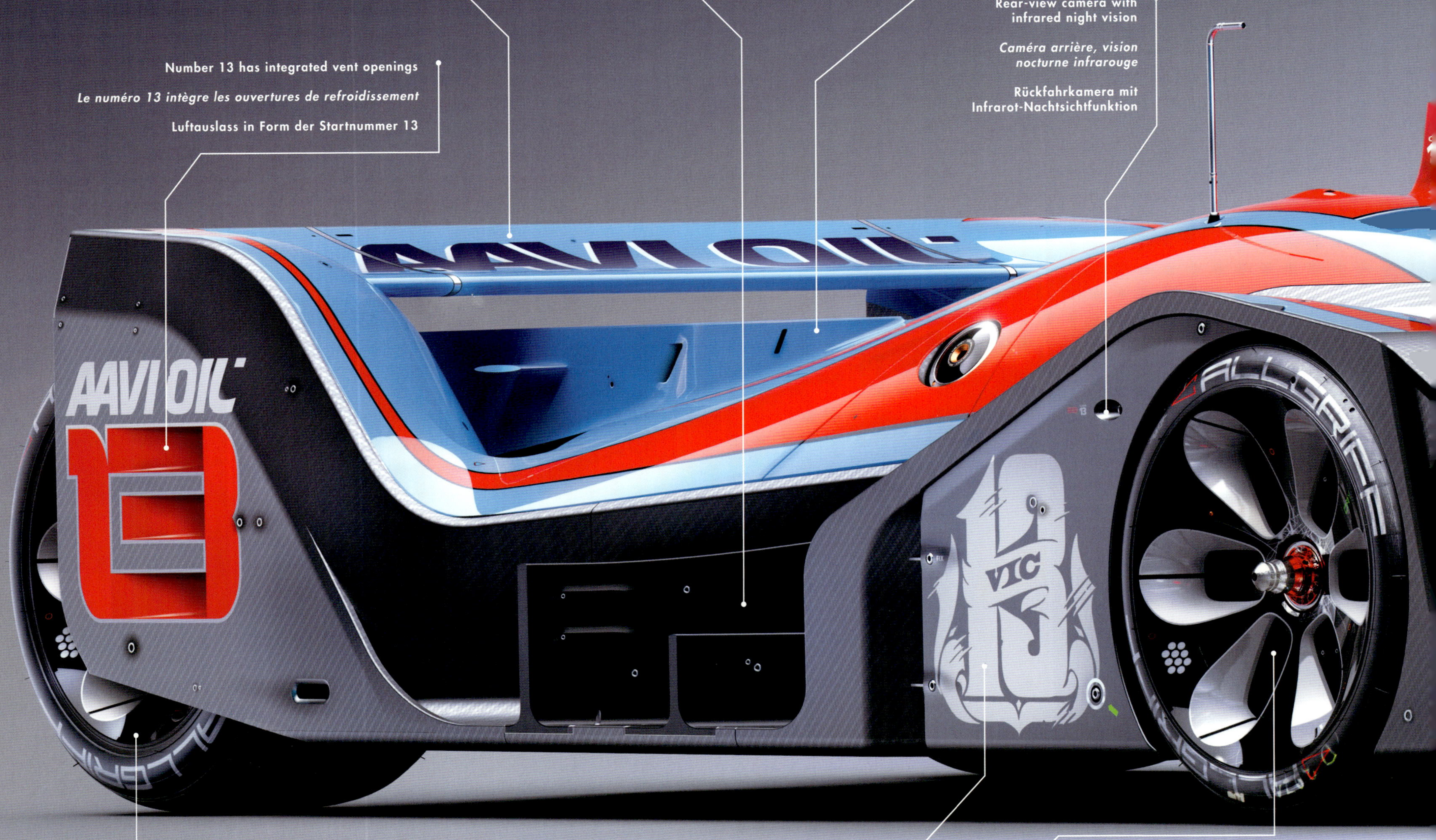

There was much work to do before the race in Southampton. Vic was eager to put in as many miles as possible after the terrible season start and the team returned quickly to Masucci's test track in Turin, but upon return things would get even worse during the second race on the iconic track in Southern England. After only one hour, both electric motors shut down due to a software failure, and two hours later Cooper was completely out of the race with a broken gearbox.

Restait un gros travail avant la deuxième course de la saison, à Southampton. Vic voulait avaler autant d'essais que possible après ces débuts difficiles, et l'équipe retourna rapidement sur la piste d'essai de Turin. Mais les choses allaient encore empirer sur le fameux circuit du sud de l'Angleterre. Après une heure de course, une défaillance du logiciel entraîna une panne des deux moteurs électriques. Et deux heures plus tard, la voiture abandonnait, boîte cassée.

Vor dem zweiten Rennen in Southampton gab es also viel zu verbessern. Auf der hauseigenen Teststrecke in Turin spulte Vic Testkilometer ohne Ende ab. Doch beim Rennen auf dem legendären Kurs am Ärmelkanal sollte es noch schlimmer kommen. Beide Elektromotoren in der Front überhitzten nach einer Stunde aufgrund eines Softwarefehlers und fielen aus. Nach weiteren zwei Stunde musste Vic den Wagen mit Getriebeschaden sogar endgültig abstellen.

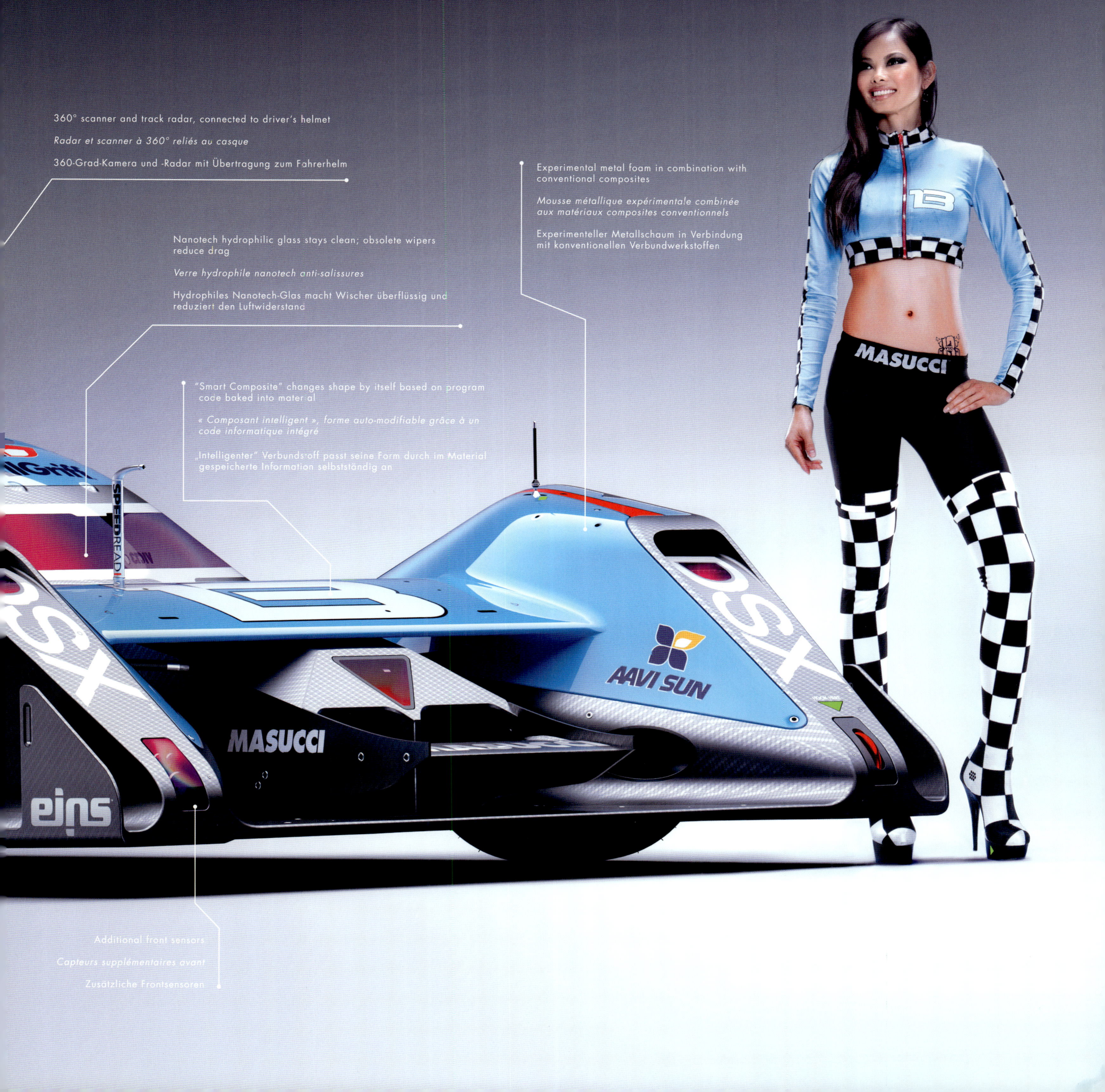

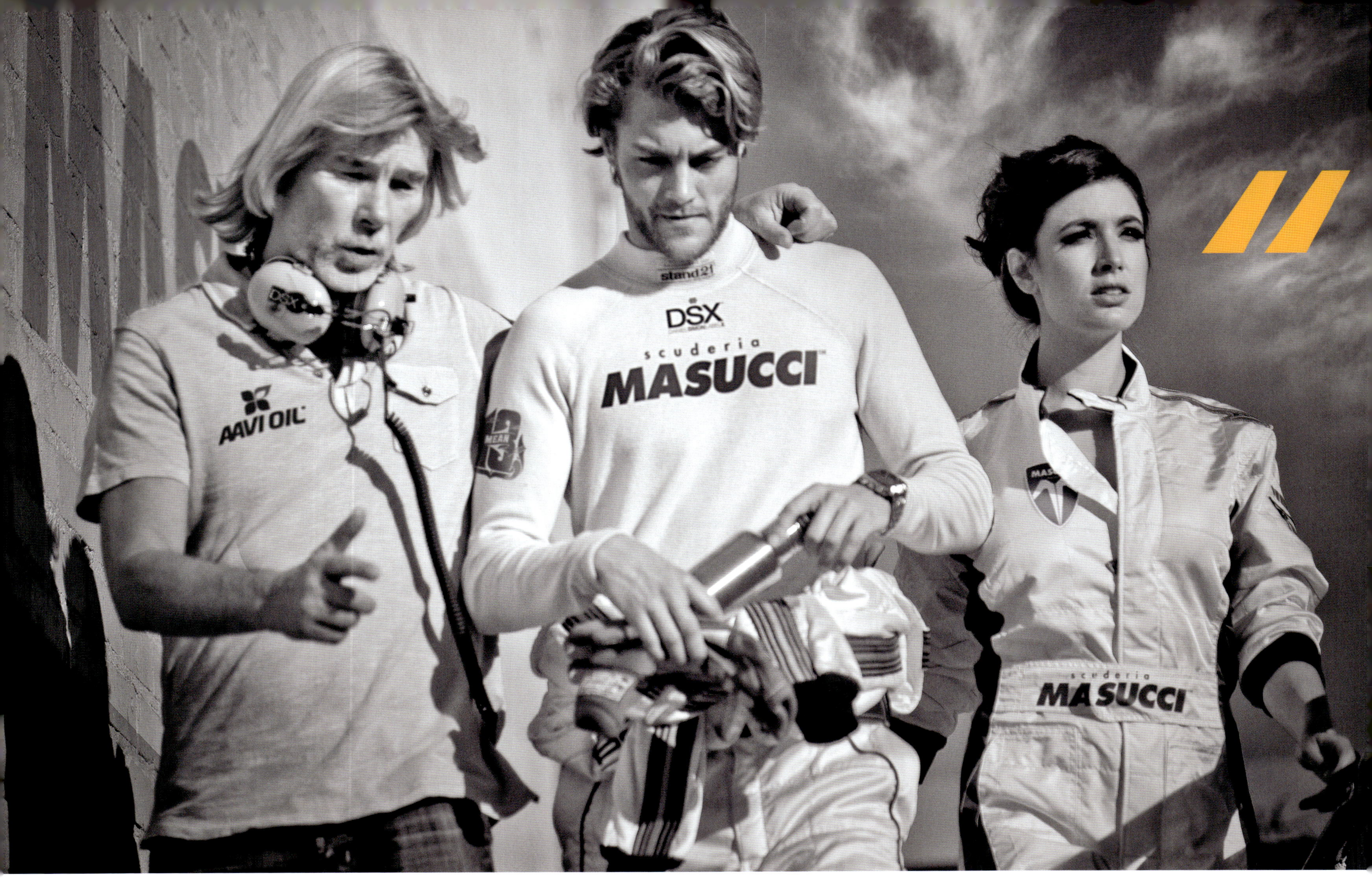

DALE **BURTON** AND **AAVI CORP.**

CHARISMA AND CASH FOR THE X-7

Charisma and cash for the X-7. Dale Burton is a man who lives his life in full swing. The phenomenal rise of his Aavi Oil Corporation allows him freedoms only few can imagine. He has invested in many boundary-pushing business adventures, including space vacation travel and postmortem mind preservation. While Burton is known for his immense philanthropic efforts, the Aavi Oil business is also the subject of many controversies and public disputes. Burton is a petrolhead and has sponsored entire racing series. He enjoys vintage racing and has the world's largest collection of classic Masucci cars, bikes, boats, and planes. He flies the stunning 1935 Masucci Aquila A-35C biplane to public appearances and is often seen in the paddocks of racing events of all kinds.

When Burton learned about the struggling X-7 project, he became interested in a successful return of Masucci into racing, after 41 years of their absence and being a personal fan of their history. He announced the large sponsorship after Cooper's third disastrous race with ". . . building a winning car in a few months seems impossible. But I know it can be done. I love Masucci and believe in their revival." The X-7B was from then on red and blue, the corporate colors of Aavi Oil.

Charisme et cash pour la X-7. Dale Burton est de ceux qui vivent leur vie à 300 km/h. Le succès de sa société Aavi lui permet des libertés imaginables par peu de gens. Son audace dans les affaires est réputée, qu'il s'agisse de tourisme spatial ou de recherche sur la préservation du cerveau post-mortem. Et si les investissements philanthropiques de Burton sont connus, dans le secteur pétrolier, Aavi fait l'objet de nombreuses controverses. Amateur de moteurs en tous genres, Burton a sponsorisé de nombreuses compétitions. Il fait courir des véhicules anciens et possède la plus grande collection au monde de Masucci anciennes (voitures, motos, bateaux et avions). Il pilote le magnifique biplan Masucci Aquila A-35C de 1935 lors de rassemblements aériens, et on le voit souvent arpenter les paddocks, quelle que soit la discipline.

Lorsque Burton eut connaissance du projet X-7 et de ses difficultés, il s'engagea pour favoriser le retour de Masucci après 41 ans d'absence. Il annonça son parrainage après la troisième course désastreuse de Cooper, précisant « ... construire une voiture gagnante en quelques mois semble impossible. Mais je sais qu'on peut le faire. J'aime Masucci et je crois en leur renaissance. » La X7-B apparut dès lors en rouge et bleu, couleurs d'Aavi Oil.

Charisma und Kohle für den X-7. Dale Burton ist ein Mann, der das Leben bis zum Anschlag auskostet. Der kometenhafte Aufstieg seines Aavi-Oil-Imperiums gestattet ihm extravagante Freiheiten. Er investiert in bahnbrechende Projekte wie Weltraum-Resorts oder postmortale Gedanken-Konservierung und spendet regelmäßig Millionenbeträge für wohltätige Zwecke. Im Kontrast dazu stehen die Geschäftspraktiken von Aavi-Oil immer wieder in der öffentlichen Kritik. Dass Burtons Blut mit ungewöhnlich viel Benzin angereichert ist hat er mehrfach bewiesen, indem er komplette Rennserien sponserte. Auch besitzt er die größte Kollektion von Autos, Motorrädern, Booten und Flugzeugen der Marke Masucci. Bei Traditionsrennen fährt er seine Vintage-Rennwagen selbst und schwebt zu öffentlichen Auftritten gerne mit einem Masucci Aquila A-35C Doppeldecker von 1935 ein.

Als Burton von der Rückkehr Masuccis in den Rennsport erfuhr, wollte er mithelfen, das Unternehmen auf die Erfolgsspur zu bringen. Nach Coopers drittem sieglosen Rennen im X-7A kündigte Burton einen Sponsorendeal mit Masucci an: „Es scheint unmöglich, in wenigen Wochen ein Siegerauto zu bauen. Aber ich weiß, dass es geht. Ich liebe Masucci und glaube an deren Rückkehr." Von diesem Tag an fuhr der X-7B in den Aavi-Farben Rot und Blau.

BUILDING A WINNING CAR IN A FEW MONTHS SEEMS IMPOSSIBLE. BUT I KNOW IT CAN BE DONE. I LOVE MASUCCI AND BELIEVE IN THEIR REVIVAL.

Dale Burton **| BUSINESS MAGNATE AND CEO OF AAVI CORP., ABOUT HIS MASSIVE FUNDING OF THE MASUCCI X-7**

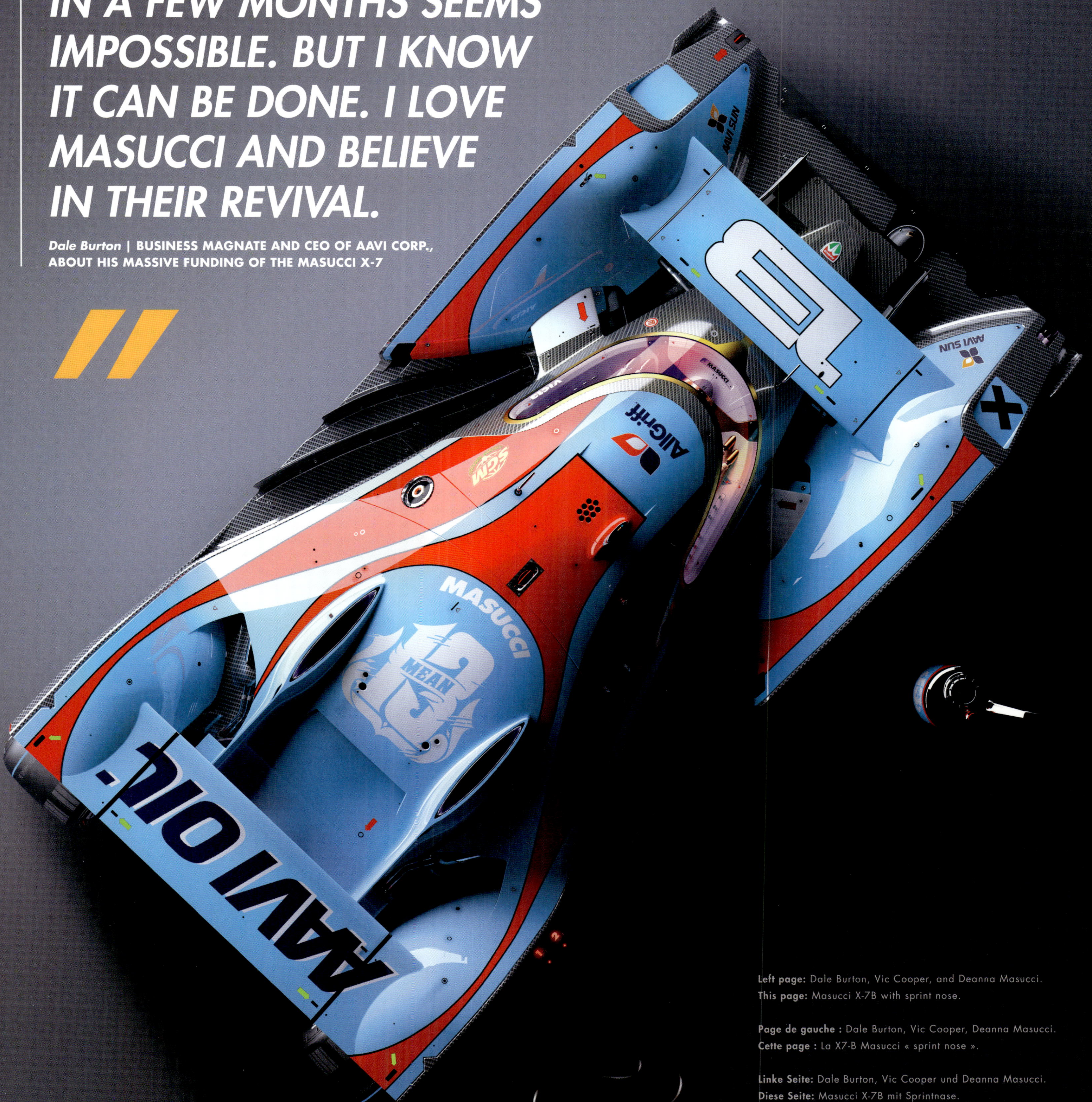

Left page: Dale Burton, Vic Cooper, and Deanna Masucci.
This page: Masucci X-7B with sprint nose.

Page de gauche : Dale Burton, Vic Cooper, Deanna Masucci.
Cette page : La X7-B Masucci « sprint nose ».

Linke Seite: Dale Burton, Vic Cooper und Deanna Masucci.
Diese Seite: Masucci X-7B mit Sprintnase.

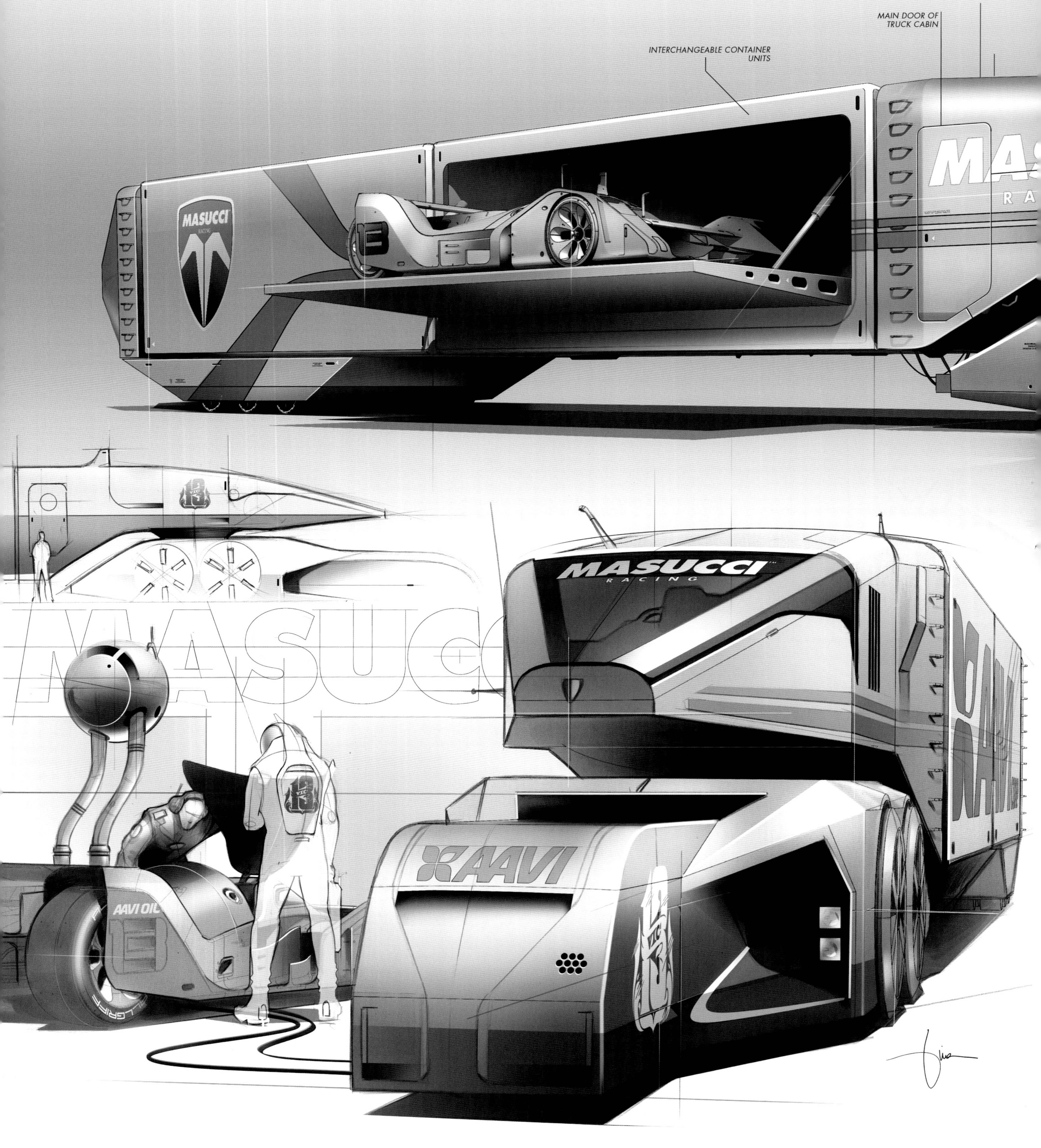
MAIN DOOR OF
TRUCK CABIN
INTERCHANGEABLE CONTAINER
UNITS
MASUCCI
MASUCCI
RACING
AAVI
AAVI OIL

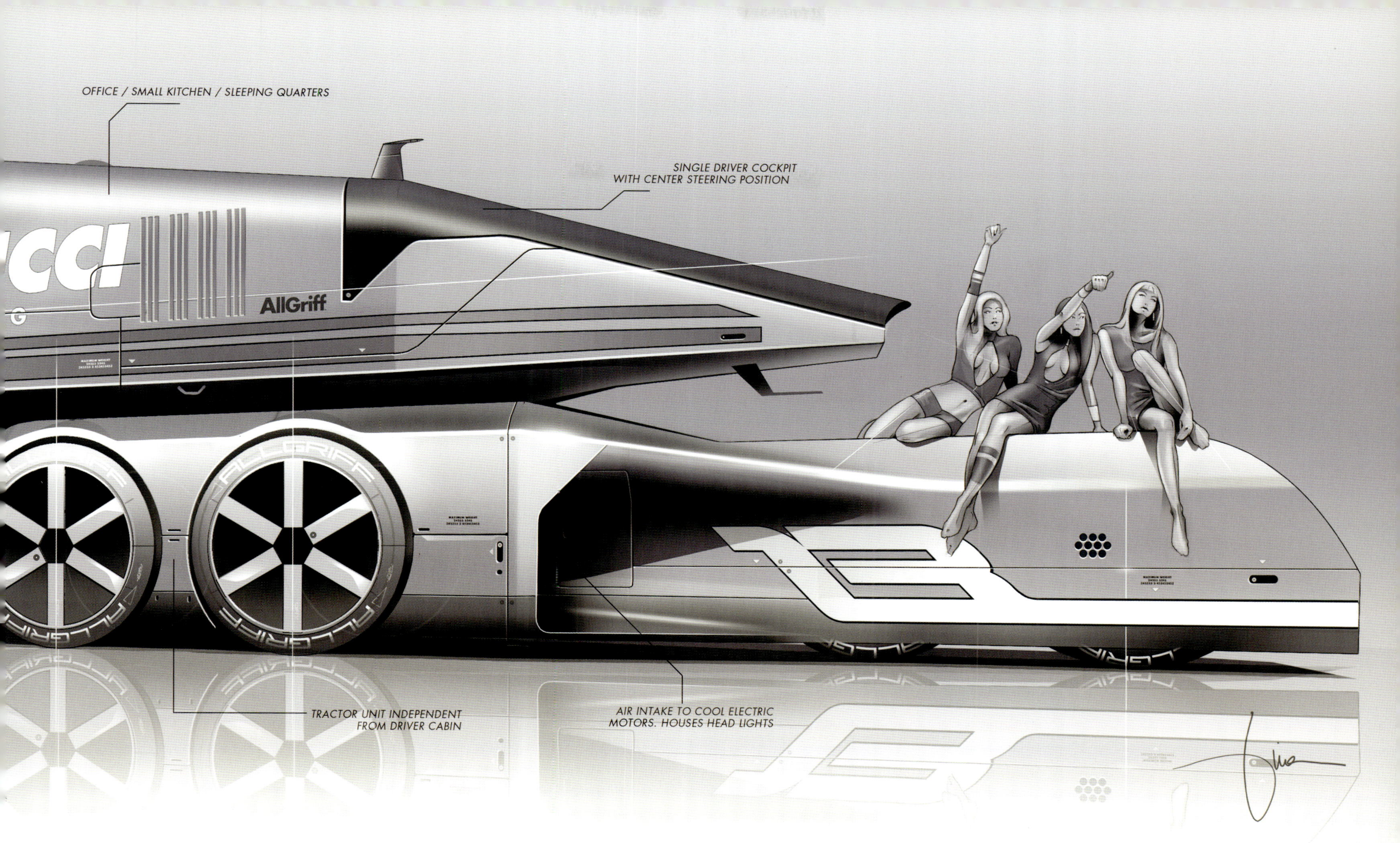

GEARINGUPTHETEAM
IT TAKES MORE THAN A CAR

It takes more than a car. If you ever went to a major motor racing event, you probably were impressed by how much equipment is necessary to make one car or one bike go around a circuit. I was always fascinated with the support efforts of teams, down to the temporary cafeterias that get set up behind the pit lane. One big part of a global racing circus is transporting everything around the world, but mostly in normal production trucks with a nice paint scheme and tailor-made trailer interiors. This fantasy world needed even more than that. So I started thinking of highway truck trains, specialized vehicles commissioned by race teams to transport their cars to tests or races.

The Masucci T5000 Superstrada was designed specifically for the Masucci Endurance Racing team and its X-7 program, financed with cash from Dale Burton's Aavi Oil Corporation. It is 82 feet long, 8.2 feet wide, and powered by six Cifiq electric motors. This long-haul machine operates on European Superspeedways, and was built with different trailers. The cabin is attached to those trailers and the electric tractor unit can be exchanged independently of the cockpit/living unit. Masucci would become a leader in off-track-equipment design and their spectacular and holistic appearance for their racing squad set new standards in the world of speed.

Il faut bien plus qu'une voiture. Si vous avez jamais assisté à une course, vous aurez pu être impressionné par la quantité de matériel nécessaire pour rendre possible un tour de piste. Les efforts fournis par les équipes me fascinent. Dans le grand cirque mondial de la compétition auto ou moto, une grande partie du travail consiste à transporter toutes sortes d'équipements à travers la planète, généralement dans des camions classiques aux peintures attrayantes. Mais le monde imaginaire a besoin de bien plus. De ce fait, j'ai commencé à penser à des « camions-trains » permettant aux écuries de transporter leurs véhicules jusqu'aux circuits.

Le Masucci T5000 Superstrada a été conçu pour l'équipe Masucci Endurance Racing, grâce aux fonds d'Aavi Oil, la société de Dale Burton : il mesure 25 mètres de long sur 2,5 mètres de large, et est propulsé par six moteurs électriques Cifiq. C'est une machine long-courrier circulant entre les plus grands circuits d'Europe. La cabine est solidaire de la remorque, tandis que la partie motrice électrique est escamotable et indépendante de la partie habitacle. Masucci allait aussi devenir leader dans la conception d'équipements de transport, et établir de nouveaux standards grâce à cette volonté de créer un environnement le plus favorable possible pour son écurie.

Ein Auto ist nicht genug. Eine immer wieder erstaunliche Beobachtung hinter den Kulissen eines Rennens ist die Materialschlacht, die nötig ist, um einen Piloten auf die Strecke schicken zu können. Der enorme Aufwand, der unsichtbar hinter den Boxenmauern betrieben wird, beeindruckt mich immer wieder. Vor allem, weil wirklich alles – vom Wagenheber bis zum Motorhome – alle paar Wochen um die Welt geschickt werden muss. Eine wichtige Rolle spielen hierbei Zugmaschinen. Doch die Fantasiewelt von *The Timeless Racer* benötigt auch hier etwas Besonderes. Zum Beispiel eine Autobahn-Langstrecken-Zugmaschine, die die Rennwagen schnell durch ganz Europa transportieren kann.

Der Masucci T5000 Superstrada wurde speziell für das eigene Endurance-Team entwickelt und von Aavi Oil finanziert. Er wird von sechs Elektromotoren angetrieben, ist 25 Meter lang und 2,5 Meter breit. Der T5000 fährt ausschließlich auf den neuen europäischen Superautobahnen und ist durch verschiedene Auflieger variabel. Die Kabine ist Teil des Aufliegers und ermöglicht so einen vom Fahrerquartier unabhängigen Austausch der Zugmaschine. Masucci setzte mit diesem spektakulären Gesamtkonzept neue Standards für den Auftritt von Rennteams und knüpfte mit dem Design an seine glamouröse Historie an.

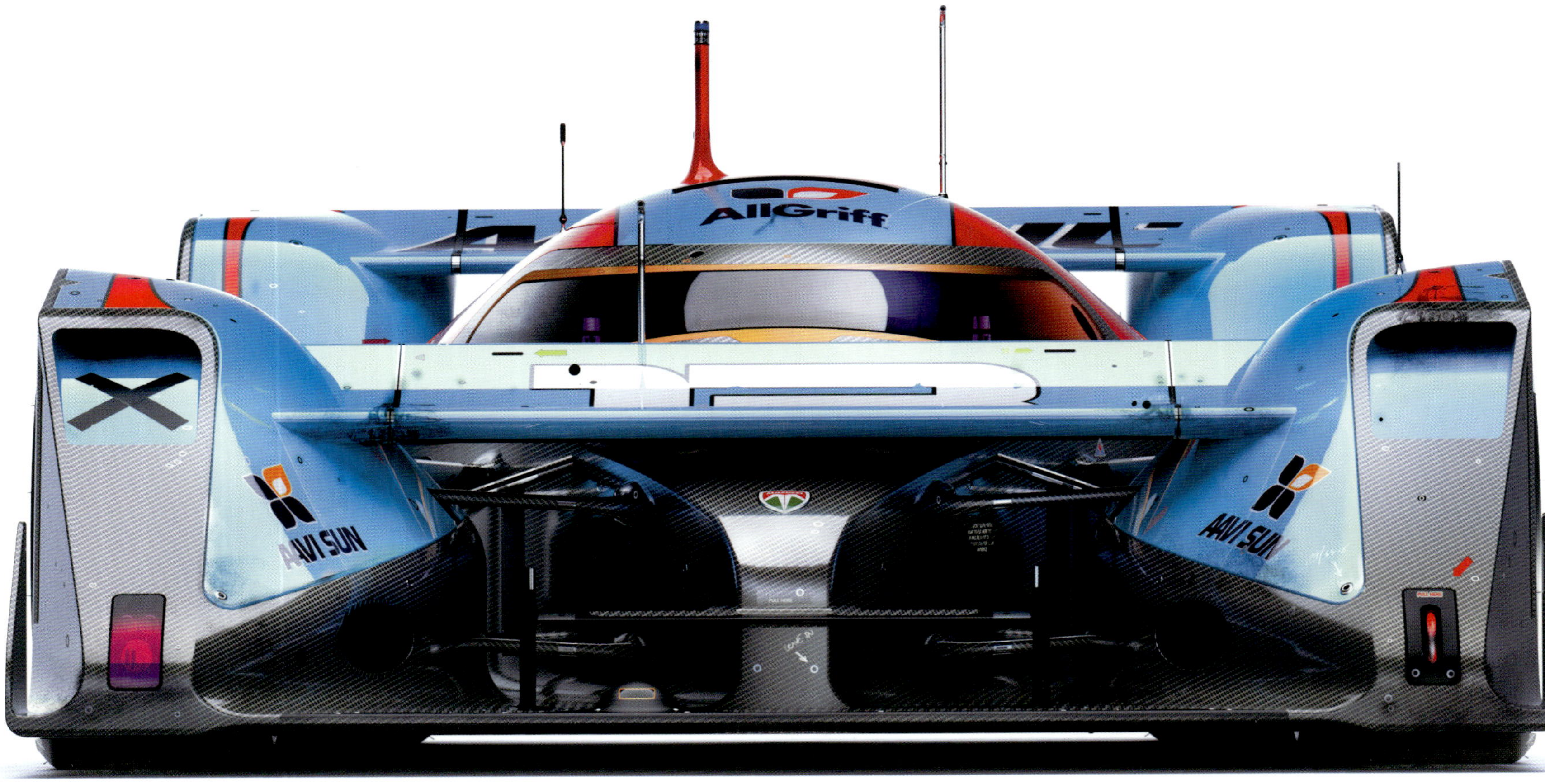

2027 MASUCCI TURBINE X7

VIC13 IS READY TO RACE

Vic13 is ready to race. Dale Burton's cash made all the difference during the summer break and Vic Cooper finished fifth in the 12 Hours of South Africa. The complex gearbox issues were tackled with a special team, the software coding for the gas turbine was entirely rewritten and the electric front motors were improved.

More work went into preparing the season finale in San Diego in November 2027, the very unique 48 Hours of California. While a driver would have a rest in the paddocks, his car would go back on track autonomously and it would be the first high-speed race with self-driving cars together on the track with human-driven cars. Each race car would be equipped with a standardized high-tech nose, packed with sensors and electronics (see the X-7S on the opposite page).

The lap times are significantly slower in autonomous mode and all cars share the same SGM-approved driving software, which has a passive attitude and always yields to a car piloted by a human. The Société Globale de Moteurs is hoping to break new ground with this type of racing and the future will tell if fans accept such hybrid events. The much improved Masucci X-7S, at least, was more than ready for this challenge. All eyes were now on the 48 Hours of California.

Vic13 est prête à courir. Les fonds de Dale Burton avaient fait toute la différence durant la pause estivale, permettant à Cooper de terminer cinquième en Afrique du Sud. Les problèmes complexes de boîte de vitesses avaient été résolus, les moteurs électriques avant améliorés, et il avait fallu refondre le logiciel de codage de la turbine à gaz.

La finale de la saison à San Diego, pour les 48 Heures de Californie de novembre 2027, demanda encore plus de travail. En effet, pendant que le pilote se reposerait dans le paddock, son bolide continuerait de tourner en piste : il s'agirait de la toute première course entre voitures avec et sans pilotes, chacune étant dotée d'un nez standard pourvu de capteurs et d'une électronique spécifiques (voir la X-7S sur la page ci-contre).

Les chronos sont sensiblement plus lents en mode autonome. Toutes les voitures partagent le même logiciel SGM à attitude passive, qui fait qu'une voiture sans pilote cèdera toujours le pas à une voiture menée par un humain. La Société Globale de Moteurs espère innover avec ce type de course, et l'avenir dira si les amateurs peuvent s'enthousiasmer pour de tels événements hybrides. La Masucci X-7S nettement améliorée était, quant à elle, plus que prête pour le défi. Tous les regards se tournaient maintenant vers les 48 heures de Californie.

Vic13 ist zum Angriff bereit. Dale Burtons Geldsegen bescherte dem Team während der Sommerpause rasche Fortschritte. Ein Spezialteam behob die Getriebeprobleme, die Software für die Turbine wurde neu geschrieben und die Elektromotoren in der Front wurden verbessert. Damit holte Cooper in Südafrika den fünften Platz.

Noch mehr Aufwand wurde in das Saisonfinale investiert, dem bahnbrechenden 48-Stunden-Rennen in San Diego im November 2027. Wenn der Fahrer hier eine Ruhepause einlegt, fährt sein Rennwagen autonom weiter. Es ist das erste Rennen der Motorsportgeschichte, in dem abschnittsweise Computer gegen Menschen antreten. Eine besondere Bedeutung besitzt hier die Frontpartie der Autos, die voller Sensoren und Elektronik steckt (siehe gegenüberliegende Seite: der X7-S).

Die Rundenzeiten der unbemannten Autos sind allerdings deutlich langsamer. Sie werden von einer SGM-Software mit einer passiven Fahrcharakteristik gesteuert, die den von Piloten gefahrenen Wagen immer ausweicht. Die SGM hofft, mit dieser Technologie eine neue Rennsport-Ära einzuläuten, doch ob die Fans sie annehmen, bleibt abzuwarten. Der Masucci X-7S jedenfalls war mehr als gerüstet: Vic Cooper begann das letzte Rennen der Saison als ernstzunehmender Herausforderer.

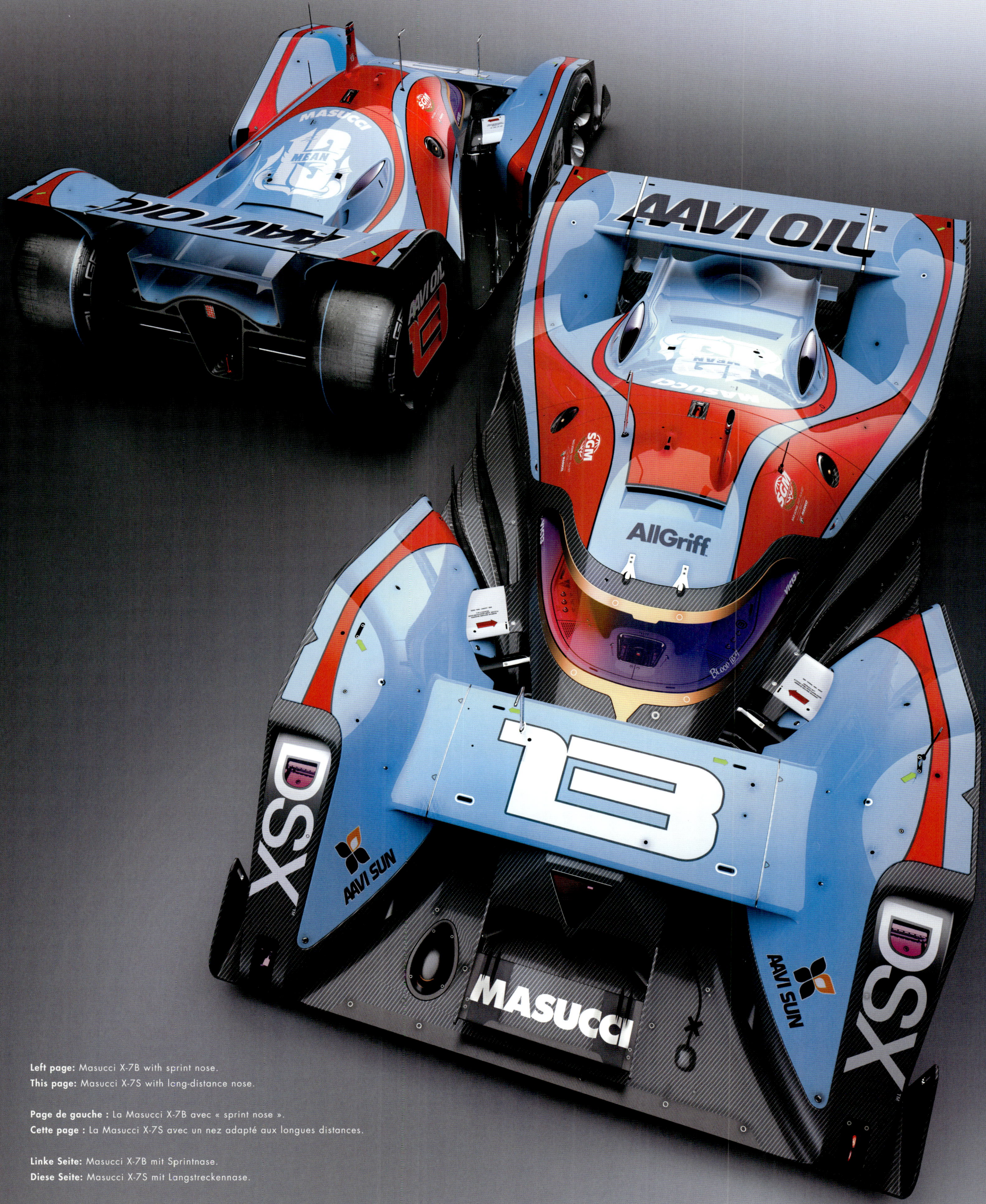

Left page: Masucci X-7B with sprint nose.
This page: Masucci X-7S with long-distance nose.

Page de gauche : La Masucci X-7B avec « sprint nose ».
Cette page : La Masucci X-7S avec un nez adapté aux longues distances.

Linke Seite: Masucci X-7B mit Sprintnase.
Diese Seite: Masucci X-7S mit Langstreckennase.

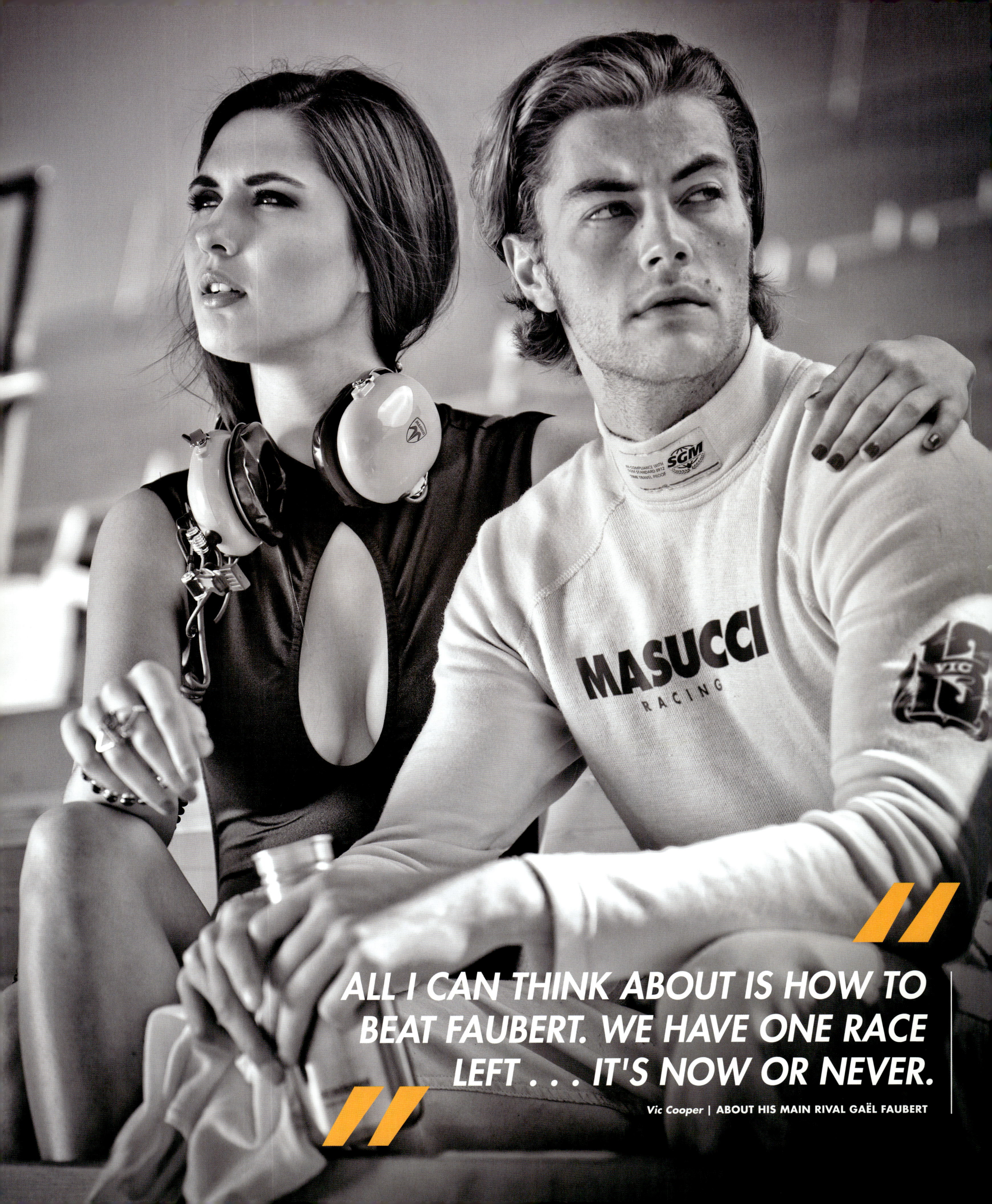

ALL I CAN THINK ABOUT IS HOW TO BEAT FAUBERT. WE HAVE ONE RACE LEFT . . . IT'S NOW OR NEVER.

Vic Cooper | **ABOUT HIS MAIN RIVAL GAËL FAUBERT**

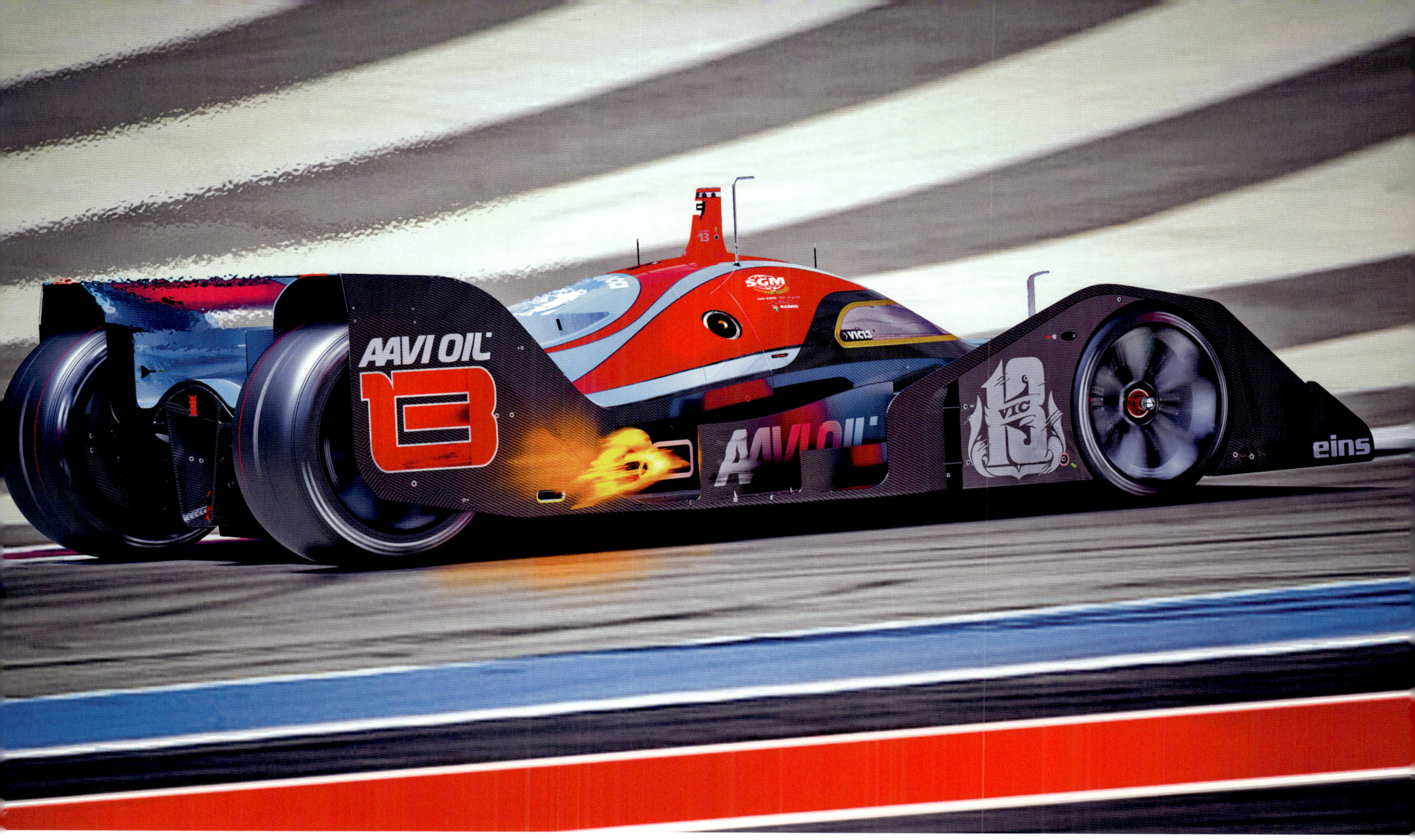

2027 VIC COOPER
AT HOME ON THE TRACK

At home on the track. "Looking at the number 13 on my car and the Masucci logo on my race suit", Cooper says with a grin on his face, "is like having arrived. It feels like home." The iconic shield with the white "M" describing the snow-covered twin mountains seen from Masucci's Turin office, has surrounded Cooper throughout his childhood. Troubled with many controversies but always silencing doubters with extraordinary success and inventive machines, the Italian team has a special place in Coopers heart: "My father and Masucci wrote motorsports history. I remember quite a bit of it, even from so long ago. Driving the X-7 now. I can understand what he must have felt. Masuccis are something else, it's hard to describe!"

Cooper's first half of the season, however, provided no memorable motorsports history at all, no podium, no points. The car was quite a mess, and even Cooper started secretly questioning the turbine concept. "It takes time to make a car competitive, but this one was a struggle." In Brazil, Cooper had his first podium finish in third and was finally confident for the last race to go for a win. "Only one race left to beat Faubert, but now, for the first time, my car is talking to me. I don't know which of our endless modifications it is, but I can really feel it now. That is what my father always said, the car has to talk to you! Now I know what he meant. I am relaxed in it, one with it. We are ready to race. All I can think about is how to beat Faubert. We have one race left. It's now or never."

Sur la piste comme chez soi. « Quand je vois le numéro 13 sur ma voiture et le logo Masucci sur ma combinaison, j'ai un sentiment d'achèvement. Comme si j'étais enfin à la maison », déclare Vic Cooper dans un large sourire. Le célèbre écusson, flanqué d'un « M » blanc figurant les deux montagnes enneigées visibles depuis le bureau de Masucci à Turin, fait partie des images ayant bercé l'enfance de Vic. Suscitant la controverse, mais faisant taire les critiques grâce aux excellents résultats de ses machines innovantes, l'écurie italienne a une place à part dans son cœur : « Mon père et Masucci ont écrit de très belles pages de l'histoire du sport automobile. Aujourd'hui, au volant de la X-7, je comprends mieux ce dont il voulait parler : les Masucci sont des machines à part. »

Pourtant, la première moitié de la saison se déroula assez mal. Ni podium, ni points marqués. La voiture semblait ratée, et Cooper s'interrogeait sérieusement sur l'intérêt de la turbine. « Il faut du temps pour rendre une voiture compétitive, mais là, c'était une vraie galère. » Au Brésil, il finit tout de même sur le podium, ce qui lui redonna l'espoir d'accrocher la victoire lors de la dernière course. « C'est ma dernière chance de battre Faubert. Et là, pour la première fois, ma voiture me « parle ». Maintenant, je comprends ce que mon père voulait dire quand il disait qu'il fallait que la machine et lui communiquent. Je me sens bien à son volant, nous ne faisons qu'un. Je veux battre Faubert. Il nous reste une course, c'est maintenant ou jamais. »

Auf der Rennstrecke zu Hause. „Wenn ich die 13 und das Masucci-Logo auf meinem Rennoverall sehe", sagt Cooper mit einem Grinsen, „dann ist es als wäre ich angekommen, ein Gefühl wie zu Hause." Unter dem Wappen mit dem weißen „M", das die schneebedeckten Zwillingsgipfel vor Masuccis Turiner Büro symbolisiert, hat Cooper buchstäblich seine Kindheit verbracht. Trotz aller Kontroversen um die waghalsigen Konstruktionen Masuccis hat das Team einen sicheren Platz in Vics Herzen: „Mein Vater und Masucci haben Renngeschichte geschrieben. Ich kann mich an vieles noch erinnern. Jetzt, wo ich selber für Masucci fahre, kann ich die Begeisterung meines Vaters gut verstehen!"

Nach Renngeschichte sah die erste Hälfte der Saison von Cooper und dem Team allerdings nicht aus. Kein Podium, keine Punkte. Das Auto war schwer zu verstehen und selbst in Cooper regten sich Zweifel am Turbinenkonzept. „Es braucht Zeit, ein Gewinnerauto zu bauen, aber das hier ist schon etwas ernüchternd." In Brasilien stand Cooper dann zum ersten Mal auf dem Podium und war wieder voller Zuversicht. „Nur noch ein Rennen diese Saison und ich kann es fühlen, ich kann das Auto endlich fühlen! Welche unserer endlosen Verbesserungen es genau war, kann ich nicht sagen, aber das Auto spricht endlich zu mir. Das ist, was mein Vater immer gesagt hat: Es muss zu dir sprechen! Jetzt denke ich nur noch daran, wie ich Faubert schlagen kann. Jetzt oder nie."

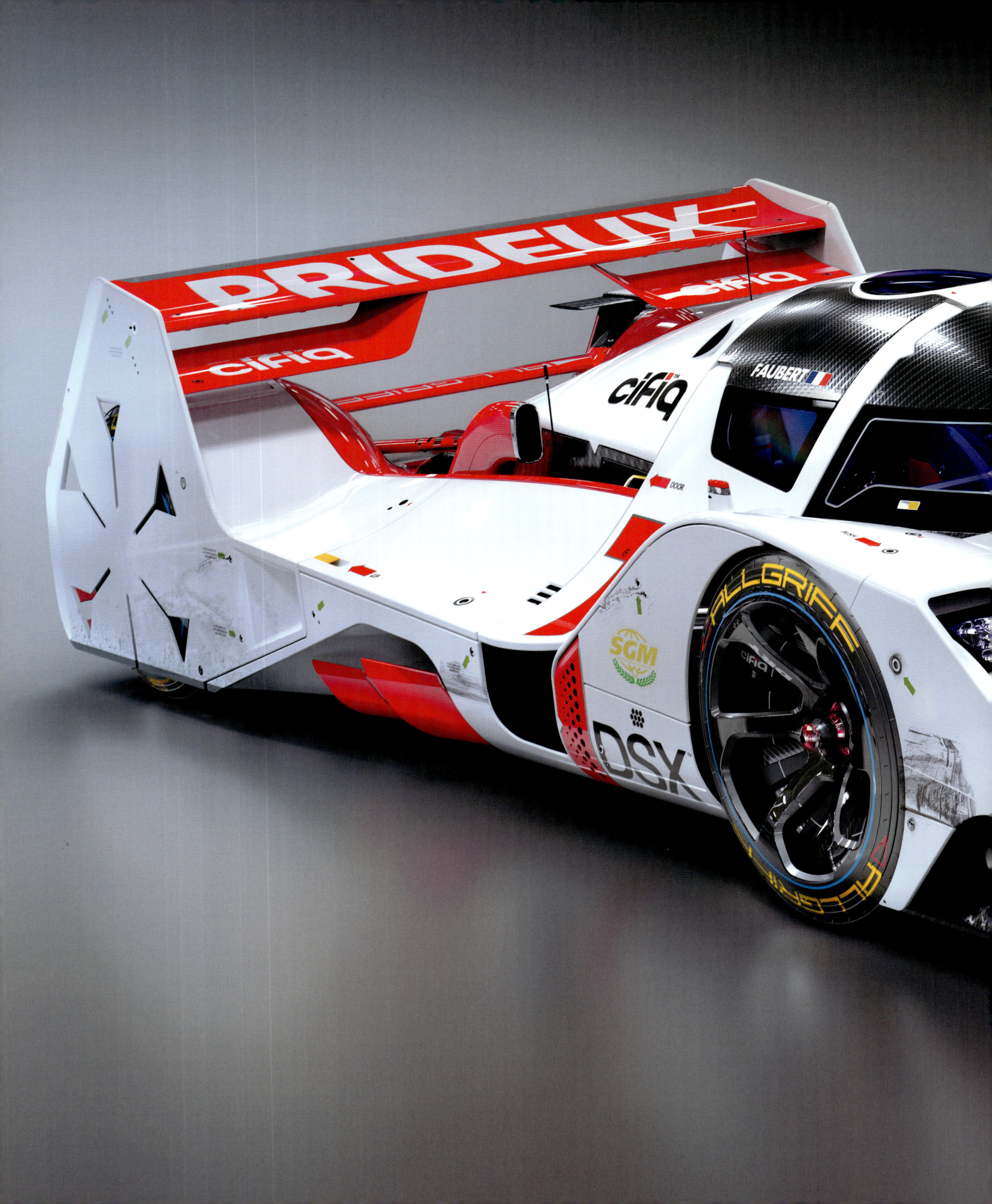
PRIDELUX
cifiq
cifiq
cifiq
FAUBERT
DOOR
SGM
DSX
ALLGRIFF

THE CAR AND MAN TO BEAT

PRIDEUX-MARTIN MF/27

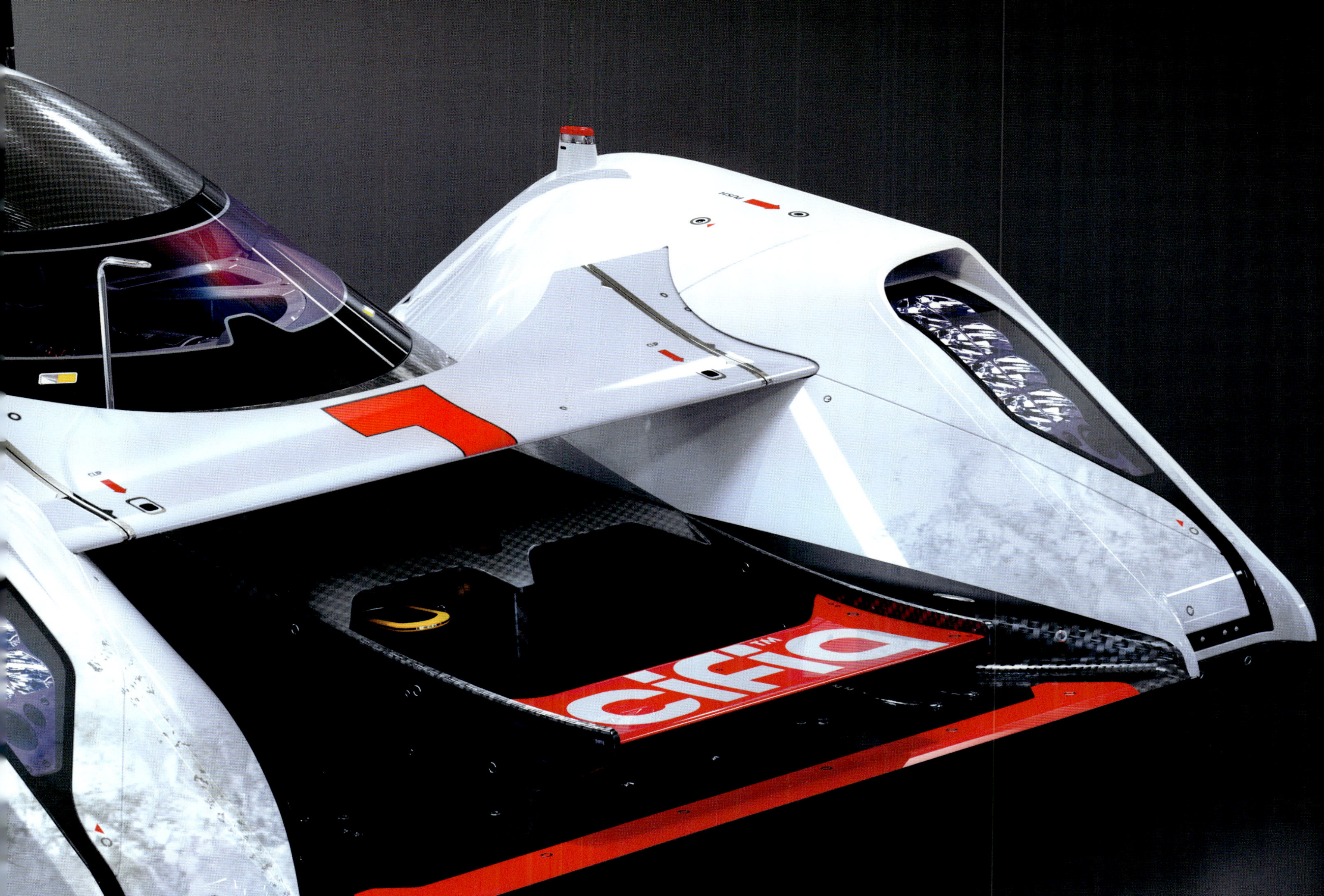

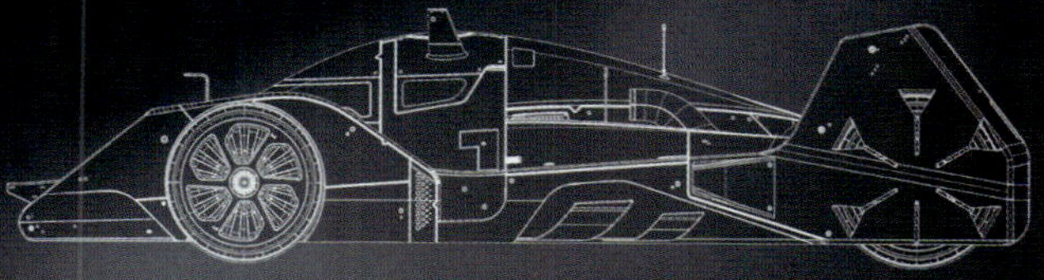

MODEL	Prideux-Martin MF / 27
TYPE	SGM Endurance World Cup
YEAR	2027
DESIGNER	Léon Prideux
ENGINE	Rear: Martin 6-cyl diesel / Front: Cifiq electric
POWER OUTPUT	807 hp
TOP SPEED	432 km/h / 268 mph
PINCIPLE DRIVER	Gaël Faubert
L / W / H	4594mm / 2034mm / 1130mm
WHEELBASE	3020mm

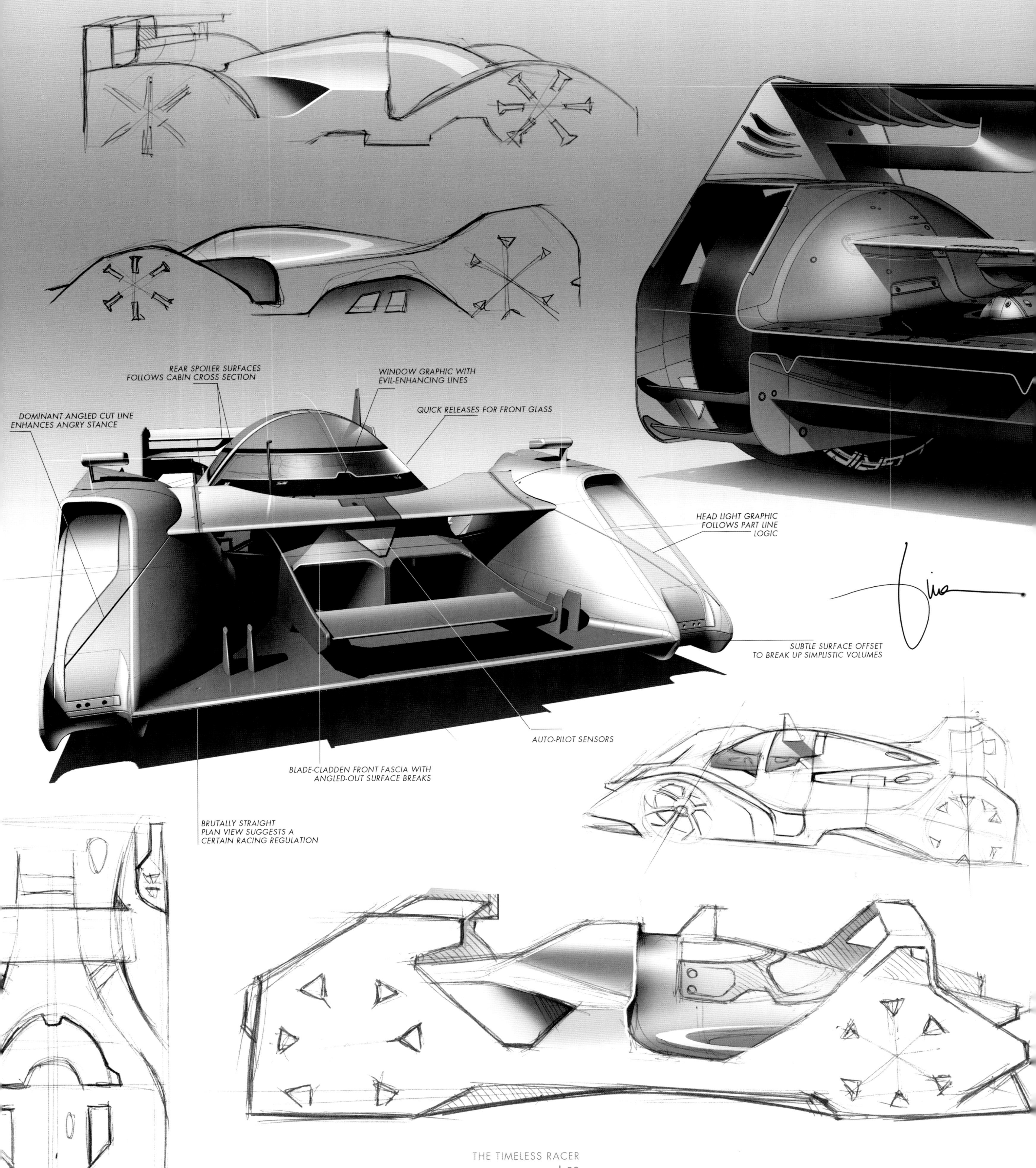
REAR SPOILER SURFACES
FOLLOWS CABIN CROSS SECTION
WINDOW GRAPHIC WITH
EVIL-ENHANCING LINES
DOMINANT ANGLED CUT LINE
ENHANCES ANGRY STANCE
QUICK RELEASES FOR FRONT GLASS
HEAD LIGHT GRAPHIC
FOLLOWS PART LINE
LOGIC
SUBTLE SURFACE OFFSET
TO BREAK UP SIMPLISTIC VOLUMES
AUTO-PILOT SENSORS
BLADE-CLADDEN FRONT FASCIA WITH
ANGLED-OUT SURFACE BREAKS
BRUTALLY STRAIGHT
PLAN VIEW SUGGESTS A
CERTAIN RACING REGULATION

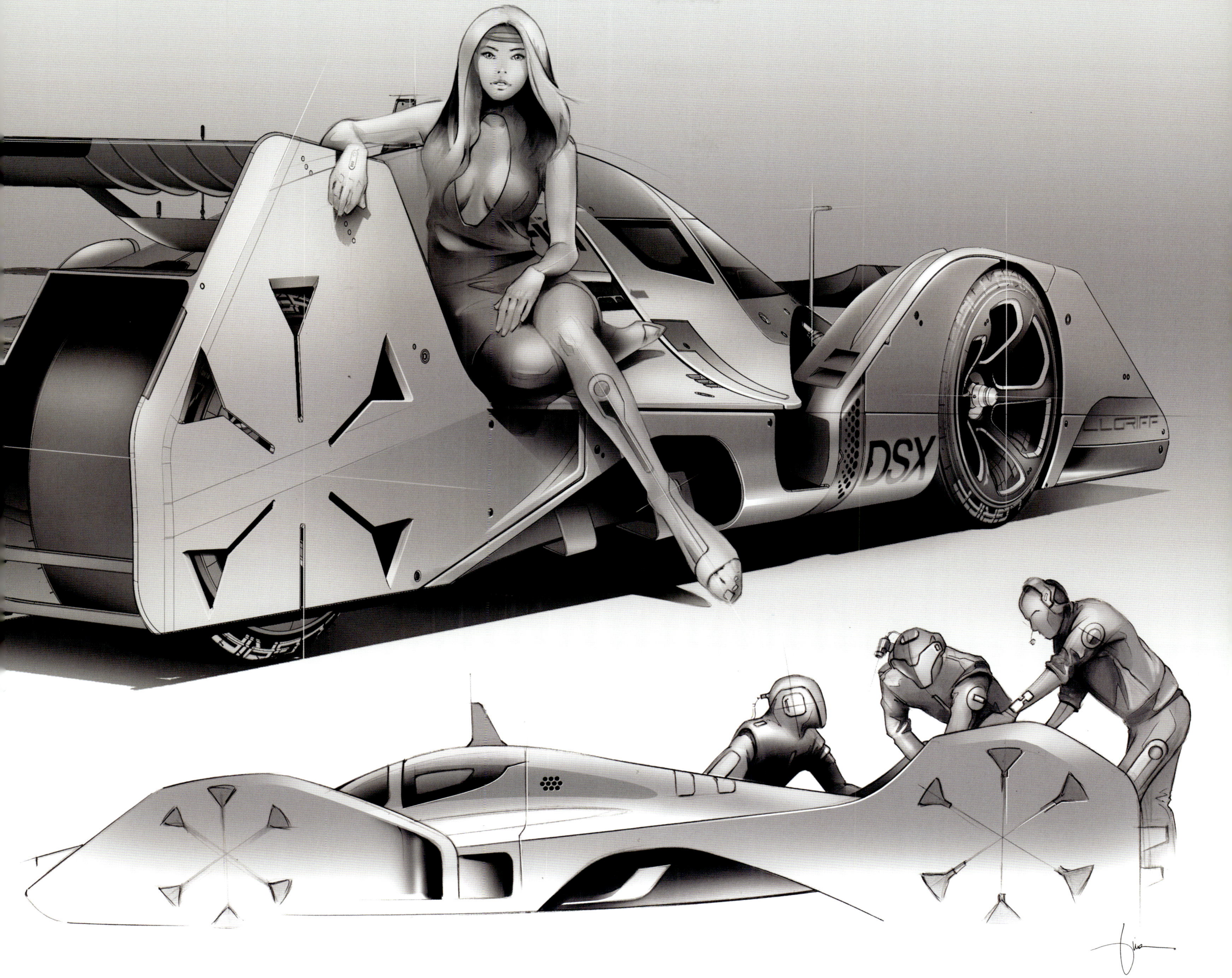

DESIGNPRIDEUXMARTINMF/27
CREATING A FRENCH CHAMPION

Creating a french champion. The car that would represent a dominating force in the SGM Endurance Cup needed an advanced and very confident look. In contrast to the quite soft-shaped Masucci cars, I was after a sharp folded architecture. The top surface breaks open right behind the cabin, revealing mechanical engine parts. In artistically approached industrial design I always enjoy the contrast of large simplistic skins that expose an underlying structure in some well-selected areas. The cooling slots on the rear fenders make your mind complete a set of wheels, and a very narrow window graphic helps to establish a sinister expression. The biggest creative challenge was the front, where I was looking for an open, abstract structure, without leaving the car faceless.

Naissance d'un champion français. La voiture dominant la Coupe d'endurance SGM doit impressionner. Contrairement aux modèles de Masucci, aux formes douces, je pensais à une architecture forte avec des plis. La surface supérieure se brise derrière le cockpit, révélant certaines parties mécaniques. Dans mon approche artistique, j'ai toujours apprécié le contraste apporté par de grandes surfaces couvrantes qui laissent néanmoins entrevoir la structure complexe de certains éléments. Les fentes de refroidissement à l'arrière laissent ainsi imaginer les roues, tandis que les étroites surfaces vitrées contribuent à donner à l'ensemble une expression plutôt sinistre. Un grand défi créatif concernait l'avant, où je devais concilier la recherche d'une certaine abstraction et la volonté de donner un visage à l'auto.

Ein französischer Champion entsteht. Um die totale Dominanz im SGM Endurance Cup darstellen zu können, musste der gegnerische Wagen Fortschrittlichkeit und Selbstbewusstsein ausstrahlen. Im Gegensatz zu den weichen Formen der Masucci-Rennwagen besitzt der Prideux eine kantige Architektur: die Dachfläche reißt abrupt hinter der Kabine auf und legt Strukturteile frei – ein designerischer Kunstgriff, den ich bei Fantasy-Fahrzeugen gerne anwende. Die Kühlschlitze an den hinteren Kotflügeln spielen mit der Wahrnehmung der verdeckten Räder und die schmale Cockpit-Verglasung vermittelt einen aggressiven Look. Als größte Herausforderung für das Design entpuppte sich die Front, die ich sehr offen und abstrakt gestalten wollte, ohne dem Auto sein Gesicht zu nehmen.

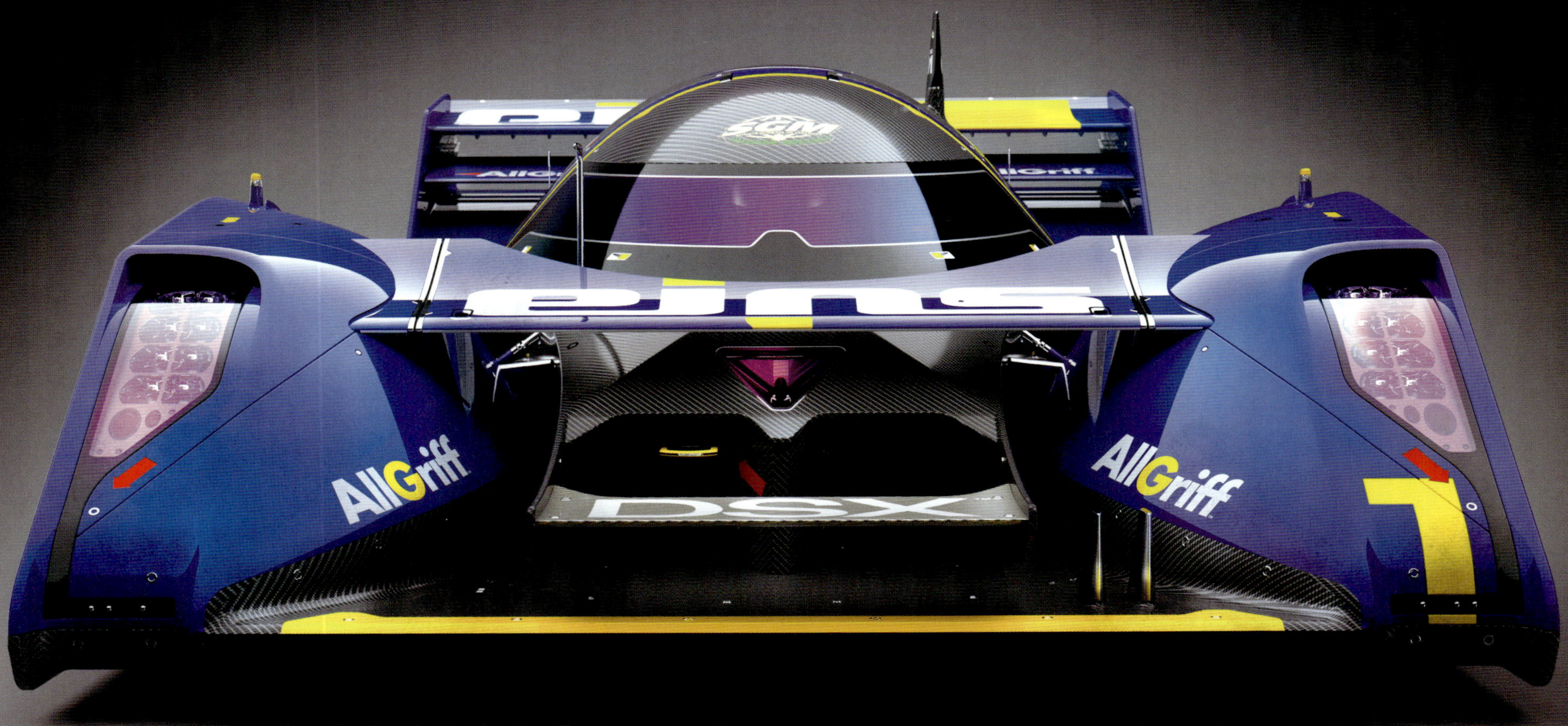

2027PRIDEUX**MARTINMF/27**
THE FLAWLESS BENCHMARK

The flawless benchmark. The French racing team Prideux joined the Endurance Cup grid in 2019. Within a few years, team manager and bean counting dictator Léon Prideux made astonishing progress and pushed his equipe to all four championships between 2023 and 2026. A key element was driver Gaël Faubert (page 56) and his collaboration with the greatest engineers and designers money can buy.

The blue car seen here is the MF/26-Eins as it started the 2027 season. A disagreement between communication multi Eins and Prideux ended the sponsorship immediately and the iconic blue and yellow was replaced by a sleek white, silver, and red livery for the next race in France. Those colors belong to Cifiq, the Canadian powerhouse in electric drive systems and battery solutions.

Léon Prideux built two different cars for the 2027 season. Car One of Faubert was a hybrid with the Martin six-cylinder diesel driving the rear and two Cifiq electric motors driving the front. A conservative but reliable solution, it created 807 hp for 50 hours. The car can be recognized by a set of exhausts on the rear hatch and star-shaped cooling slots on the rear fenders. Car Two, an all-electric test mule for the 2028 season, collected valuable data for the following season, when combustion engines would be banned from the SGM Extreme class. This "visionary" move by Prideux opened new discussion about Léon's relationship to Société Globale de Moteurs president Jacques Castel.

La référence absolue. L'écurie française Prideux rejoint la Coupe d'Endurance SGM en 2019. De 2023 à 2026, sous la houlette du redouté Léon Prideux, l'équipe s'illustre quatre fois d'affilée. Elément-clé de cette réussite, le pilote Gaël Faubert (p. 56), qui tire le meilleur parti de sa collaboration avec des ingénieurs et concepteurs parmi les plus compétents au monde.

La voiture bleue figurant ici est la MF/26-Eins dans sa robe de début de saison 2027. A la suite d'un profond désaccord entre le sponsor Eins et Prideux, la livrée bleue et jaune devint pour la course suivante en France un élégant blanc, argent et rouge, couleurs de la Cifiq, société canadienne spécialisée dans les systèmes d'entraînement électriques et les solutions pour batteries.

Prideux construisit deux voitures pour 2027. La numéro 1 de Faubert était une hybride : un six cylindres diesel Martin était relié aux roues arrière, alors que deux moteurs électriques Cifiq entraînaient l'avant. Solution conservatrice mais fiable, délivrant 807 ch pendant 50 heures. La deuxième voiture, un mulet de test tout-électrique, permit de recueillir de précieux enseignements pour la saison 2028 à venir, quand les moteurs à combustion seraient interdits dans la catégorie SGM Extrême. Cette disposition due à Prideux suscita la polémique quant à sa relation avec la Société Globale de Moteurs et son président Jacques Castel.

Das Maß aller Dinge. Der französische Rennstall Prideux begann sein Engagement im Endurance Cup in der Saison 2019. Innerhalb weniger Jahre verbuchte Léon Prideux erstaunliche Erfolge: Das Team gewann zwischen 2023 und 2026 alle Meistertitel. Dies ist in erster Linie dem Fahrer Gaël Faubert (siehe Seite 56) zu verdanken sowie den teuersten Ingenieuren und Designern der Welt.

Hier ist der blaue MF/26-Eins abgebildet, mit dem Faubert das erste Saisonrennen in Japan klar dominierte. Aufgrund von wachsenden Spannungen zwischen dem Kommunikationskonzern Eins und Prideux wurde der langjährige Sponsorenvertrag aufgelöst und der blau-gelbe Anstrich wich den Farben Weiß, Silber und Rot des kanadischen Elektro- und Batteriegiganten Cifiq.

Léon Prideux baute für die Saison 2027 zwei Fahrzeuge auf. Fauberts Wagen 1 war ein Hybrid mit einem Martin-Sechs-Zylinder-Diesel für die Hinterachse und zwei Cifiq-E-Motoren vorn. Diese Lösung stellte bis zu 807 PS zuverlässig über 50 Stunden bereit. Der Wagen ist an den Zwillingsendrohren und den sternförmigen Kühlschlitzen an den hinteren Radabdeckungen zu erkennen. Wagen 2 war ein komplett elektrisch getriebener Erprobungsträger für 2028 – der Saison, in der Verbrennungsmotoren von der SGM-Extreme-Klasse ausgeschlossen werden würden. Dieser „weitsichtige" Schachzug Prideux entfachte einmal mehr Diskussionen über dessen Beziehung zu SGM-Präsident Jacques Castel.

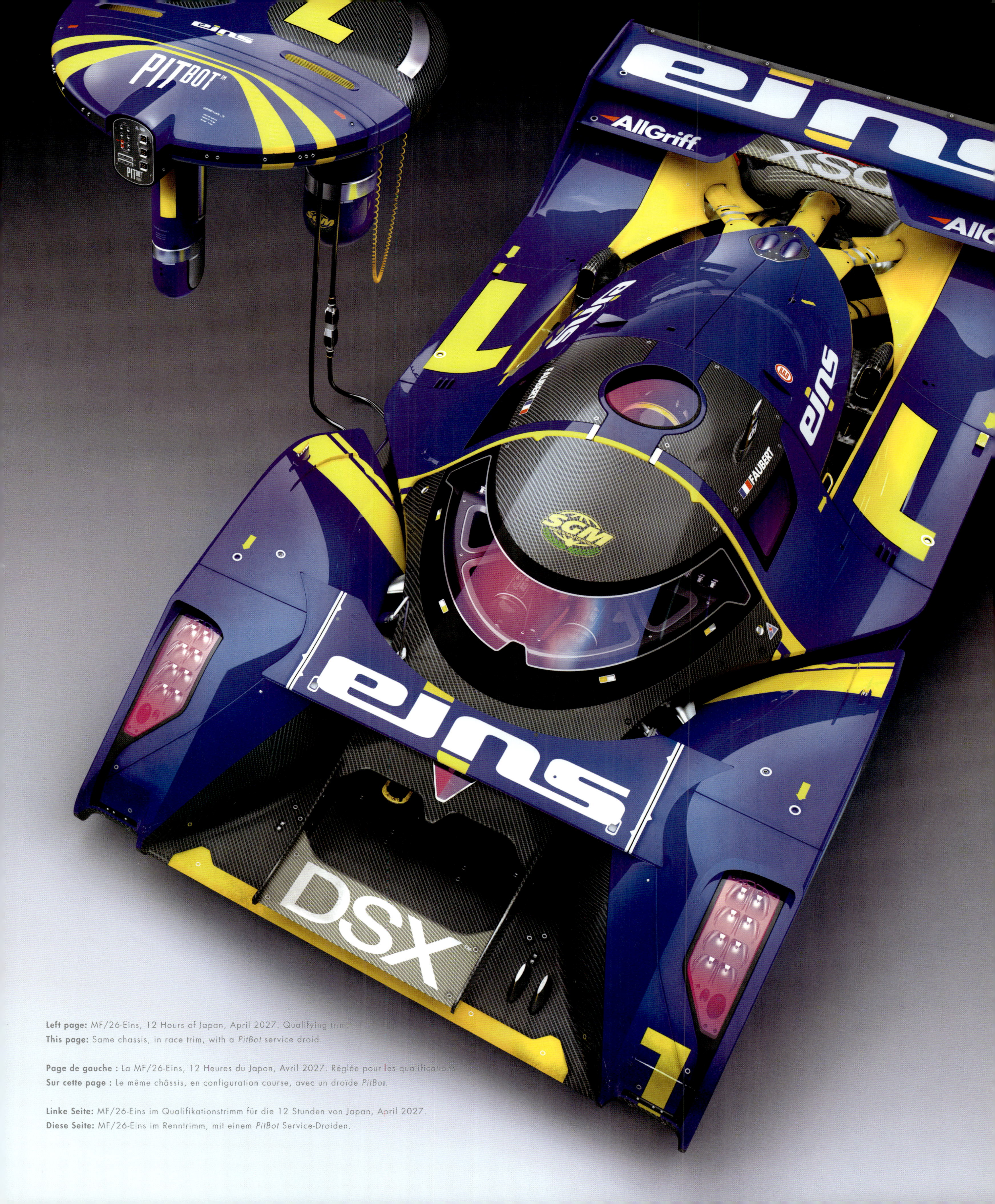

Left page: MF/26-Eins, 12 Hours of Japan, April 2027. Qualifying trim.
This page: Same chassis, in race trim, with a *PitBot* service droid.

Page de gauche : La MF/26-Eins, 12 Heures du Japon, Avril 2027. Réglée pour les qualifications.
Sur cette page : Le même châssis, en configuration course, avec un droïde *PitBot*.

Linke Seite: MF/26-Eins im Qualifikationstrimm für die 12 Stunden von Japan, April 2027.
Diese Seite: MF/26-Eins im Renntrimm, mit einem *PitBot* Service-Droiden.

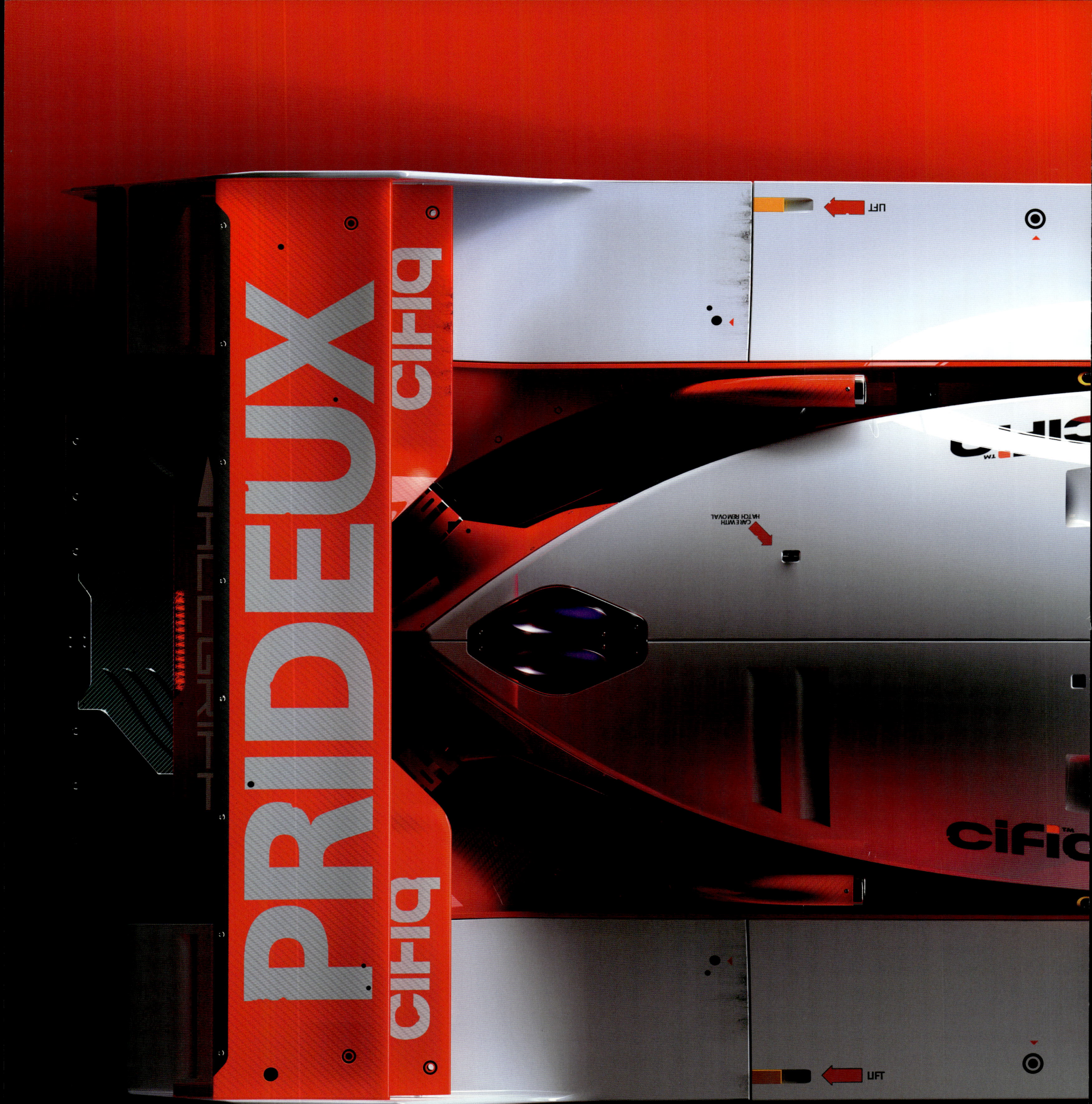
PRIDEUX
LIFT

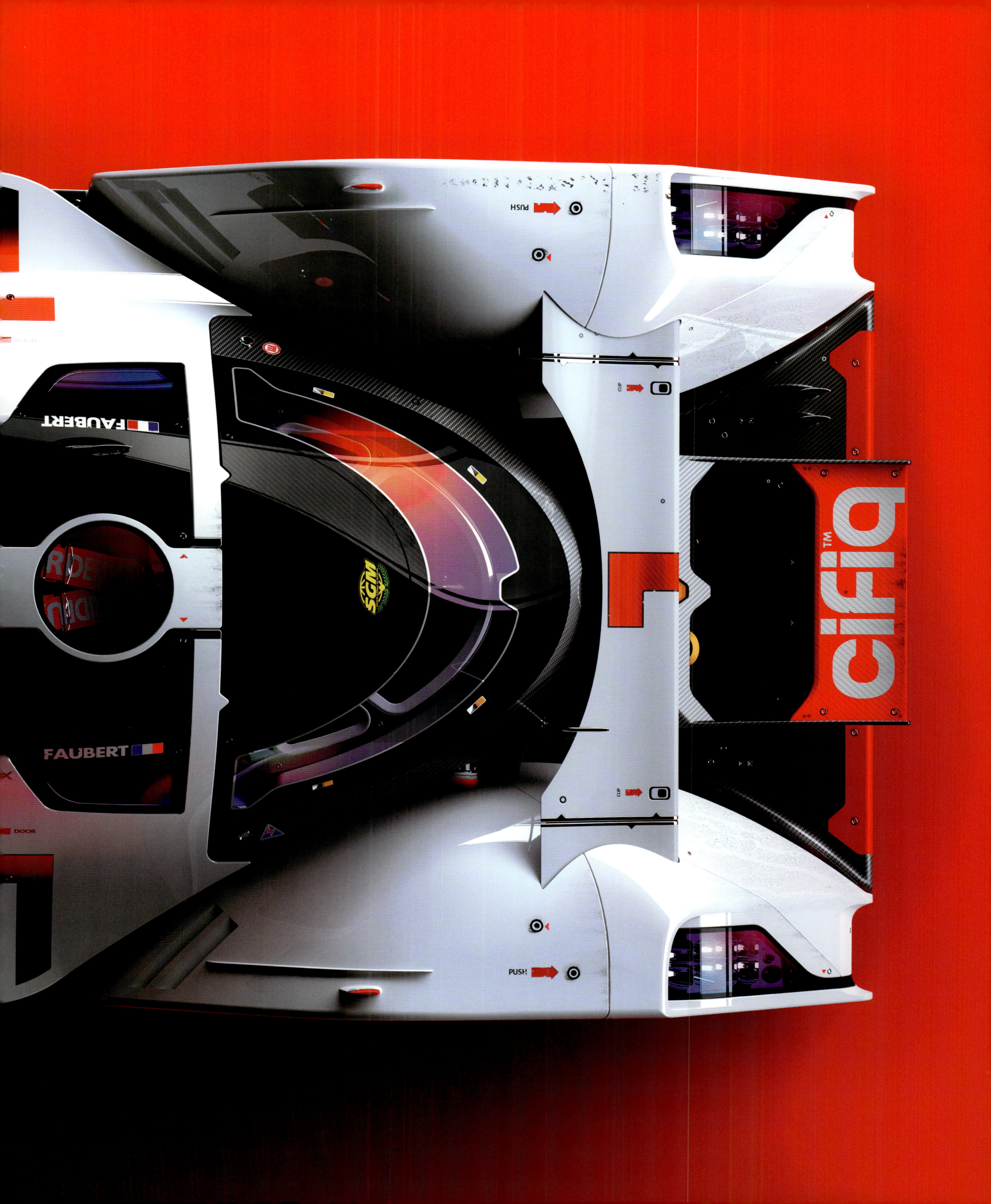

PUSH
FAUBERT
SGM
cifia™
DOOR
FAUBERT
PUSH

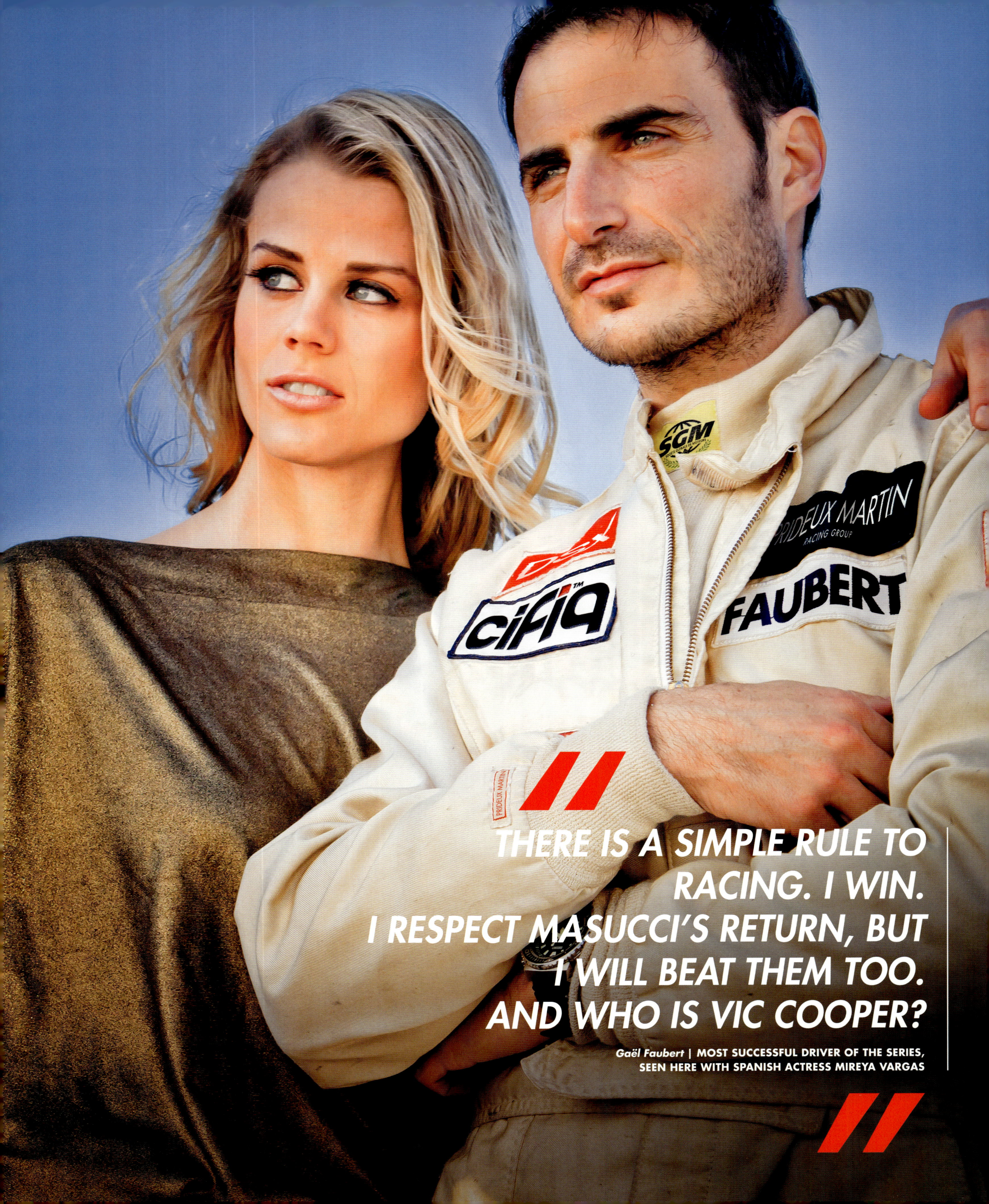

THERE IS A SIMPLE RULE TO RACING. I WIN. I RESPECT MASUCCI'S RETURN, BUT I WILL BEAT THEM TOO. AND WHO IS VIC COOPER?

Gaël Faubert | MOST SUCCESSFUL DRIVER OF THE SERIES, SEEN HERE WITH SPANISH ACTRESS MIREYA VARGAS

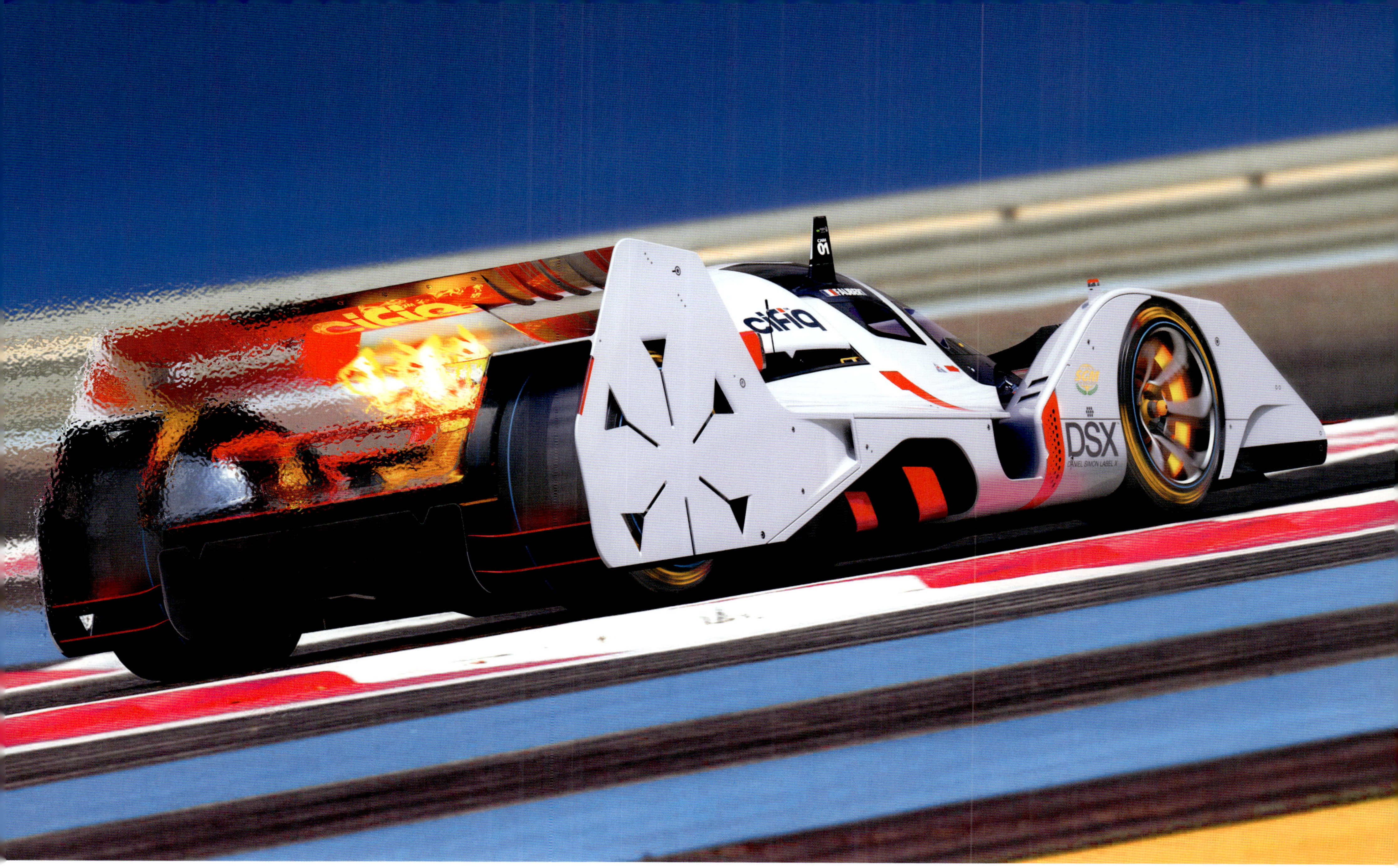

2027 GAËL FAUBERT
THE FLYING FRENCHMAN

The flying frenchman. Gaël Faubert is the most successful racing driver in the SGM Endurance Cup. Adopted and raised by a French motor sport clan, he was exposed to the sport from an early age. His adoptive father, Gilles Faubert, is a famous racer and businessman who won championships on land and in the air, including the Formula Zero and the Peregrine Cup.

Faubert joined Prideux in 2019 as a test driver. He constantly outperformed the Prideux factory drivers in the Prideux-Coste MF/19, and was promoted to lead driver after only two months. His first season was plagued with mechanical problems, but since 2023 Faubert has won the championship an unprecedented four times. His 2027 MF/27 is the second evolution of the fast MF/26 chassis and was developed partly by Faubert, with all other drivers of the French Prideux team having to adjust to his driving characteristics.

A personal friendship between Faubert and Société Globale de Moteurs president and rule maker Jacques Castel was long a secret. Faubert's statement about Cooper sounds deceitful in that context: "There is a simple rule to racing. I win. I respect Masucci's return, but I will beat them too. And who is Vic Cooper?" Faubert is engaged to Spanish actress Mireya Vargas. They live in Nice, France.

Le Français volant. Gaël Faubert est le pilote ayant remporté le plus de victoires en Coupe d'Endurance SGM. Il a été adopté et élevé par une dynastie française du sport mécanique. Son père adoptif, Gilles Faubert, célèbre pilote de course et homme d'affaires, a remporté des compétitions sur terre et dans les airs, comme le Championnat de Formule Zero et la Peregrine Cup.

Faubert rejoint l'écurie française Prideux en 2019 comme pilote d'essai. Surpassant constamment les pilotes titulaires de la Prideux-Coste MF/19, il est promu numéro 1 en deux mois seulement. Si sa première saison aura été gâchée par de nombreux problèmes mécaniques, à partir de 2023 Faubert remportera quatre fois le championnat, un fait sans précédent. Sa MF/27 2027, seconde évolution de la très rapide MF/26, a été mise au point par lui et pour lui, les autres pilotes devant s'adapter à ses consignes techniques.

L'amitié entre Faubert et le Président de la SGM, Jacques Castel, auteur de la réglementation, resta longtemps secrète. Dans ce contexte, cette déclaration de Faubert à propos de Cooper semble suspecte : « Il y a une règle simple en course. Je gagne. Je respecte le retour de Masucci, mais je vais les battre aussi. Et qui est Vic Cooper ? » Faubert est fiancé à l'actrice espagnole Mireya Vargas. Ils vivent en France, à Nice.

Der fliegende Franzose. Gaël Faubert ist der erfolgreichste Fahrer des SGM Endurance Cups. Das Adoptivkind, groß geworden in einer französischen Renndynastie, kam schon früh mit dem Rennsport in Berührung: Sein Adoptivvater Gilles Faubert, ein bekannter Pilot und Geschäftsmann, gewann Weltmeistertitel zu Lande (Formel Zero) und in den Lüften (Peregrine Cup).

Faubert kam 2019 als Testfahrer zu Prideux, wo er bei Runden auf dem Prideux-Coste MF/19 den Werksfahrern regelmäßig die Sekunden abnahm. Nach nur zwei Monaten wurde Gaël von Prideux als Hauptfahrer verpflichtet. Seine erste Saison war noch von Mechanikproblemen geplagt, doch ab 2023 konnte Faubert die Meisterschaft beispiellose vier Mal gewinnen. Fauberts MF/27 von 2027 ist eine Evolution des Vorjahreswagens und ausschließlich auf ihn abgestimmt – sehr zum Ärger seiner Teamkollegen.

Eine enge Freundschaft Fauberts zu SGM-Präsident und Regelpapst Jaques Castel blieb lange geheim. Fauberts berühmtestes Zitat erscheint daher ziemlich link: „Es gibt eine einfache Regel. Ich gewinne. Masuccis Rückkehr zum Rennsport respektiere ich, werde aber auch sie schlagen. Und wer ist Vic Cooper?" Faubert lebt mit seiner Verlobten, der spanischen Schauspielerin Mireya Vargas, in Nizza.

All eyes were on the final race of the season, the 48 Hours of California in November 2027. Vic Cooper had qualified in second place, right behind Faubert. Forty-eight hours are long, but every second counts. The radical X-7 gas turbine concept was finally reliable and Cooper gave Faubert a run for his money, changing the lead with him a stunning 97 times. Cooper won, by the length of a car. It was Faubert's first defeat in years and many records were broken that weekend, including the first win of a gas turbine car, first 48-hour win for a rookie driver, and the longest distance raced of an unmanned car. Sponsor Dale Burton had his money well spent and in celebration of the win took the entire Masucci crew to his orbital holiday space resort.

Tous les yeux se braquaient désormais vers les 48 Heures de Californie, en novembre 2027. Vic Cooper s'était qualifié en deuxième position, juste derrière Faubert. 48 heures, c'est long et chaque seconde compte. La turbine à gaz de la X-7 se révéla fiable. Cooper livra une rude opposition à Faubert, les deux hommes s'échangeant la tête de la course à 97 reprises. Cooper s'imposa finalement, gagnant d'une longueur de voiture. Première défaite de Faubert depuis des années, et nombreux records battus : première victoire d'une voiture à turbine à gaz, première course de 48 heures remportée par un débutant, et distance la plus longue parcourue par une voiture sans pilote. Dale Burton avait bien investi son argent et, pour fêter la victoire, invita toute l'écurie Masucci dans son club de vacances spatial.

Im November 2027 gab es nur ein Thema: das Finale von Kalifornien. Cooper qualifizierte sich auf Zwei, direkt hinter Faubert. Auch über 48 Stunden sollte es auf jede Sekunde ankommen. Masuccis radikaler Gasturbinen-X-7 war endlich zuverlässig. Cooper lieferte sich mit Faubert einen erbitterten Kampf mit unglaublichen 97 Führungswechseln. Nach 48 Stunden gewann Cooper mit einer Autolänge Vorsprung. Es war nicht nur Fauberts erste Niederlage seit Jahren, sondern auch die Stunde weiterer Rekorde: der erste Sieg eines Gasturbinenwagens, der erste Rookie-Sieg in einem 48-Stunden-Rennen und die längste per Autopilot gefahrene Renndistanz. Auch Sponsor Dale Burton befand, er habe sein Geld gut angelegt und spendierte der Masucci-Crew einen Urlaub in seinem Weltraumferienresort.

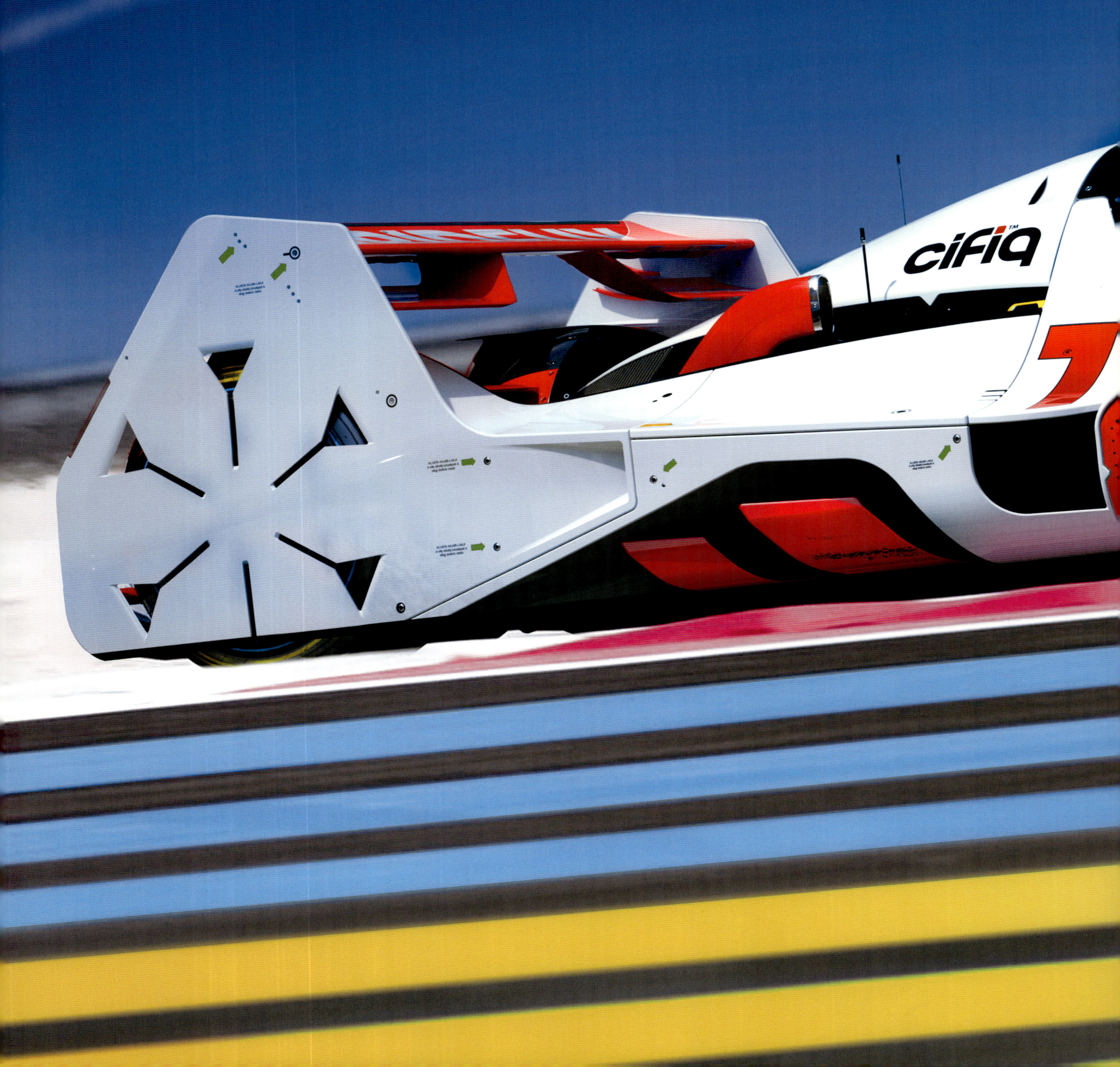

Masucci Racing was finally back in the motorsports history books, with 95-year-old Filomeno Masucci joyfully watching. It had been over 41 years since the last win of a Masucci car, with Cooper's father Jay McQuade behind the wheel. What a moment, what a feeling. Vic Cooper felt like he could become the greatest racer who has ever lived, when he suddenly collapsed under a stinging pain . . . He was back in the real world, but further away from it than ever before. Confused and overwhelmed, he knew one thing: he would have to return.

Masucci Racing était de retour dans les livres d'histoire du sport, pour la plus grande joie de Filomeno, 95 ans. Il s'était écoulé 41 ans depuis la dernière victoire d'une Masucci. Quel grand moment !
Alors qu'il s'imaginait déjà devenir le plus grand pilote de tous les temps, Vic s'effondra soudain, saisi d'une douleur fulgurante… Il était maintenant de retour dans le vrai monde, vis-à-vis duquel jamais il ne s'était senti aussi déphasé. A la fois confus et sonné, au moins avait-il une certitude : il lui faudrait revenir.

Masucci Racing stand wieder in den Motorsport-Geschichtsbüchern, zur großen Freude des mittlerweile 95-jährigen Filomeno Masucci. Den letzten Sieg hatte Vic Coopers Vater Jay McQuade vor mehr als 41 Jahren geholt! Welch ein triumphaler Moment, welch ein Gefühl. Cooper war erfüllt von dem Glauben, dass er einer der besten Rennfahrer aller Zeiten werden könnte, als er plötzlich wie vom Blitz getroffen zusammenbrach … Er war zurück. Zurück in der wahren Welt - und fühlte sich weiter von ihr entfernt als je zuvor. Verwirrt und überwältigt wusste er sofort: Er musste zurück.

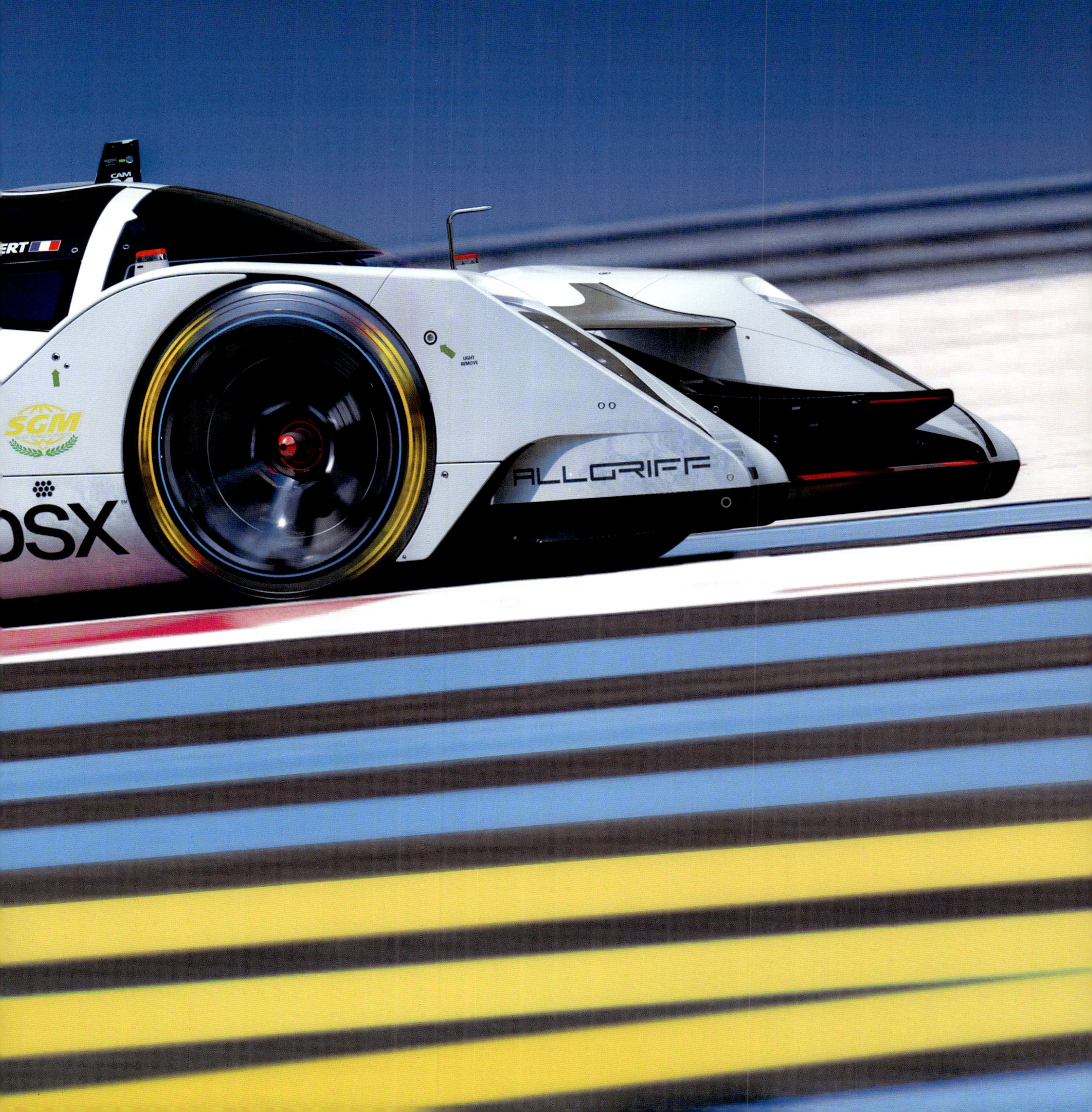

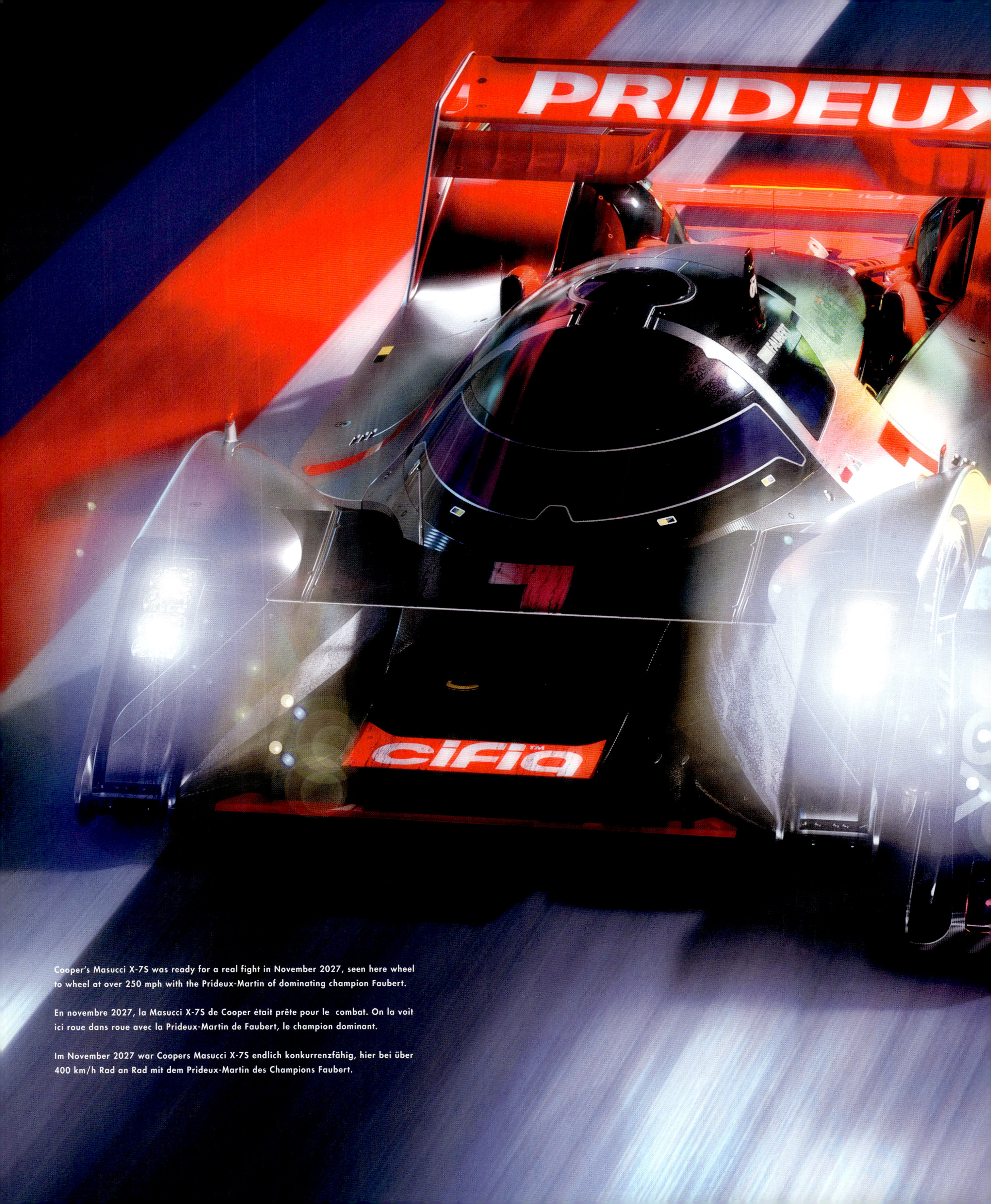

Cooper's Masucci X-7S was ready for a real fight in November 2027, seen here wheel to wheel at over 250 mph with the Prideux-Martin of dominating champion Faubert.

En novembre 2027, la Masucci X-7S de Cooper était prête pour le combat. On la voit ici roue dans roue avec la Prideux-Martin de Faubert, le champion dominant.

Im November 2027 war Coopers Masucci X-7S endlich konkurrenzfähig, hier bei über 400 km/h Rad an Rad mit dem Prideux-Martin des Champions Faubert.

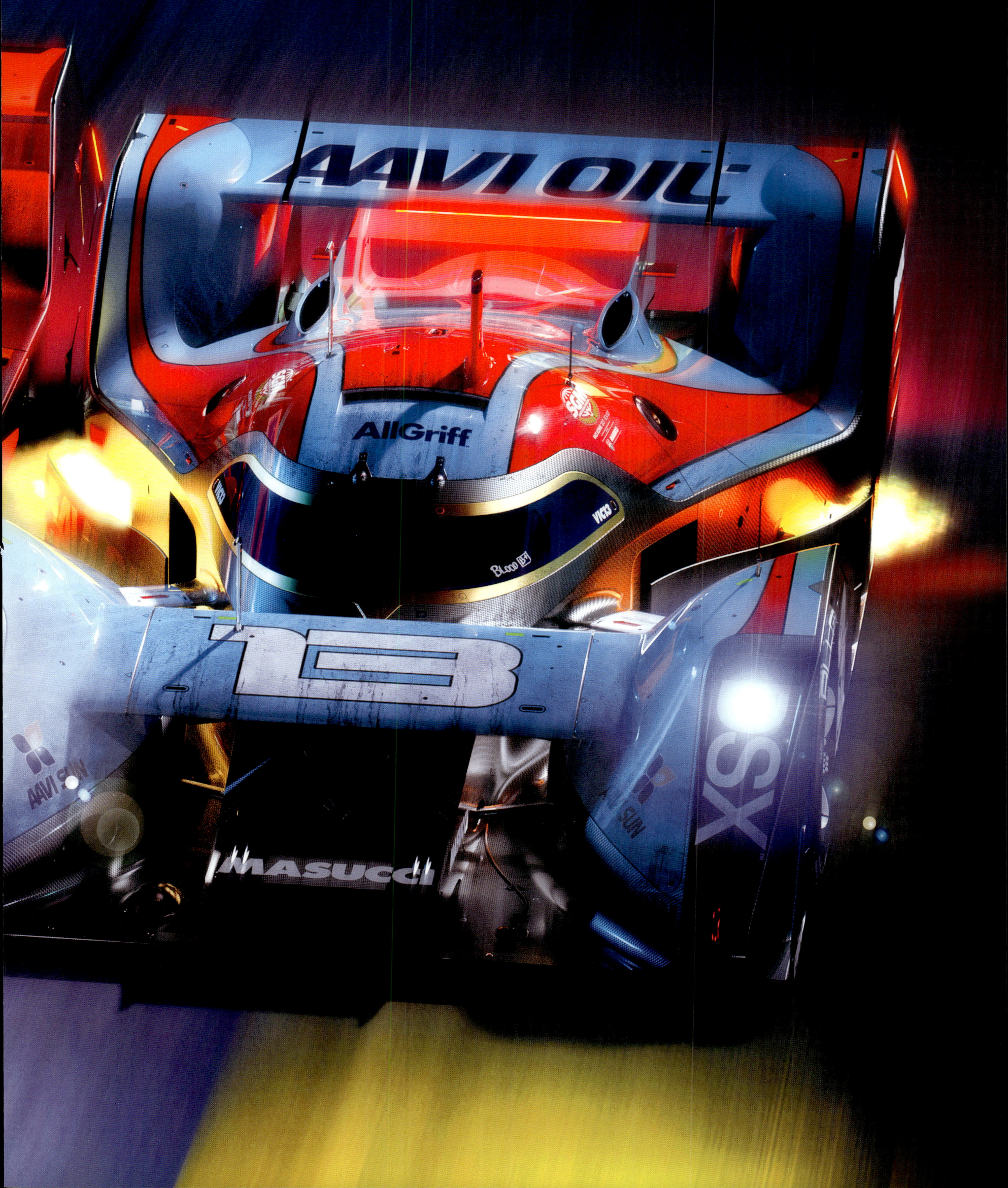
AAVI OIL
AllGriff
13
MASUCCI
AAVI SUN

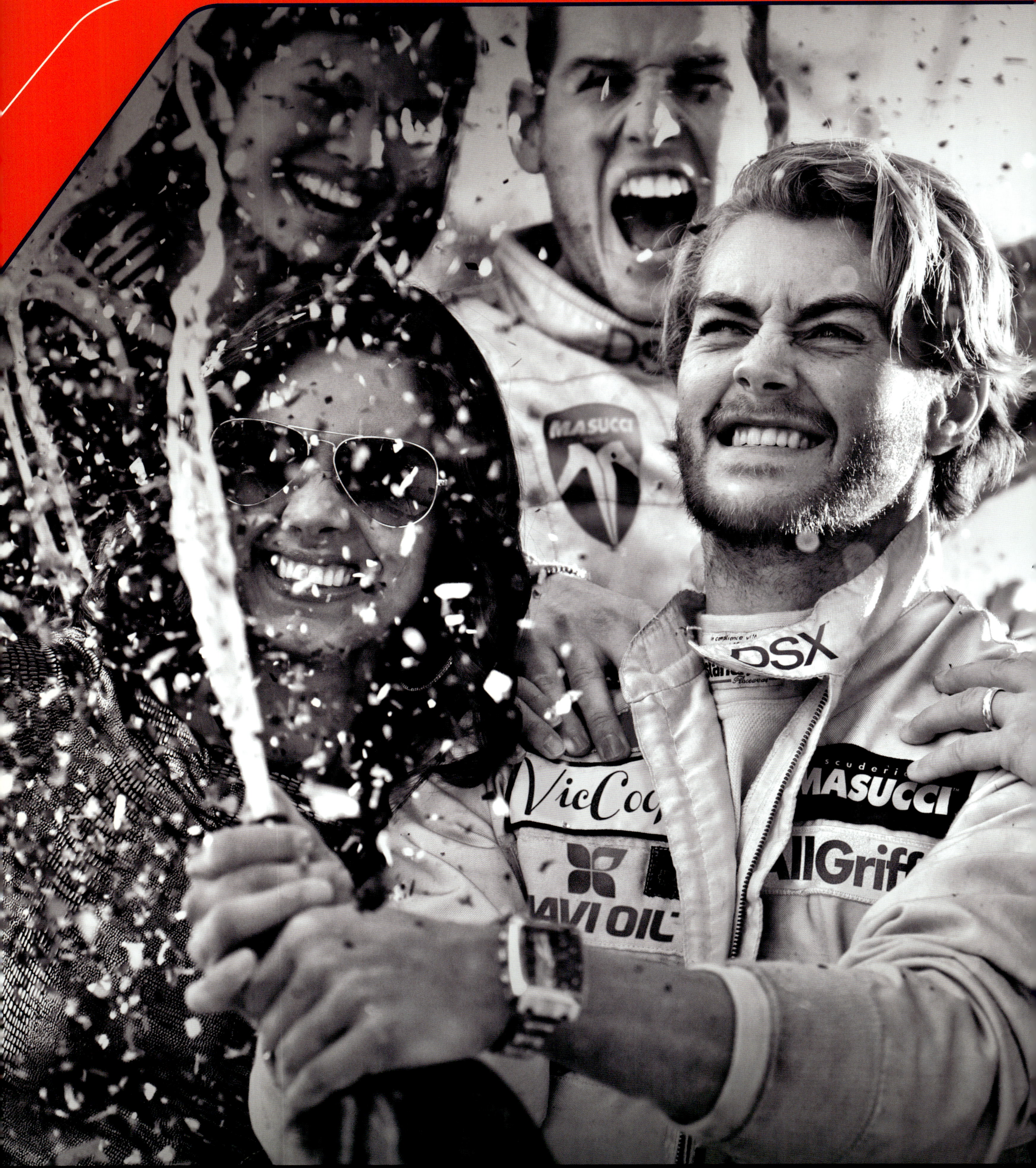

« Masucci Racing voudrait dédier cette victoire à tous ceux qui prétendaient qu'elle serait impossible. » | Novembre 2027, 48 Heures de Californie. Vic Cooper l'emporte sur une Masucci X-7

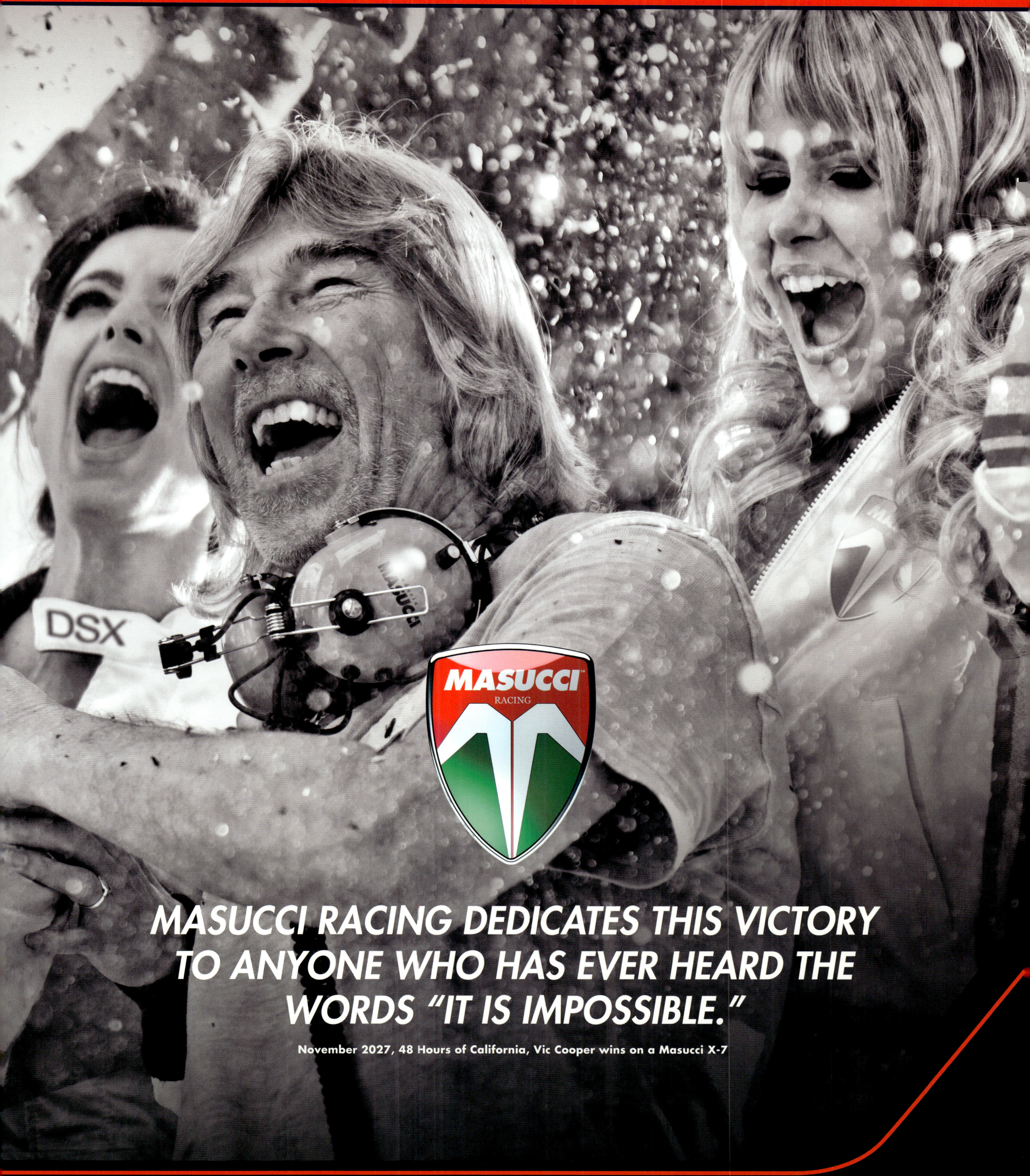

Masucci widmet diesen Sieg allen, denen jemals gesagt wurde: „Es ist unmöglich." | November 2027, 48 Stunden von Kalifornien, Vic Cooper gewinnt auf dem Masucci X-7

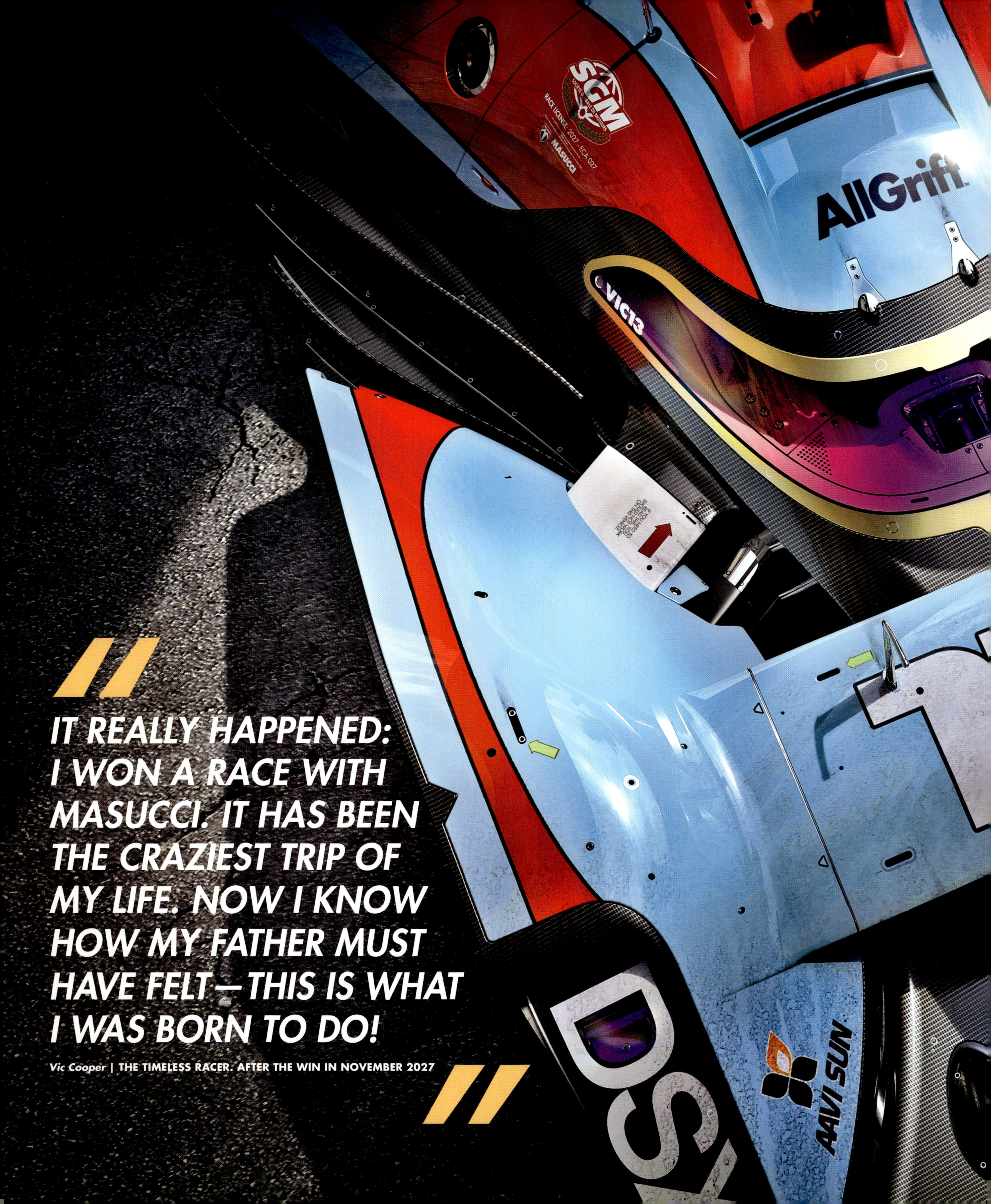

"IT REALLY HAPPENED: I WON A RACE WITH MASUCCI. IT HAS BEEN THE CRAZIEST TRIP OF MY LIFE. NOW I KNOW HOW MY FATHER MUST HAVE FELT—THIS IS WHAT I WAS BORN TO DO!"

Vic Cooper | THE TIMELESS RACER. AFTER THE WIN IN NOVEMBER 2027

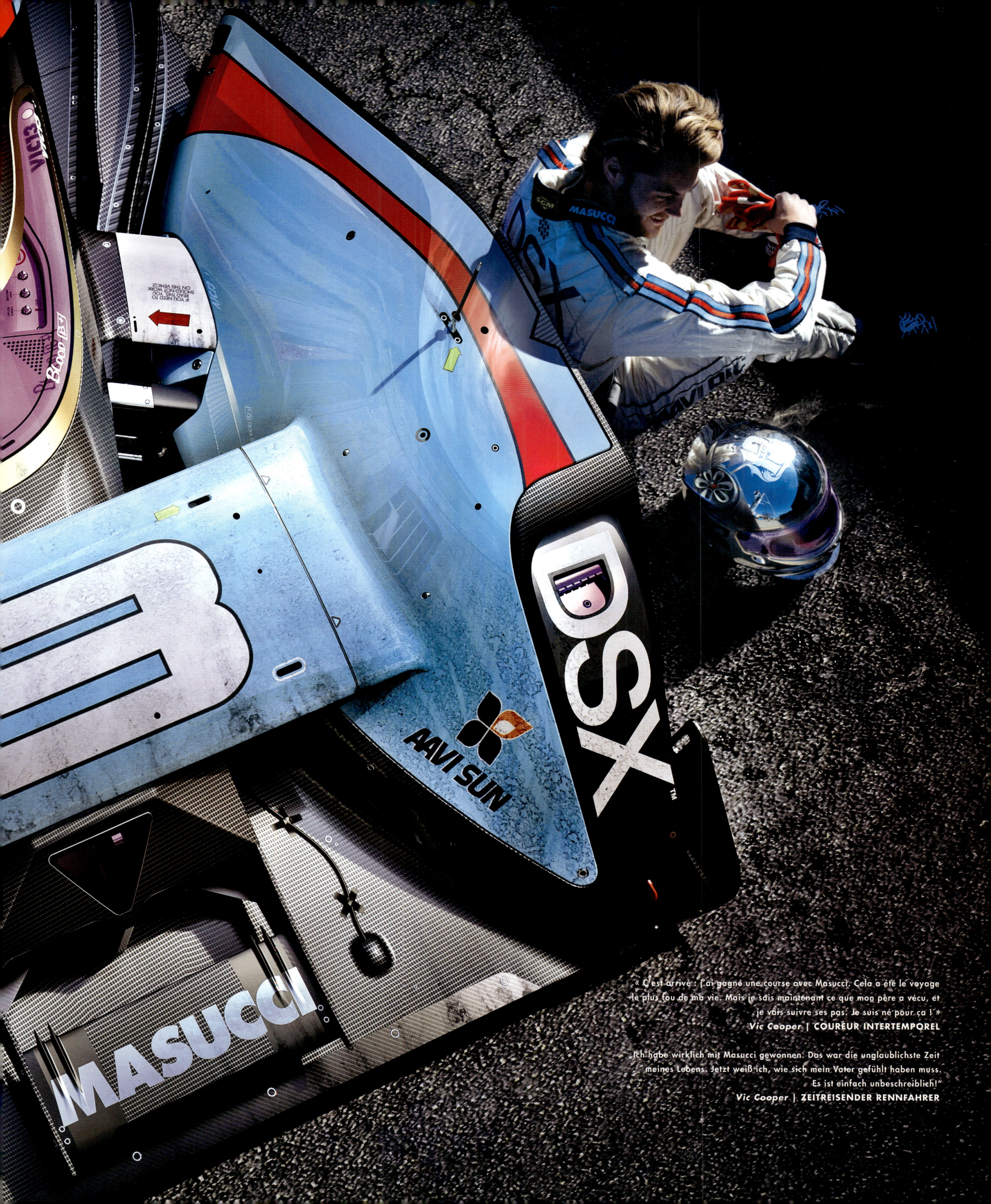

« C'est arrivé : j'ai gagné une course avec Masucci. Cela a été le voyage le plus fou de ma vie. Mais je sais maintenant ce que mon père a vécu, et je vais suivre ses pas. Je suis né pour ça ! »
Vic Cooper | **COUREUR INTERTEMPOREL**

„Ich habe wirklich mit Masucci gewonnen. Das war die unglaublichste Zeit meines Lebens. Jetzt weiß ich, wie sich mein Vater gefühlt haben muss. Es ist einfach unbeschreiblich!"
Vic Cooper | **ZEITREISENDER RENNFAHRER**

MASUCCI X-5P

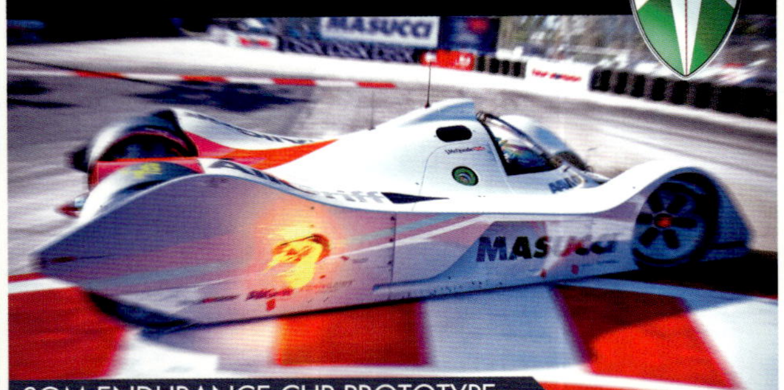

SGM ENDURANCE CUP PROTOTYPE

YEAR	POWER OUTPUT	TOP SPEED	TOP SPEED	TEAM / ENGINE
1981	886 HP	448 KM/H	278 MPH	TEAM: MASUCCI ENGINE: MASUCCI

MODEL .... Masucci X-5P Prototipo
TYPE .... SGM Endurance Cup Prototype
DESIGNER .... Filomeno Masucci
PRINCIPLE DRIVER .... Pia Saravese / Jay McQuade
ENGINE .... **Masucci V12 5998 cc**
L / W / H METRIC .... 4146 mm / 2000 mm / 957 mm
WHEELBASE METRIC .... 2970 mm
L / W / H IMPERIAL .... 163.2 in / 78.7 in / 37.7 in
WHEELBASE IMPERIAL .... 117 in

MASUCCI X-6A

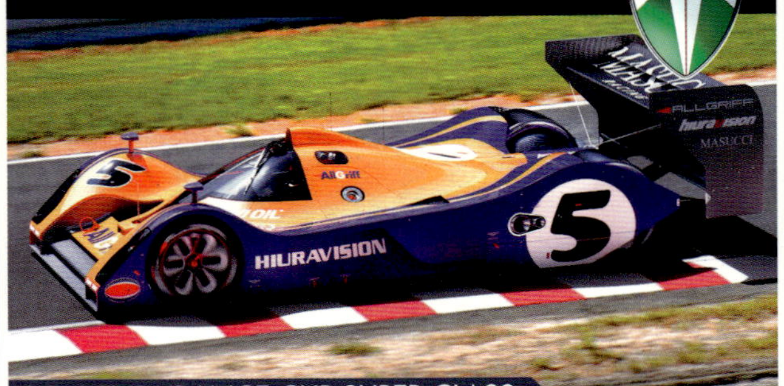

SGM ENDURANCE CUP SUPER CLASS

YEAR	POWER OUTPUT	TOP SPEED	TOP SPEED	TEAM / ENGINE
1982	990 HP	373 KM/H	232 MPH	TEAM: MASUCCI ENGINE: MASUCCI

MODEL .... Masucci X-6A
TYPE .... SGM Endurance Cup Super Class
DESIGNER .... Filomeno Masucci
PRINCIPLE DRIVER .... Jay McQuade / G.Masucci / J.Hiura
ENGINE .... **Masucci V12 5998 cc**
L / W / H METRIC .... 4766 mm / 2000 mm / 1200 mm
WHEELBASE METRIC .... 2970 mm
L / W / H IMPERIAL .... 187.6 in / 78.7 in / 47.2 in
WHEELBASE IMPERIAL .... 117 in

MASUCCI X-6D

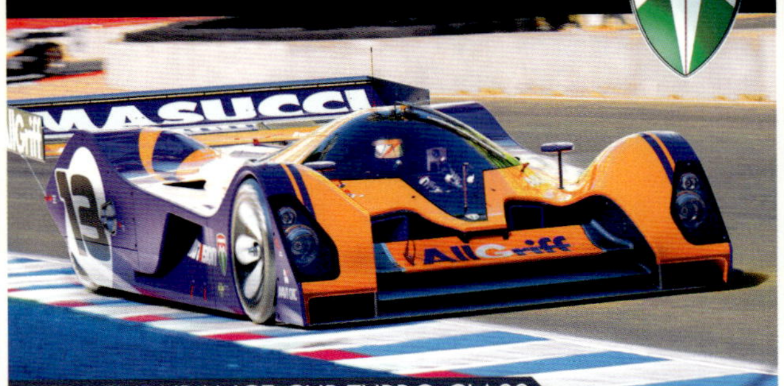

SGM ENDURANCE CUP TURBO CLASS

YEAR	POWER OUTPUT	TOP SPEED	TOP SPEED	TEAM / ENGINE
1985	1620 HP	469 KM/H	291 MPH	TEAM: MASUCCI ENGINE: MASUCCI

MODEL .... Masucci X-6D Turbo
TYPE .... SGM Endurance Cup Turbo Class
DESIGNER .... Filomeno Masucci
PRINCIPLE DRIVER .... Jay McQuade / G.Masucci / J.Hiura
ENGINE .... **Masucci V12 6998cc, 4 turbos**
L / W / H METRIC .... 5172 mm / 2000 mm / 957 mm
WHEELBASE METRIC .... 2971 mm
L / W / H IMPERIAL .... 203.6 in / 78.7 in / 37.7 in
WHEELBASE IMPERIAL .... 117 in

MASUCCI X-7P

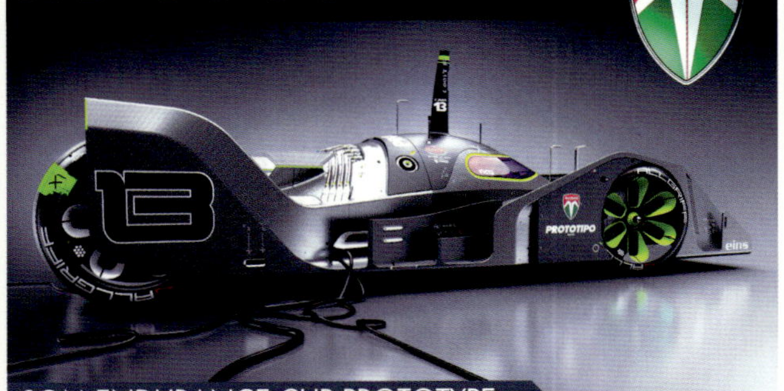

SGM ENDURANCE CUP PROTOTYPE

YEAR	POWER OUTPUT	TOP SPEED	TOP SPEED	TEAM / ENGINE
2027	670 HP	375 KM/H	233 MPH	TEAM: MASUCCI ENGINE: MASUCCI

MODEL .... Masucci X-7P Prototipo
TYPE .... SGM Endurance Cup Prototype
DESIGNER .... Luca Masucci
PRINCIPLE DRIVER .... Vic Cooper
ENGINE .... **Masucci Gas Turbine 'Ciri' 4498cc / electric**
L / W / H METRIC .... 4445 mm / 2200 mm / 1542 mm
WHEELBASE METRIC .... 3056 mm
L / W / H IMPERIAL .... 175 in / 86.6 in / 60.7 in
WHEELBASE IMPERIAL .... 120.3 in

MASUCCI X-7A

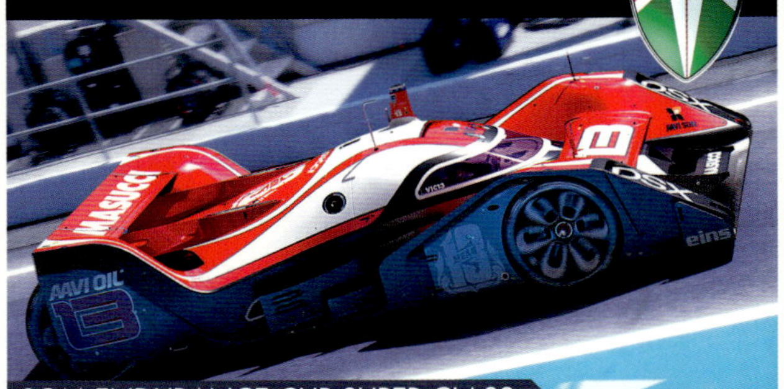

SGM ENDURANCE CUP SUPER CLASS

YEAR	POWER OUTPUT	TOP SPEED	TOP SPEED	TEAM / ENGINE
2027	780 HP	398 KM/H	247 MPH	TEAM: MASUCCI ENGINE: MASUCCI

MODEL .... Masucci X-7A
TYPE .... SGM Endurance Cup Super Class
DESIGNER .... Luca Masucci
PRINCIPLE DRIVER .... Vic Cooper
ENGINE .... **Masucci Gas Turbine 'Ciri' 4998cc / electric**
L / W / H METRIC .... 4445 mm / 2200 mm / 1180 mm
WHEELBASE METRIC .... 3056 mm
L / W / H IMPERIAL .... 175 in / 86.6 in / 46.5 in
WHEELBASE IMPERIAL .... 120.3 in

MASUCCI X-7S

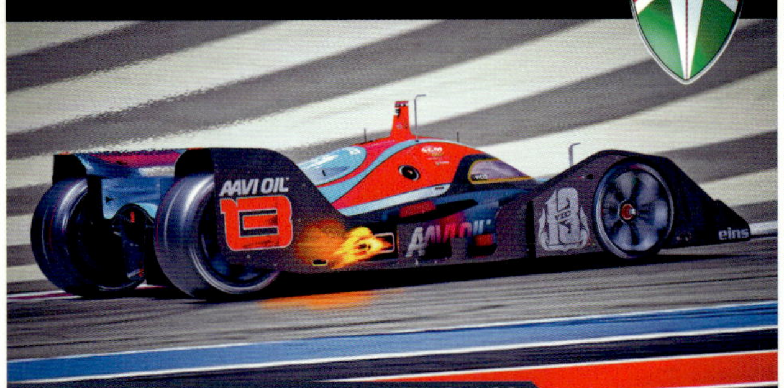

SGM ENDURANCE CUP SUPER CLASS

YEAR	POWER OUTPUT	TOP SPEED	TOP SPEED	TEAM / ENGINE
2027	835 HP	435 KM/H	270 MPH	TEAM: MASUCCI ENGINE: MASUCCI

MODEL .... Masucci X-7S
TYPE .... SGM Endurance Cup Super Class
DESIGNER .... Luca Masucci / Dale Burton
PRINCIPLE DRIVER .... Vic Cooper
ENGINE .... **Masucci Gas Turbine 'Ciri' 4998cc / electric**
L / W / H METRIC .... 4445 mm / 2200 mm / 1180 mm
WHEELBASE METRIC .... 3056 mm
L / W / H IMPERIAL .... 175 in / 86.6 in / 46.5 in
WHEELBASE IMPERIAL .... 120.3 in

PRIDEUX-EINS **MF/26**

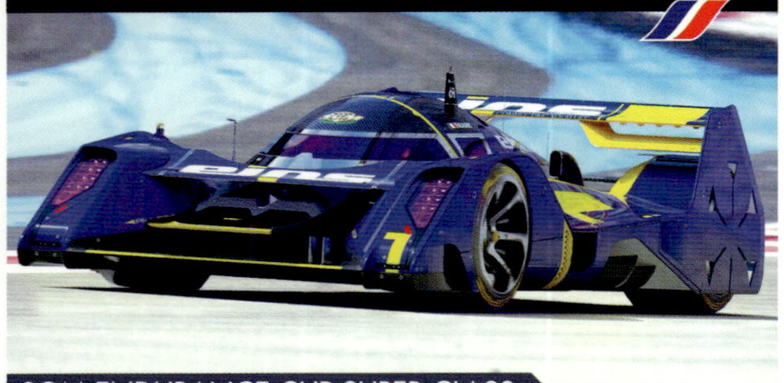

SGM ENDURANCE CUP SUPER CLASS

YEAR	POWER OUTPUT	TOP SPEED	TOP SPEED	TEAM / ENGINE
2026	805 HP	415 KM/H	258 MPH	TEAM: PRIDEUX ENGINE: MARTIN

MODEL .... Prideux-Eins MF/26 MF/27
TYPE .... SGM Endurance Cup Super Class
DESIGNER .... Léon Prideux
PRINCIPLE DRIVER .... Gaël Faubert
ENGINE .... **Rear: Martin 6-cyl diesel / Front: Cifiq electric**
L / W / H METRIC .... 4594 mm / 2034 mm / 1130 mm
WHEELBASE METRIC .... 3020 mm
L / W / H IMPERIAL .... 180.9 in / 80 in / 44.5 in
WHEELBASE IMPERIAL .... 118.9 in

PRIDEUX-MARTIN **MF27**

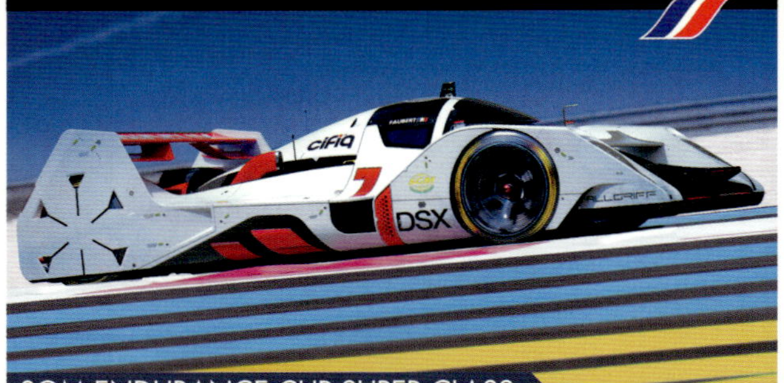

SGM ENDURANCE CUP SUPER CLASS

YEAR	POWER OUTPUT	TOP SPEED	TOP SPEED	TEAM / ENGINE
2027	807 HP	432 KM/H	268 MPH	TEAM: PRIDEUX ENGINE: MARTIN

MODEL .... Prideux-Martin MF/27
TYPE .... SGM Endurance Cup Super Class
DESIGNER .... Léon Prideux
PRINCIPLE DRIVER .... Gaël Faubert
ENGINE .... **Rear: Martin 6-cyl diesel / Front: Cifiq electric**
L / W / H METRIC .... 4594 mm / 2034 mm / 1130 mm
WHEELBASE METRIC .... 3020 mm
L / W / H IMPERIAL .... 180.9 in / 80 in / 44.5 in
WHEELBASE IMPERIAL .... 118.9 in

PRIDEUX-CIFIQ **MF/28**[H]

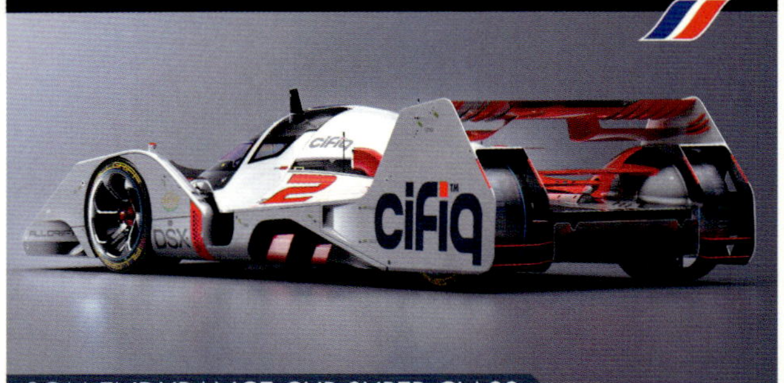

SGM ENDURANCE CUP SUPER CLASS

YEAR	POWER OUTPUT	TOP SPEED	TOP SPEED	TEAM / ENGINE
2028	940 HP	439 KM/H	273 MPH	TEAM: MASUCCI ENGINES: CIFIQ

MODEL .... Prideux-Cifiq MF/28[H]
TYPE .... SGM Endurance World Cup
DESIGNER .... Léon Prideux
PRINCIPLE DRIVER .... Raphaël Rousseau
ENGINE .... **4 x Cifiq electric hub mount**
L / W / H METRIC .... 4594 mm / 2034 mm / 1130 mm
WHEELBASE METRIC .... 3019 mm
L / W / H IMPERIAL .... 180.9 in / 80 in / 44.5 in
WHEELBASE IMPERIAL .... 118.9 in

12 HOURS OF JAPAN

APRIL 15-18, 2027

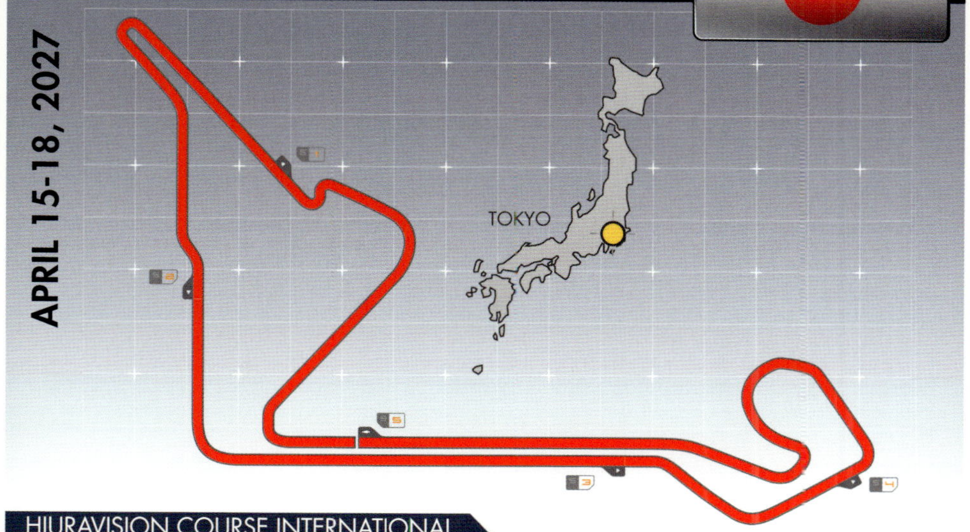

HIURAVISION COURSE INTERNATIONAL

RACE	LENGTH	TURNS	LAP RECORD	TOP SPEED RECORD	DISTANCE RECORD
1	7.273 km 4.519 mi	19	01:46:863 245 KM/H AVERAGE SPEED 2025 GAËL FAUBERT	402 km/h 250 mph	2691 km 1672 mi

12 HOURS OF BRITAIN

MAY 20-23, 2027

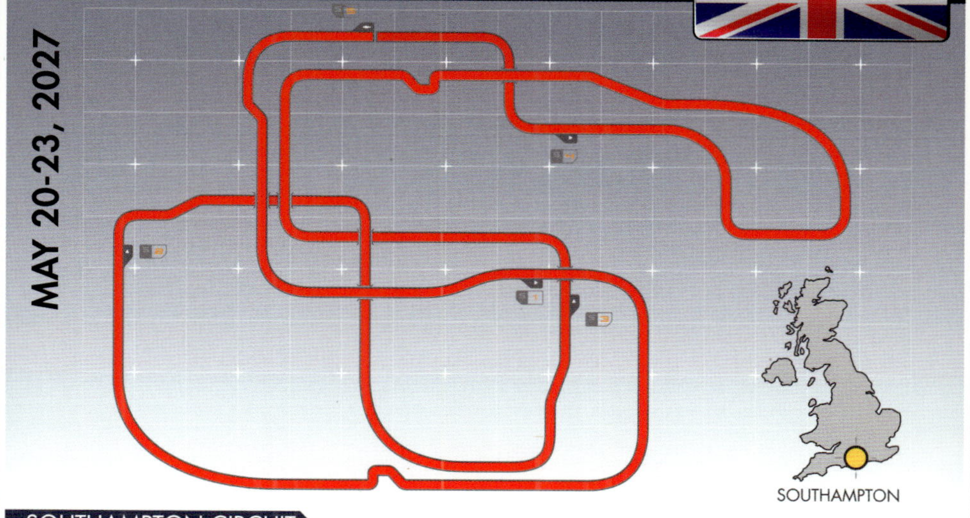

SOUTHAMPTON CIRCUIT

RACE	LENGTH	TURNS	LAP RECORD	TOP SPEED RECORD	DISTANCE RECORD
2	11.265 km 7.001 mi	36	03:36:866 187 KM/H AVERAGE SPEED 2023 RAPHAËL ROUSSEAU	331 km/h 206 mph	2003 km 1245 mi

18 HOURS OF RUSSIA

JUNE 03-06, 2027

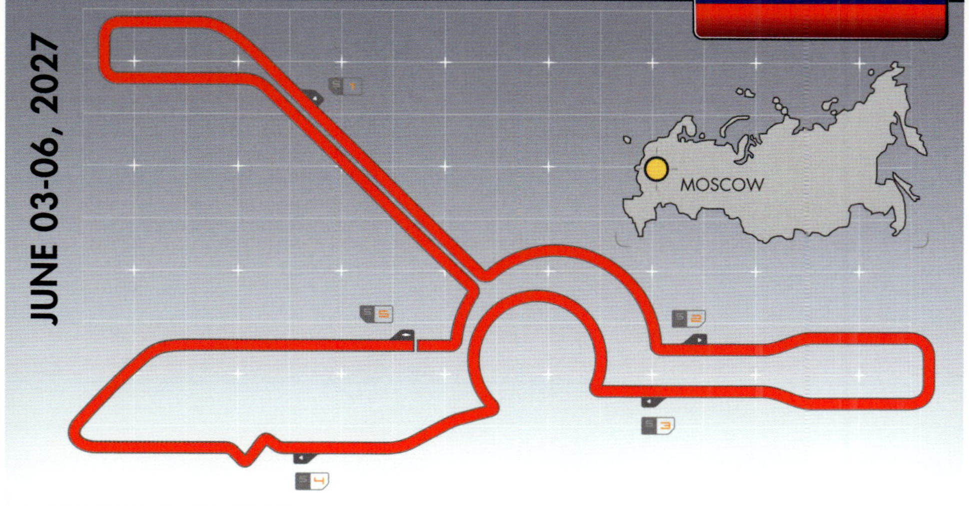

EURASIA SUPER SPEEDWAY

RACE	LENGTH	TURNS	LAP RECORD	TOP SPEED RECORD	DISTANCE RECORD
3	9.502 km 5.904 mi	26	02:45:252 207 KM/H AVERAGE SPEED 2025 GAËL FAUBERT	368 km/h 229 mph	3487 km 2167 mi

12 HRS OF SOUTH AFRICA

SEPTEMBER 16-19, 2027

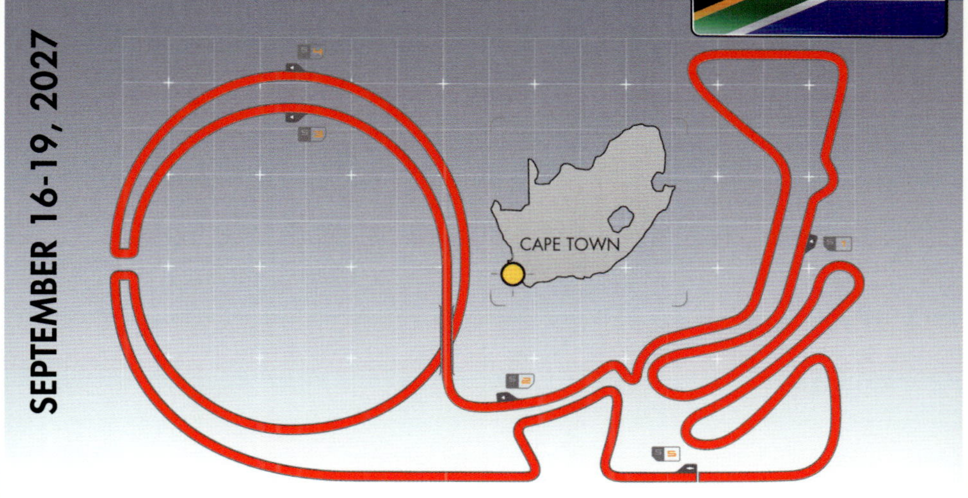

WESTERN CAPE CIRCUIT

RACE	LENGTH	TURNS	LAP RECORD	TOP SPEED RECORD	DISTANCE RECORD
4	12.679 km 7.889 mi	28	03:42:971 205 KM/H AVERAGE SPEED 2023 RAPHAËL ROUSSEAU	417 km/h 259 mph	2205 km 1370 mi

24 HOURS OF BRAZIL

OCTOBER 13-17, 2027

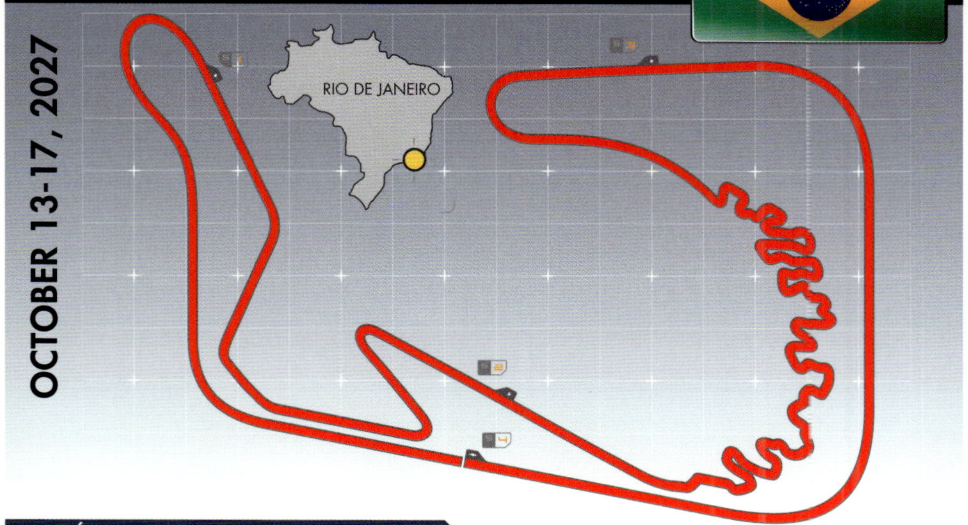

AUTÓDROMO CIDADE MARAVILHOSA

RACE	LENGTH	TURNS	LAP RECORD	TOP SPEED RECORD	DISTANCE RECORD
5	18.405 km 11.436 mi	65	06:34:392 168 KM/H AVERAGE SPEED 2027 GAËL FAUBERT	422 km/h 262 mph	3868 km 2403 mi

48 HOURS OF CALIFORNIA

NOVEMBER 10-14, 2027

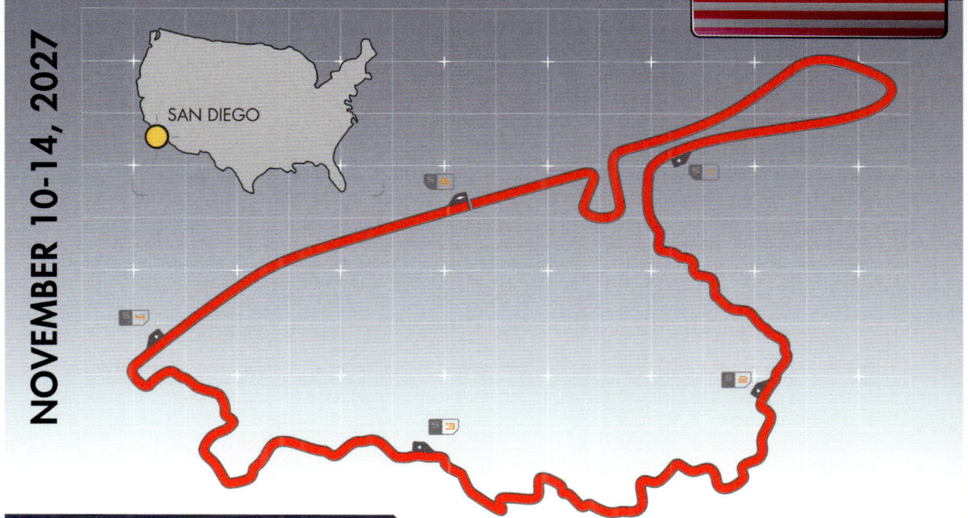

ALLGRIFF RACEWAY CALIFORNIA

RACE	LENGTH	TURNS	LAP RECORD	TOP SPEED RECORD	DISTANCE RECORD
6	25.288 km 15.713 mi	61	07:19:791 215 KM/H AVERAGE SPEED 2027 VIC COOPER	435 km/h 270 mph	8762 km 5444 mi

BEHIND**THEPAGES**
A NEW CHALLENGE

A new challenge. I was born in 1975 and worked as a senior designer for Volkswagen and Bugatti until 2005. After the success of my first book, *Cosmic Motors*, published and encouraged by Scott Robertson of Design Studio Press, I got a magic call from director Joe Kosinski to join his team for *Tron: Legacy*. I could not resist and moved from Germany to California. Ever since, I was able to design for Marvel's *Captain America*, spend amazing weeks with Alien director Ridley Scott on *Prometheus*, and return to the great Joe Kosinski for Universal's *Oblivion* with Tom Cruise. Always open to new challenges, I penned the livery for the 2011 *HRT F1* team and the 2012 *Lotus LMP2* team.

When I work on Hollywood films, I disappear for up to 14 months, completely emmersing myself into the world of my director, leaving little to no space for personal projects. So at the end of 2011, I felt it would be good timing for a break and to start something I had dreamed of for a long time: *The Timeless Racer*. In January 2012 I glued a first little prototype of this book together, a little over two inches in size. And it promised that the idea for this oversize picture book series could work. It then took over 4,500 hours to finish what you are now holding in your hands.

The biggest challenge was the realism. I take fantasy space ship design very seriously, but creating believable cars for a very educated and critical audience requires tedious research. I studied many books about endurance racing, visited races, and met great drivers. These personal conversations were by far the greatest inspiration! Armed with all this input, three fully original race cars were designed and built in 3D, with support by digital design guru Joe Hiura, whom I met on *Tron: Legacy*. No detail is from stock; each screw is custom-built. Meaningful names had to be found for each character and machine. Sponsors and their histories had to be invented, with the great help of designer Leslie Lau, who also created the tracks. The Brazil circuit is still giving me the chills! Rendering all the final car models was the next challenge, with a resolution up to 50 Megapixels, to bring you the best detail and resolution possible. And finally, an intense photo shoot in Hollywood, a few days before going to print. What a fun journey it all was!

I am very excited about this new series, and I hope you will follow hero Vic Cooper, the Masucci team, and me through time. There is much to discover, and much to enjoy. Welcome to the world of *The Timeless Racer*.

Un nouveau défi. Je suis né en 1975. J'ai été senior designer pour Volkswagen et Bugatti jusqu'en 2005. Devant le succès de mon premier livre, *Cosmic Motors*, publié et soutenu par Scott Robertson du Design Studio Press, Hollywood me proposa de travailler sur *Tron: L'Héritage* (Disney). Comment résister ? J'ai déménagé en Californie. Depuis, j'ai travaillé sur *Captain America* (Marvel) et passé des semaines incroyables avec Ridley Scott, le réalisateur de *Alien*, sur *Prometheus*, pour revenir vers le grand Joe Kosinski pour *Oblivion* (Universal). Aimant les défis, j'ai aussi collaboré avec l'équipe *HRT F1* en 2011 pour créer son identité visuelle. Idem en 2012, avec l'écurie *Lotus* en LMP2.

Quand je m'implique dans un film, je disparais jusqu'à 14 mois. Fin 2011, j'ai estimé une pause nécessaire et lancé un projet personnel, *The Timeless Racer*. En janvier 2012, le prototype d'un ouvrage à grand format et d'un peu plus de 6 cm d'épaisseur était prêt, et me semblait extrêmement prometteur. Le résultat final, que vous tenez entre les mains, m'aura demandé 4500 heures d'efforts.

Le plus grand défi tient à ma recherche de réalisme. Car même si j'aime les vaisseaux spatiaux, l'enjeu est d'un tout autre ordre: ici, il faut créer des voitures qui convainquent des lecteurs au niveau d'exigences très élevé. Le travail reprend. Sur l'histoire elle-même du *Timeless Racer*, par de nombreuses lectures sur la course d'endurance, en assistant à des épreuves et en rencontrant des pilotes. Les idées affluent, germent, combinant l'histoire avec l'actualité. Trois voitures de course, avec tous les détails, doivent être conçues et construites en 3D, avec l'aide de Joe Hiura, gourou de la création numérique. Aucun élément n'est tiré d'archives, chaque vis est créée sur mesures, il faut des noms significatifs pour chaque personnage, chaque engin. Les sponsors, leurs histoires, sont imaginés avec l'aide précieuse de Leslie Lau, qui a aussi dessiné les circuits. Celui du Brésil, notamment, me donne le frisson ! Autre défi : finaliser les derniers modèles de voitures avec une résolution jusqu'à 50 mégapixels pour une précision maximale. Vint enfin l'intense séance de photos à Hollywood, précédant de peu la mise sous presse. Au final, quelle aventure passionnante !

J'espère que vous allez suivre les héros, Vic Cooper, l'équipe Masucci et moi-même dans ce voyage. Il y a encore tant à découvrir, tant à partager... Bienvenue dans le monde du *Timeless Racer*.

Eine neue Herausforderung. Ich bin 1975 geboren und habe bis 2005 als Senior Designer bei Volkswagen und Bugatti gearbeitet. Nachdem mein erstes Buch *Cosmic Motors* – ermutigt durch Scott Robertson von Design Studio Press – erfolgreich angelaufen war, kam ein magischer Anruf aus Hollywood – ich sollte für den Regisseur Joe Kosinski an *Tron: Legacy* mitwirken! Ich machte mich also auf nach Kalifornien, wo seither eine Menge Traumjobs warteten: Ich durfte für Marvels *Captain America* designen, mit Ridley Scott an *Prometheus* arbeiten und für Tom Cruise das Fluggerät in *Oblivion* entwerfen. Dazwischen gestaltete ich den Look für das Formel-1-Team von *HRT* (Saison 2011) und das *Lotus LMP2* Team (Saison 2012 und 2013).

All die Jahre gab es jedoch etwas, das mir keine Ruhe ließ, und es war nur eine Frage der Zeit, wann ich mich diesem 'Etwas' in meinem Kopf widmen könnte; schliesslich verschlingen mich intensive Hollywoodproduktionen für bis zu 14 Monate. Dieses 'Ding' erschien mir so reizvoll, dass es dann Ende 2011 nicht mehr warten konnte – es war *The Timeless Racer*. 4500 Arbeitsstunden später können Sie es nun als erstes Buch einer neuen Serie in den Händen halten.

Auch wenn mich Fantasie-Raumschiff-Design unendlich fasziniert – dieses Projekt war zu Beginn nahezu furchteinflößend. Autos gehören zu den schwierigsten Designthemen überhaupt und ich wollte auch Motorsportfans – die bekannt sind für ihr detailliertes Fachwissen – nicht enttäuschen. Während ich also an der Geschichte der Masucci-Dynastie feilte, las ich Bücher, besuchte Rennen und sprach mit Fahrern. Aus diesen persönlichen Gesprächen konnte ich mit Abstand die meisten Ideen schöpfen. Dazu entstanden drei komplette Fantasie-Rennwagen in 3-D. Mit Hilfe von Joe Hiura, den ich bei Tron: Legacy kennenlernte, wurde die Autos samt jeder Schraube komplett konstruiert. Die so entstandenen virtuellen Boliden wurden dann in 50 Megapixeln gerendert, damit Ihnen, liebe Leser, kein Detail entgeht. Auch klangvolle Namen für Menschen, Unternehmen, Sponsoren und Maschinen mussten gefunden werden, und Designer Leslie Lau half, Logos und Rennstrecken zu entwerfen. Das große Finale war ein Fotoshooting in Hollywood, wenige Tage, bevor das Buch in Druck ging. Was für ein wunderbarer Höllenritt!

Ich freue mich auf diese neue Serie und hoffe, dass Sie den zeitreisenden Vic Cooper, das Masucci-Team und mich dabei begleiten. Es gibt viel zu entdecken. Willkommen in der Welt von *The Timeless Racer*.

01) The first text is written during a vacation weekend, away from hectic L.A.
02) Working on the livery of the Formula 1 HRT F111, in the Barcelona pit lane.
03) The 2012 Lotus LMP2 with my logo and livery at the Fuji Speedway, Japan.
04) Exciting moment: sharing first pages with Audi Sport Team Joest pilots Allan McNish, André Lotterer, and Tom Kristensen in Japan.
05) Daily notes to myself to progress the design of the cars.
06) Not the driver: learning about race cars, here in a Porsche 962 at Laguna Seca.
07) The first test version of this book, in April 2012.
08) Two legends: Jacky Ickx contributed the foreword and photographer Rainer W. Schlegelmilch his timeless shots.
09) Creative times with 3D-modeling guru Joe Hiura.
10) Over 1,000 hours: designing the fantasy cars to the smallest detail in 3D.
11) Delightful moments: with legendary driver Derek Bell and the iconic Porsche 917.
12) My dream girl promoting my project in the pit lane of the Formula 1 Monaco Grand Prix. Or: just having fun.
13) Most importantly—designing cars and finding good lines. Here, the Masucci X-7.
14) A great crew and models for the main photo shoot.
15) The real Filomeno Masucci—my amazing grandfather-in-law.
16) California sun all year: shooting model Derek Jaeschke and Danielle Burt.
17) The best part? Designing the hero cars on paper, the old school way.
18) Choosing pages with publisher Scott Robertson and graphic designer Cecilia Zo at Design Studio Press.
19) Stopping street traffic in Hollywood for the shot on page 62—what a day.

01) Premières lignes, un week-end loin de l'agitation de Los Angeles.
02) Travail sur la Formule 1 HRT F111, circuit de Barcelone.
03) La LMP Lotus 2012 arborant mon logo. Fuji Speedway, Japon.
04) Partage excitant des premières pages. Avec les pilotes Audi Sport Team Joest : Allan McNish, André Lotterer et Tom Kristensen, au Japon.
05) Prise de notes quotidienne, pour améliorer ma conception des voitures.
06) Etude de près d'un modèle, en l'occurrence une Porsche 962 à Laguna Seca.
07) Version test du livre, avril 2012.
08) Deux légendes : Jacky Ickx, qui signe l'avant-propos de ce livre, et Rainer W. Schlegelmilch, auteur de photos intertemporelles.
09) Séance de modélisation 3D numérique, avec le gourou Joe Hiura. Excellents moments.
10) Plus de 1000 heures à concevoir les voitures et leurs moindres détails en 3D.
11) Je redeviens un simple fan : chapeau bas pour la Porsche 917 et son célèbre pilote, Derek Bell.
12) Ma fille de rêve, en pleine promotion de mon projet lors du Grand Prix de Monaco.
13) Le plus important : concevoir des voitures et en trouver les lignes. Ici, la X-7.
14) Une super équipe et d'excellents modèles pour la séance photo principale.
15) Filomeno Masucci, le formidable père de ma belle-mère, qui a inspiré l'un des principaux personnages de l'histoire.
16) Séance photo avec les modèles Derek et Danielle, sous l'éternel soleil de Californie.
17) Le meilleur : la conception des voitures sur papier, à l'ancienne.
18) Choix des pages avec l'éditeur Scott Robertson, la graphiste Cecilia Zo, chez DSP.
19) Hollywood. Nous faisons stopper la circulation routière. Journée de plaisir.

01) Während eines Kurzurlaubs in Palm Springs entsteht der erste Text.
02) Letzte Justierungen an der Grafik des Formel 1 HRT F111 in Barcelona.
03) Die Arbeit mit dem 2012 Lotus LMP2 eröffnete viele Einblicke in den Sport.
04) Straßentest: erste Buch-Einblicke mit Allan McNish, André Lotterer und Tom Kristensen von Audi Sport Team Joest in Japan. Eine große Ehre.
05) Tägliche, persönliche Notizen während des Designprozesses.
06) Nur mal gucken: Geschichtsunterricht im Cockpit eines Porsche 962 in Laguna Seca.
07) Das erste Buchmodell aus dem April 2012.
08) Zwei Legenden: Jacky Ickx steuerte das Vorwort bei, Fotograf Rainer W. Schlegelmilch stellte den Kontakt her und beeindruckt mit einmaligen Fotos.
09) Mit 3-D-Modell Guru Joe Hiura während der Designphase in meinem Studio.
10) Über 1000 Stunden nur dieser Anblick: CAD bis ins kleinste Detail.
11) Ein schöner Moment mit Fahrerlegende Derek Bell im sagenhaften Porsche 917.
12) Meine Traumfrau im Cosmic Motors-Outfit in der Boxengasse beim Großen Preis von Monaco. Was für ein Tag.
13) Das Wichtigste: Autos entwerfen und gute Linien finden, hier am Masucci X-7.
14) Gruppenbild vom ersten Fotoshooting, hektisch und aufregend.
15) Der echte Filomeno Masucci – mein toller Schwiegergroßvater.
16) Mit Models Derek Jaeschke und Danielle Burt in der ewigen Sonne Kaliforniens.
17) Die Autos auf Papier zu entwerfen ist ein Genuss. Hier entsteht der X-5.
18) Mit Verleger, Freund und Inspirationsquelle Scott Robertson und Grafikerin Cecilia Zo bei Design Studio Press.
19) Seite 62 entsteht – riskant mit echtem Sekt – auf den Straßen von Hollywood.

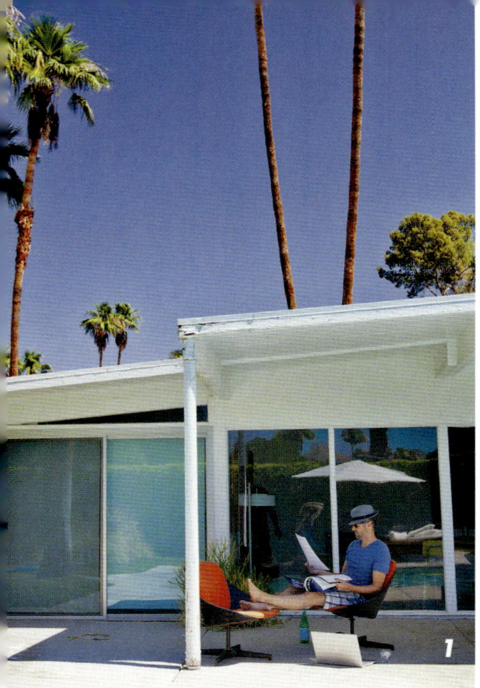
1

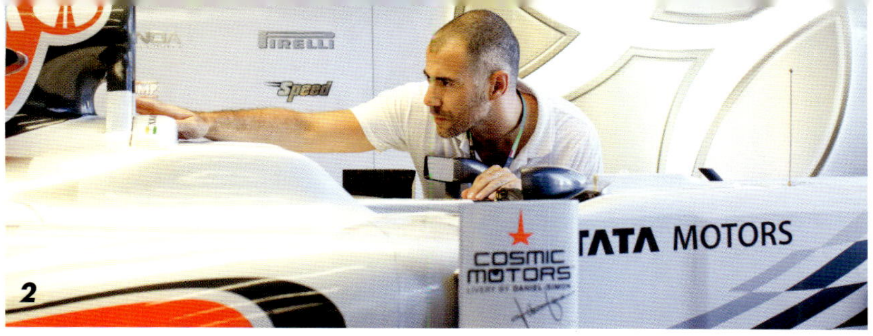

2

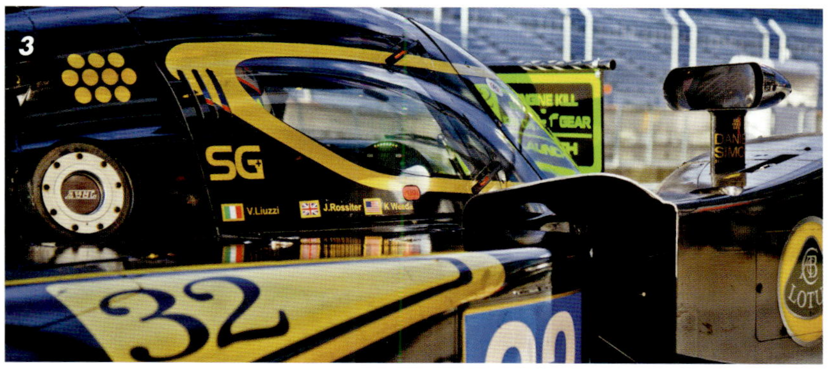

3

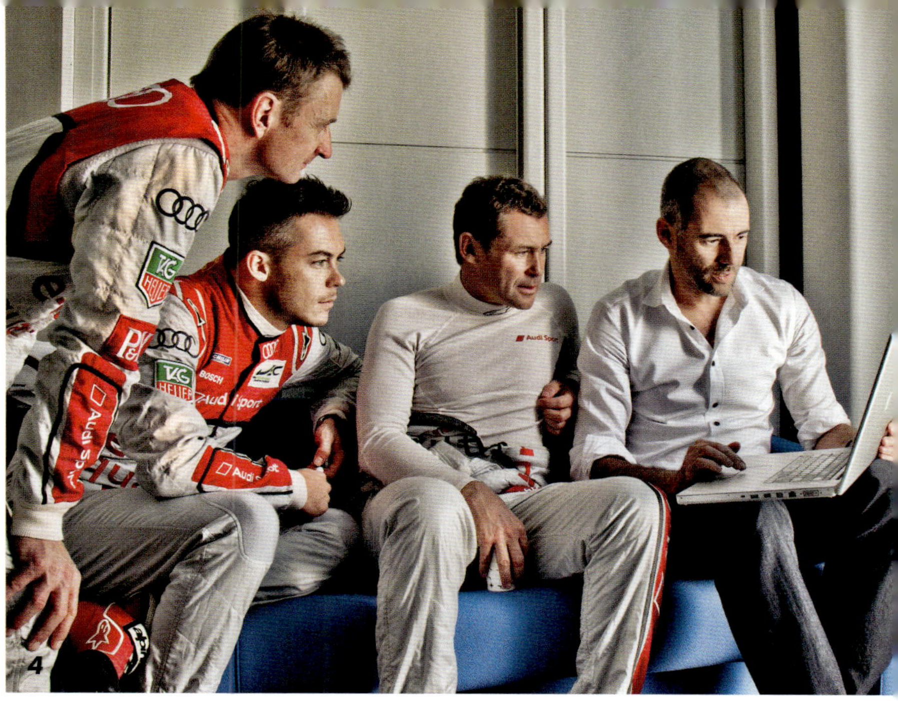
4

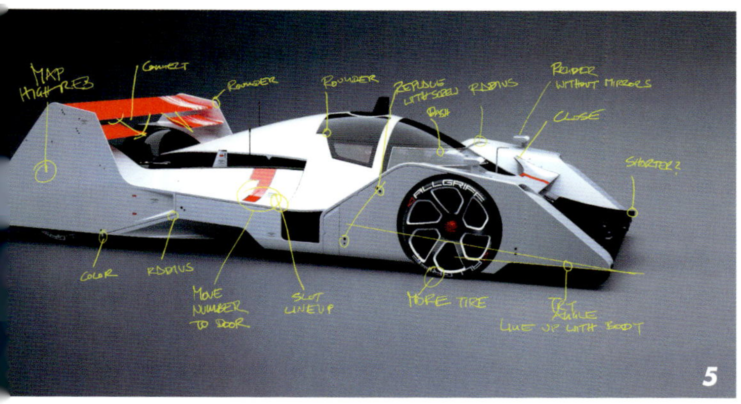
5

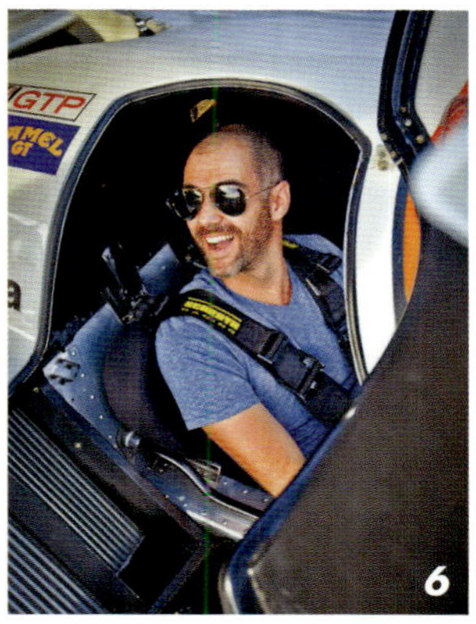
6

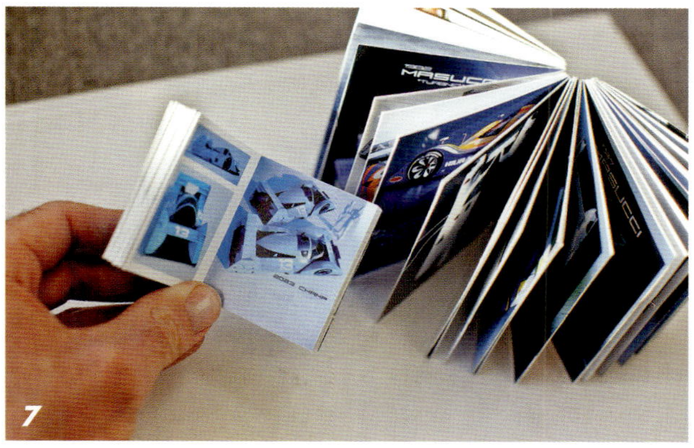
7

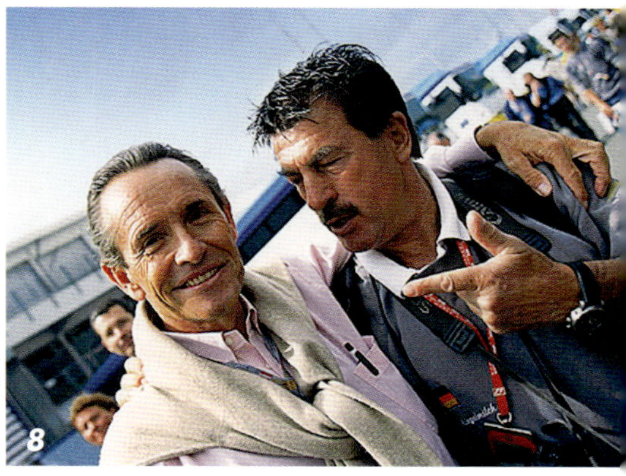
8

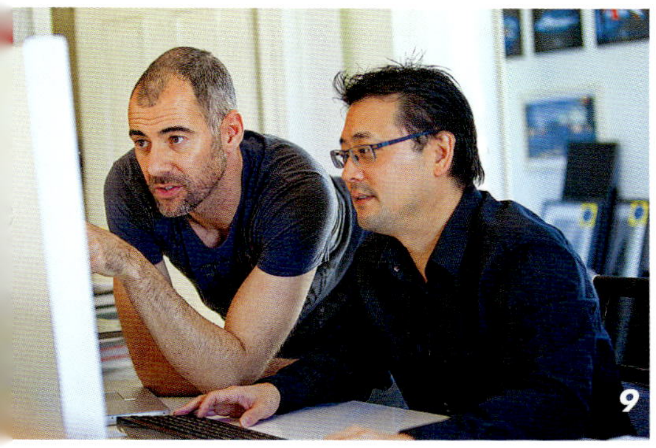
9

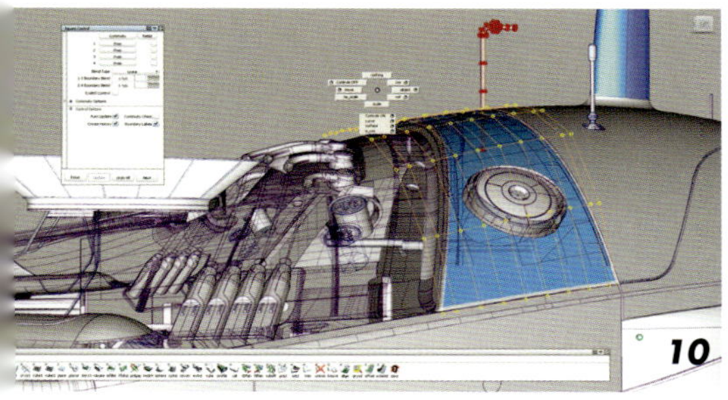
10

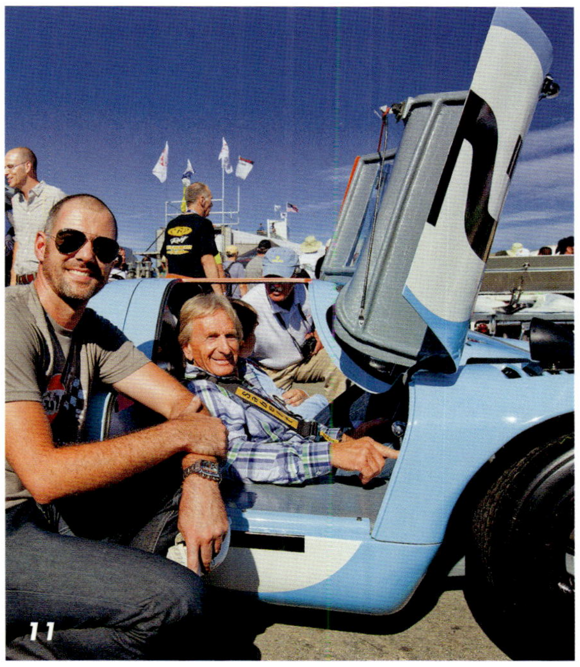
11

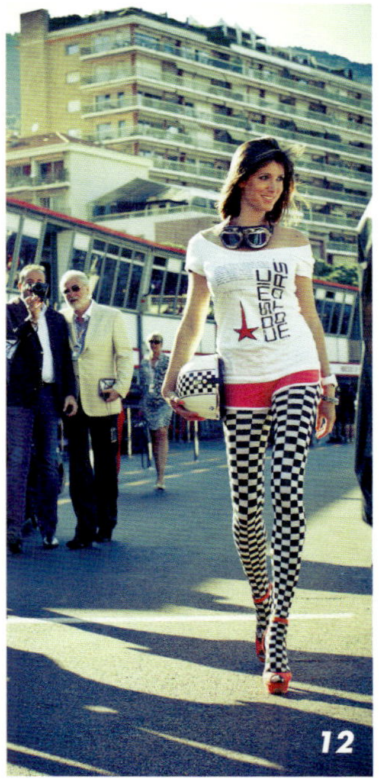
12

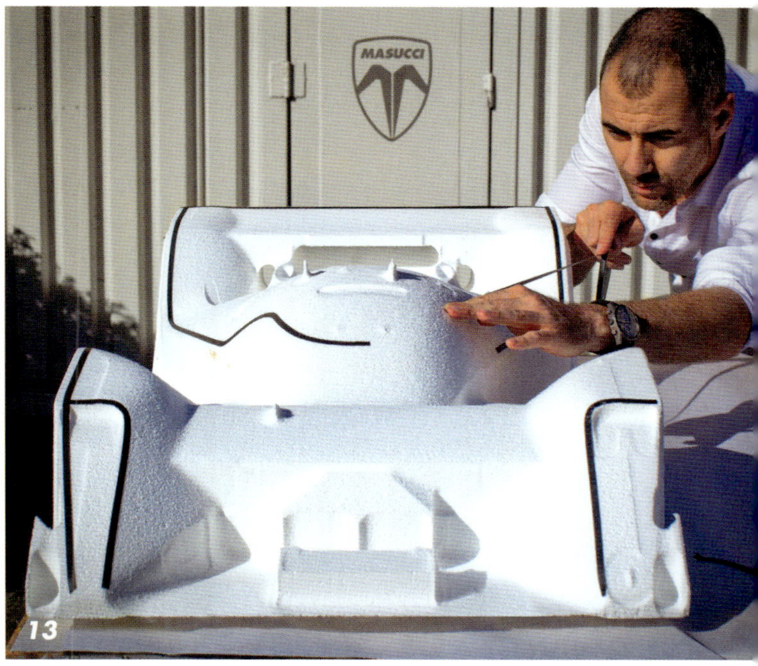

13

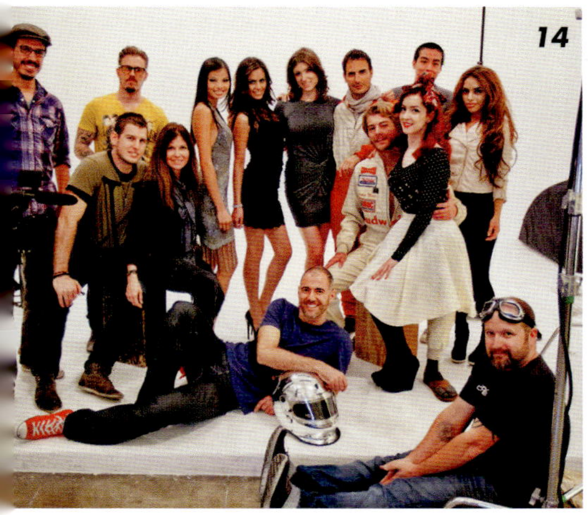
14

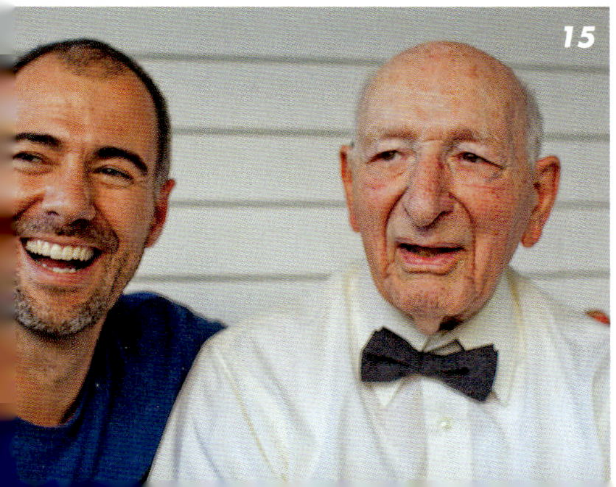
15

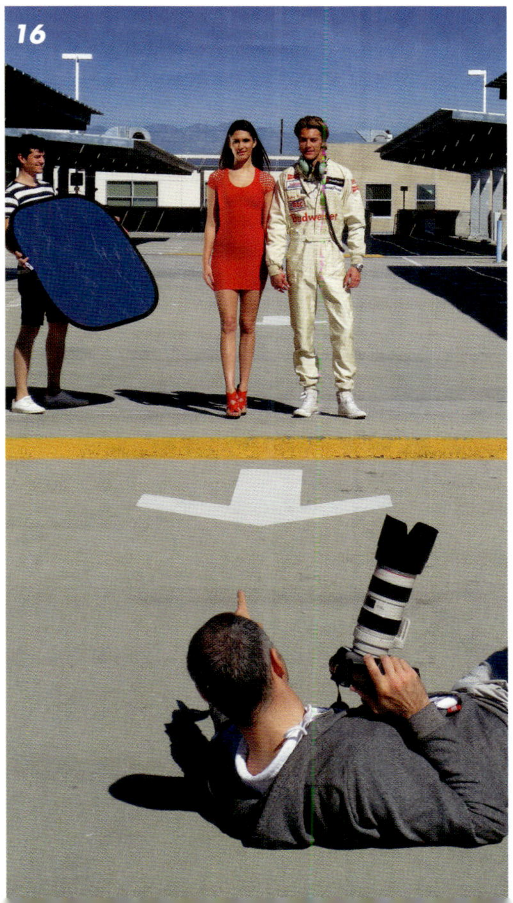
16

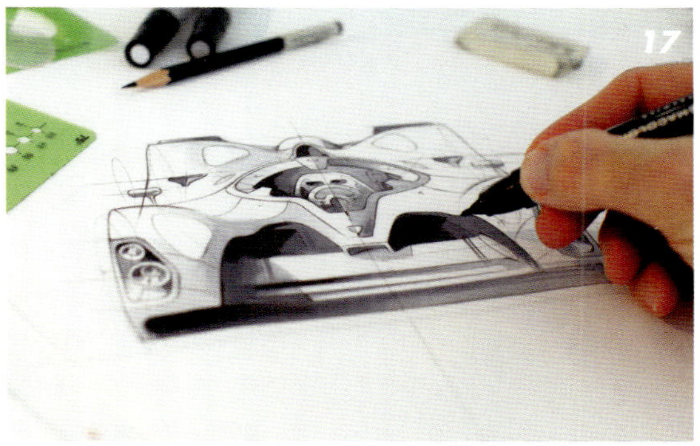
17

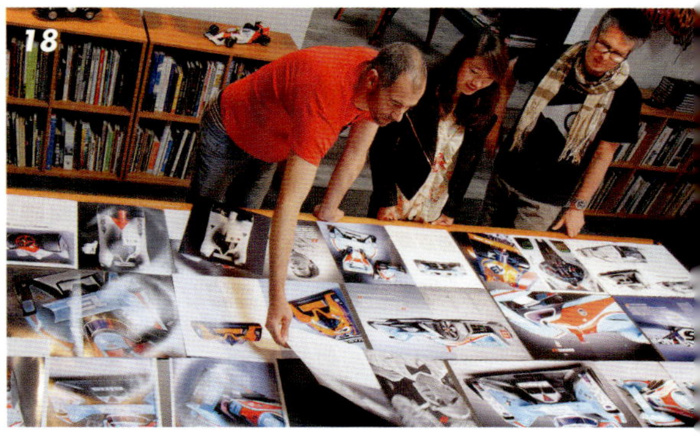
18

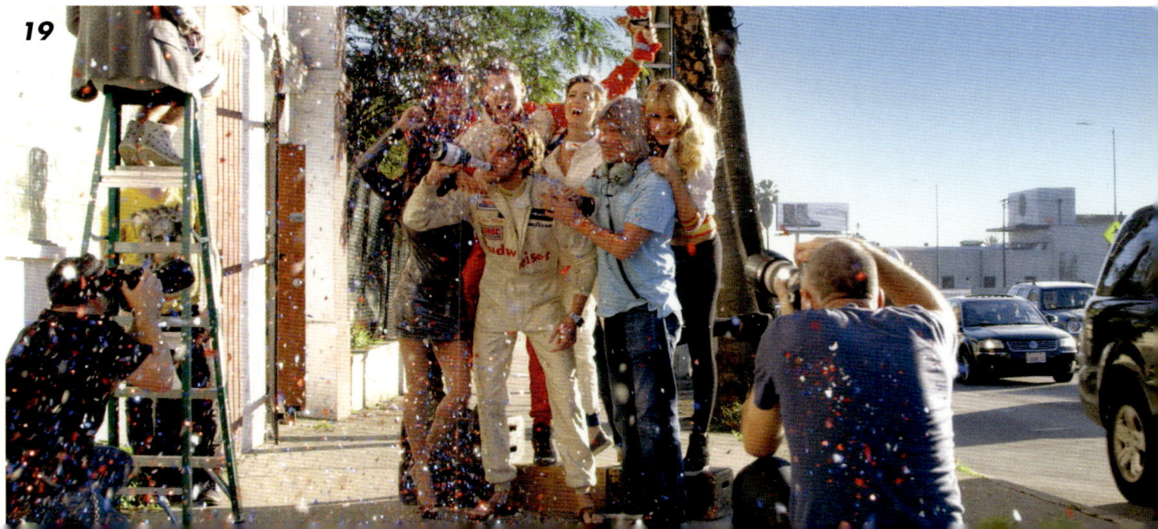
19

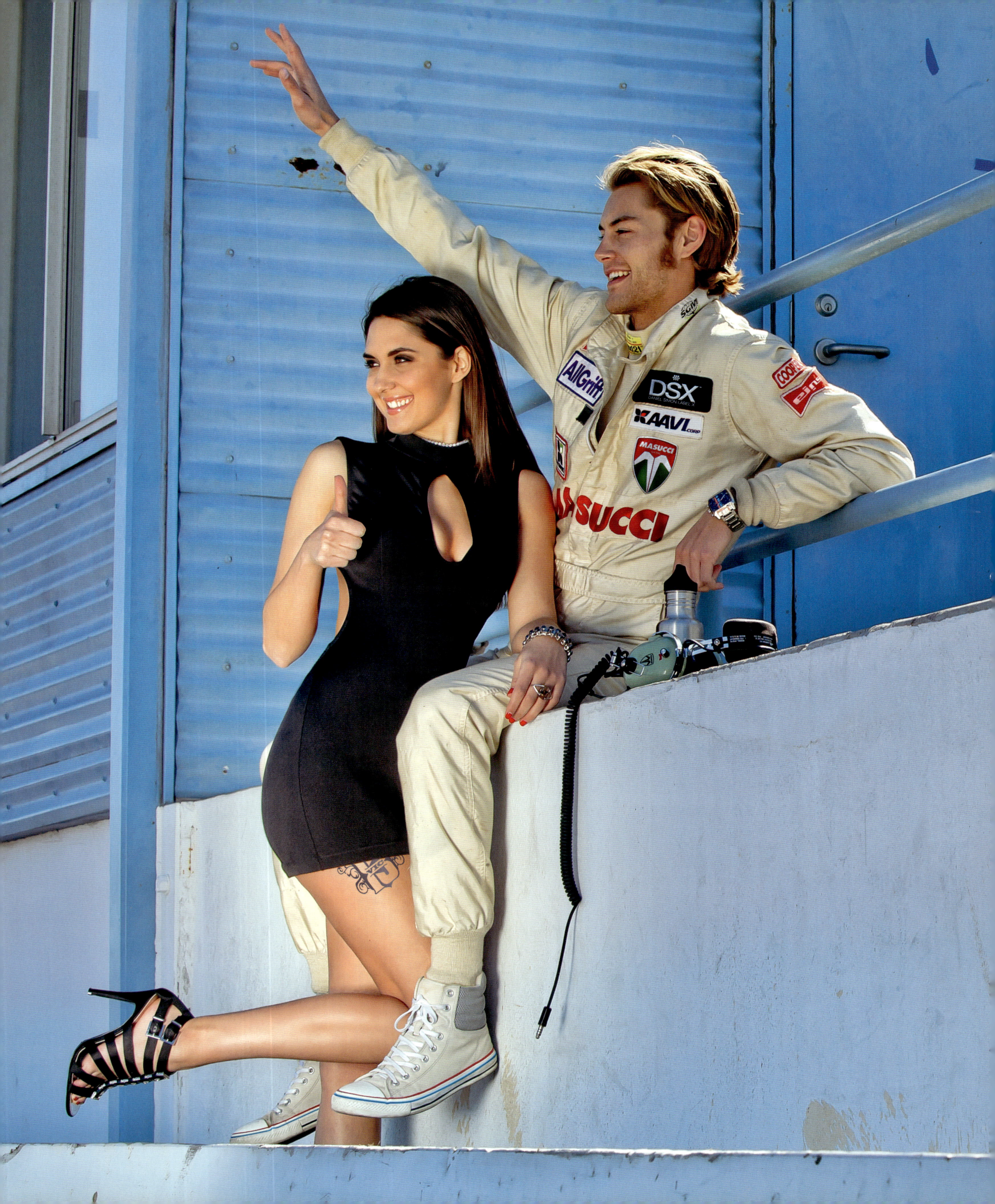
DSX
KAAVI
MASUCCI

THE **timeless racer**®

MACHINES OF A TIME TRAVELING SPEED JUNKIE

THANK YOU

There are many names to mention. I would like to thank **Scott Robertson** at *Design Studio Press* for his unstoppable support; without him this book would not exist as it is, and his wide range of advice is ever so wonderful. **Tinti Dey** for pulling invisible strings behind book making. **Cecilia Zo** for setting the layout. Digital 3D artist **Joe Hiura** for being unstoppable at what he does and jumping on board. Fellow designers **Achim Anscheidt, Alex Earle, Andre Franco Luis, Soomin Choe, Patrick Faulwetter, Jordan Meadows, Nick Gronenthal, Sasha Selipanov, Derek Jenkins, Markus Haub** and **Felix Fabian** for sharing their honest opinions and guiding me into better directions. **Sina Brückmann** for opening my mind to typography. Designer **Leslie Lau** for playing with me on logos and race tracks. **Luca Ionescu** in Australia, whose vision in graphics is stunning. **Hans Lapine** for answering my questions about racing and sharing his racing gear. **Mathieu Hayaud** at *Stand21* for sharing phenomenal race suits. Check out their catalog. **Matt Beard** for his wonderful studio photography. **Jere Hietala** for flying out to shoot with us. **Philipp Haban** and **Roman Moor** for assisting. **Lauren Michelle** and **Diana McCallister** for makeup. **Jill McDonald** for wardrobe. Thank you to all the models for being on time and patient, in particular **Derek Jaeschke** (as Vic Cooper), **Corinne Saffell** (p.18/40/63), **Danielle Burt** (p.46/70), **Jessica Just** (p.56), **Mary Tran** (p.39/62), **Lena Hakim** (p.34/62), **Candice Lorraine** (p.63), **Gaël Buzyn** (as Gaël Faubert), **Jess Harder** (as Dale Burton) and of course the amazing **Felix Masucci** (as Filomeno Masucci). **Natalie Backman** for finding talent. **David Randle** at *Bunkspeed* for answering render questions after midnight. **Kevin Ketchum** at *Alias* for answering software questions before midnight. **Justin Boitano** at *Nvidia*. **Shoaib Mohammad** at *Boxx Technologies*. **Emily Cheung** for listening to my stories. **Jason Barlow** for beefing up my text and being awesome. **Charlie Turner** from *Top Gear* for being at *Top Gear*. **Jan Wilms** for the German editorial consultancy. **Pierre-Olivier Marie** for the French translation. **Charlie Bean** for bouncing around story ideas—and your *Tron: Uprising* rocks. **Adam Gourley** and *Wildfactory* for milling strange things. Thank you to double Le Mans winner **André Lotterer** for finding time between 24-Hour race victories. To *Ferrari* Senior Vice President **Flavio Manzoni** for his kind words. To **Peter Collins** for contacting my heroes. To **Rainer W. Schlegelmilch** for inspiring me with his books and being so supportive. To his brother **Boris Schlegelmilch** for helping. To **Jacky Ickx,** for being wonderfully kind and contributing a foreword. I feel incredibly honored. The **Saffells** for their wonderful support. To my parents **Bruni** and **Dietmar** and my sister **Antje** for unleashing their inner poets. To my wonderful future wife **Corinne**, I love you so much. And to all who will read this book—thank you!

CREATED, WRITTEN, DESIGNED & PRODUCED BY .... DANIEL SIMON

FOREWORD BY .... JACKY ICKX

3D MODELING .... JOE HIURA, DANIEL SIMON

VISUALIZATION .... DANIEL SIMON

LOGO DESIGN .... LESLIE LAU, LUCA IONESCU, DANIEL SIMON

PHOTOGRAPHY .... DANIEL SIMON

PHOTOGRAPHY COVER / p.39 .... MATT BEARD, JERE HIETALA

HERO MODEL VIC COOPER .... DEREK JAESCHKE

JACKY ICKX PHOTOGRAPHY .... RAINER W. SCHLEGELMILCH

PUBLISHING PARTNER .... SCOTT ROBERTSON

PUBLISHED BY .... DESIGN STUDIO PRESS

THE TIMELESS RACER. TO BE CONTINUED . . .

MASUCCI™ RACING

VIC 13™

PRIDEUX-MARTIN™ RACING GROUP

DSX DANIELSIMONLABELX

AAVI™ CORP

DANIELSIMON™ STYLE FOR ALL GALAXIES

SGM SOCIETE GLOBALE DE MOTEURS

AllGriff™

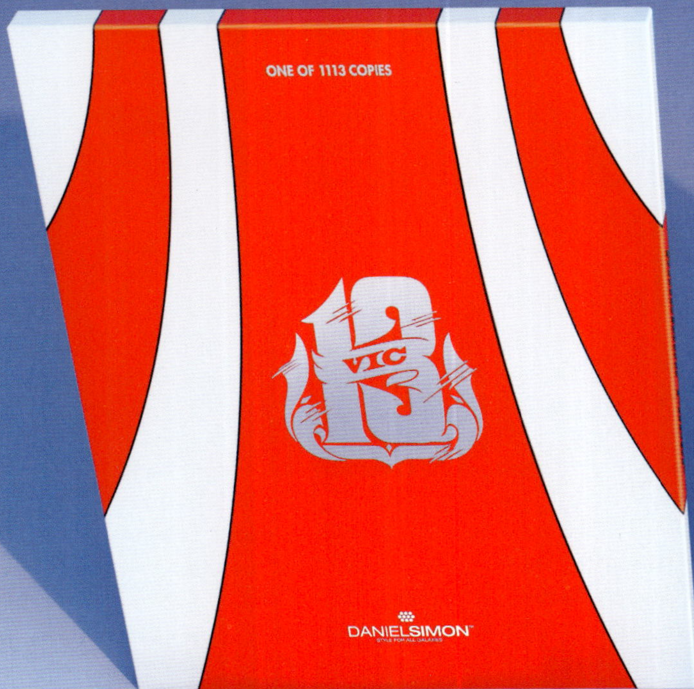

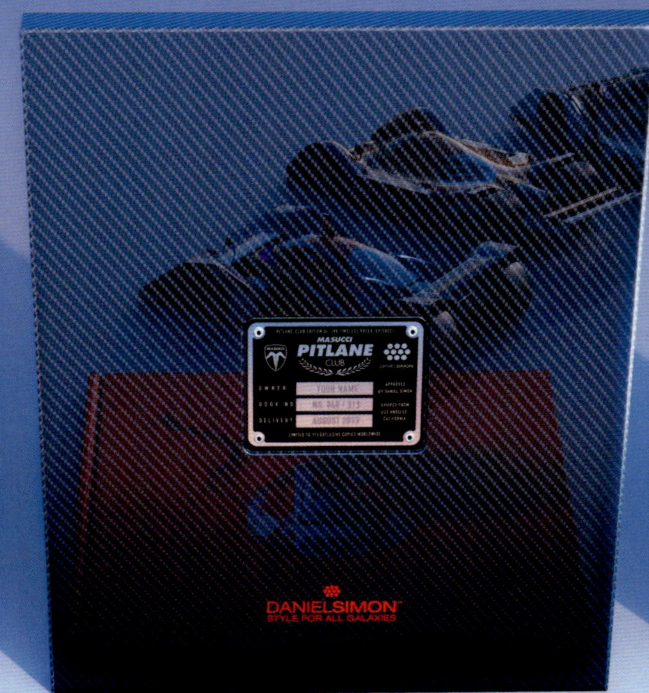

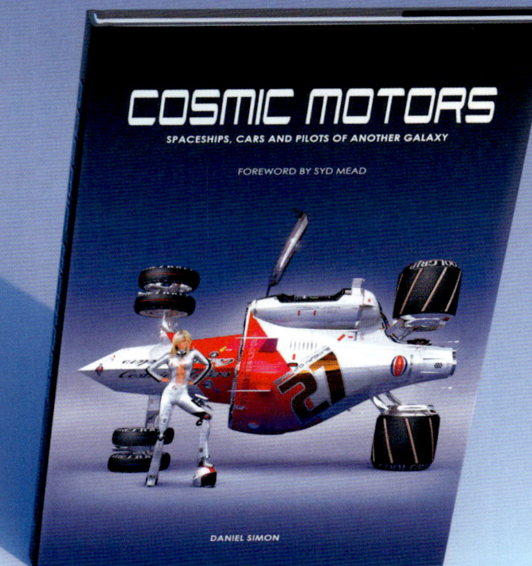

COSMIC MOTORS SOFTCOVER
- Daniel Simon's classic
- English, German
- ISBN: 978-1-933492-27-8

COSMIC MOTORS HARDCOVER
- Beautiful dust jacket
- Unique inside cover
- English, German
- ISBN: 978-1-933492-28-5

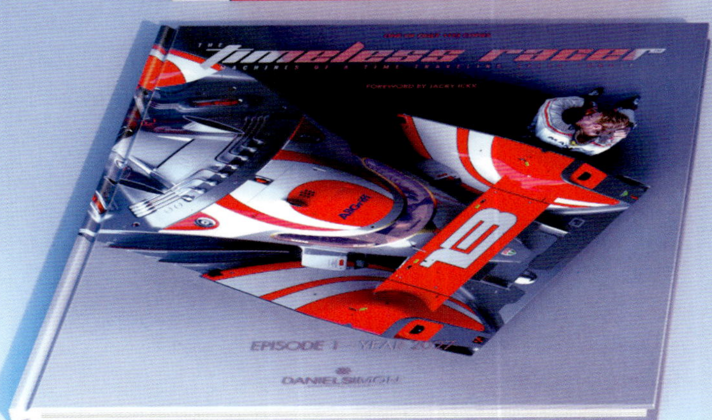

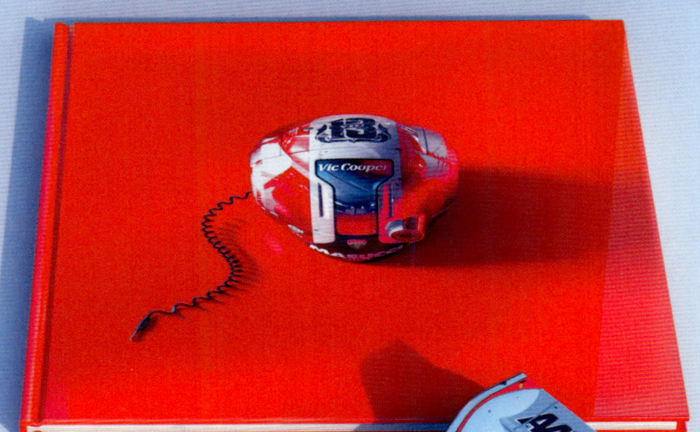

LIMITED EDITION

- Beautiful slip case
- Unique cover art
- **Limited to *1113 copies***
- English, French, German
- ISBN: 978-1-62465-111-3

Final design may vary.

PITLANE-CLUB EDITION

- Lavish slip case
- Metal plate with **your name** and **book number** debossed
- Inside hand-numbered, **signed** and individualized per request
- High gloss, heavyweight paper
- Fifth metallic color
- 11" x 13" poster
- **Limited to *only 313 copies***
- English, French, German
- Only on www.designstudiopress.com
- ISBN: 978-1-62465-013-0

Final design may vary.

VIRTUAL 1:18 MODELS
- Experience the cars from all angles through augmented reality on your device, in true 1:18 scale
- Available for iOS and Android
- Any 12"x14" Timeless Racer Eps.1 Edition required as marker

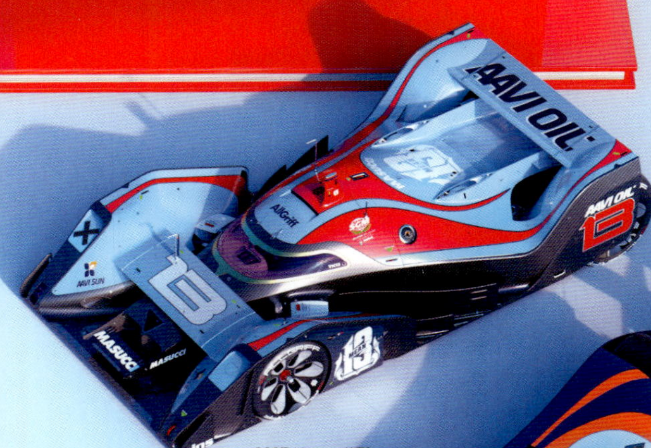

2027 Masucci X-7S

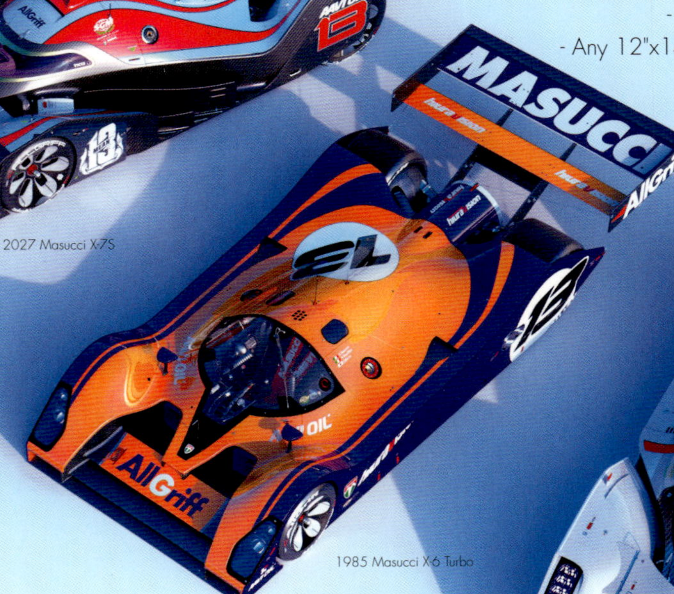

1985 Masucci X-6 Turbo

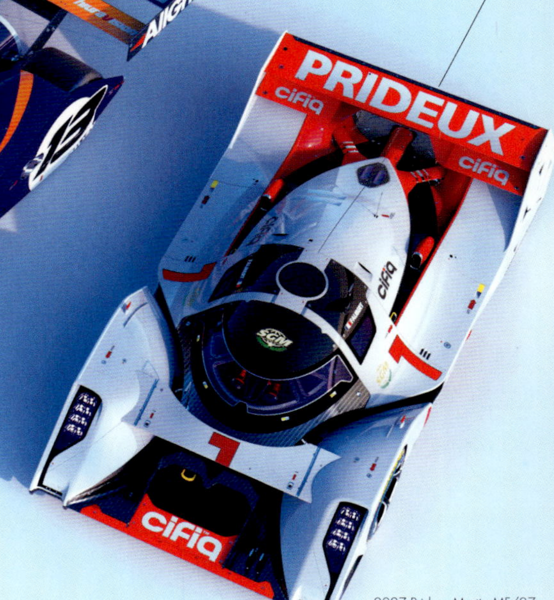

2027 Prideux-Martin MF/27

Products may change or not be available.

ABOUT THE AUTHOR: WWW.DANIELSIMON.COM

Published by Design Studio Press
8577 Higuera Street
Culver City, CA 90232
http://www.designstudiopress.com
E-mail: Info@designstudiopress.com

designstudio PRESS

English text: © Daniel Simon
English editorial consulting: **Jason Barlow**
English text copy editor: Jessica Hoffmann
French translation: **Pierre-Olivier Marie**
German text: © Daniel Simon
German consulting: The Simon family
German editorial consulting: **Jan Wilms**
Book and layout design: Daniel Simon
Production layout: Cecilia Zo

10 9 8 7 6 5 4 3 2 1

Printed in China
First Edition, October 2013

Library Of Congress Control Number:
2013935805

ISBN-13: 978-193349257-5

STAY CONNECTED TO THE MASUCCI SAGA

f /danielsimonstudio

THETIMELESSRACER.COM

DANIELSIMON™
STYLE FOR ALL GALAXIES

1916 1917 1918 1919 1920 1921 1922 1923 1924
1935 1936 1937 1938 1939 1940 1941 1942 1943
1954 1955 1956 1957 1958 1959 1960 1961 1962
1973 1974 1975 1976 1977 1978 1979 1980 1981
1992 1993 1994 1995 1996 1997 1998 1999 2000
2011 2012 2013 2014 2015 2016 2017 2018 2019
2030 2031 2032 2033 2034 2035 2036 2037 2038
2049 2050 2051 2052 2053 2054 2055 2056 2057
2068 2069 2070 2071 2072 2073 2074 2075 2076
2087 2088 2089 2090 2091 2092 2093 2094 2095
2106 2107 2108 2109 2110 2111 2112 2113 2114
2125 2126 2127 2128 2129 2130 2131 2132 2133
2144 2145 2146 2147 2148 2149 2150 2151 2152
2163 2164 2165 2166 2167 2168 2169 2170 2171
2182 2183 2184 2185 2186 2187 2188 2189 2190
2201 2202 2203 2204 2205 2206 2207 2208 2209
2220 2221 2222 2223 2224 2225 2226 2227 2228
2239 2240 2241 2242 2243 2244 2245 2246 2247
2258 2259 2260 2261 2262 2263 2264 2265 2266
2277 2278 2279 2280 2281 2282 2283 2284 2285
2296 2297 2298 2299 2300 2301 2302 2303 2304
2315 2316 2317 2318 2319 2320 2321 2322 2323
2334 2335 2336 2337 2338 2339 2340 2341 2342
2353 2354 2355 2356 2357 2358 2359 2360 2361
2372 2373 2374 2375 2376 2377 2378 2379 2380
2391 2392 2393 2394 2395 2396 2397 2398 2399
2410 2411 2412 2413 2414 2415 2416 2417 2418
2429 2430 2431 2432 2433 2434 2435 2436 2437
2448 2449 2450 2451 2452 2453 2454 2455 2456
2467 2468 2469 2470 2471 2472 2473 2474 2475
2486 2487 2488 2489 2490 2491 2492 2493 2494
2505 2506 2507 2508 2509 2510 2511 2512 2513
2524 2525 2526 2527 2528 2529 2530 2531 2532
2543 2544 2545 2546 2547 2548 2549 2550 2551
2562 2563 2564 2565 2566 2567 2568 2569 2570
2581 2582 2583 2584 2585 2586 2587 2588 2589
2600 2601 2602 2603 2604 2605 2606 2607 2608